Summer of the Geek

ALSO BY PIPER BANKS

Geek High
Geek Abroad

Summer of the Geek

Piper Banks

 New American Library

NEW AMERICAN LIBRARY
Published by New American Library,
a division of Penguin Group (USA) Inc.,
375 Hudson Street, New York, New York 10014, USA
Penguin Group (Canada), 90 Eglinton Avenue East, Suite 700, Toronto,
Ontario M4P 2Y3, Canada (a division of Pearson Penguin Canada Inc.)
Penguin Books Ltd., 80 Strand, London WC2R 0RL, England
Penguin Ireland, 25 St. Stephen's Green, Dublin 2,
Ireland (a division of Penguin Books Ltd.)
Penguin Group (Australia), 250 Camberwell Road, Camberwell,
Victoria 3124, Australia (a division of Pearson Australia Group Pty. Ltd.)
Penguin Books India Pvt. Ltd., 11 Community Centre,
Panchsheel Park, New Delhi - 110 017, India
Penguin Group (NZ), 67 Apollo Drive, Rosedale, North Shore 0632,
New Zealand (a division of Pearson New Zealand Ltd.)
Penguin Books (South Africa) (Pty.) Ltd., 24 Sturdee Avenue,
Rosebank, Johannesburg 2196, South Africa

Penguin Books Ltd., Registered Offices:
80 Strand, London WC2R 0RL, England

First published by New American Library,
a division of Penguin Group (USA) Inc.

First Printing, May 2010
3   5   7   9   10   8   6   4   2

NAL
REGISTERED TRADEMARK—MARCA REGISTRADA

LIBRARY OF CONGRESS CATALOGING-IN-PUBLICATION DATA:
Banks, Piper.
Summer of the geek / Piper Banks.
p.   cm.
ISBN 978-0-451-22984-7
[1. Au pairs—Fiction. 2. Ability—Fiction. 3. Self-esteem—Fiction. 4. Dating (Social customs)—Fiction.
5. Stepfamilies—Fiction. 6. Genius—Fiction. 7. Florida—Fiction.] I. Title.
PZ7.G2128Sum 2010
[Fic]—dc22   2009051304

Set in Bulmer • Designed by Elke Sigal

Printed in the United States of America

For Jane, who loves to read

Summer of the Geek

Chapter One

"I don't understand why this is so hard for you. I thought you were supposed to be a genius, Miranda," Dex teased me.

"Shush," I growled as I again tried to shift the car from first to second gear. This was met by a horrible grinding sound that made Dex flinch.

"The clutch! You have to step down on the clutch!" Dex said, pointing wildly at the pedals.

I stomped down on the clutch, but the car just lurched forward and stalled.

"Gah! What am I doing wrong?" I turned to look at Dex. The corners of his mouth were twitching into a smile.

"It helps if you step down on the clutch at the same time that you're shifting gears," Dex suggested.

"I give up," I said. "I told you I'd never be able to drive a standard transmission car! I can barely drive an automatic, and this is three trillion times harder."

I opened the car door and climbed out. Dex already had both his driver's license and his own car—an ancient red Honda Civic, which I now officially hated—so he'd driven me over to the empty parking lot at Orange Cove High to practice for my driving test. It was less than three weeks away, and I was pretty sure I was going to fail. It would be the greatest humiliation of my life. Even Hannah, my stepsister, who thought Albert Einstein was a member of a German boy band, had passed her driving test on the first try.

I leaned back against the car and crossed my arms over my chest. Dex walked around the car and stood in front of me.

"You can't just give up," he said.

Dex's pale blue eyes were squinting against the sun. He had lightly freckled skin, red hair that curled back from his face, and when he grinned, as he was doing now, his smile was slightly crooked. I felt a zing right in the center of my stomach every time he looked at me like that.

"I don't want to kill your car," I said.

"I don't want you to kill my car either," Dex said. "But I know you can do this."

"How do you know?" I said.

"I know."

He put his hands on my waist and leaned toward me. My heart began to rocket around inside my chest, thumping so loudly, I was amazed he couldn't hear it. Dex's lips were warm and soft against mine, and suddenly all of my frustration at not being able to master a simple stick shift transmission melted away. I reached up and encircled my arms around his neck.

After a long moment, Dex leaned back and looked at me. I loved the way he smelled, a clean scent that reminded me of soap and laundry fresh from the dryer. It made me want to nestle closer to him.

"Do you want to give it another try?" he asked.

At first, I thought he meant the kiss, so I nodded happily. It wasn't until Dex grinned at me, and turned to walk back around the car, that I realized he meant the driving lesson. I sighed. I'd already humiliated myself enough for one day. But I also knew Dex wasn't about to let me give up, so I reluctantly climbed back into the car and, once we were both safely buckled in, turned the key in the ignition. There was an awful grinding noise. Dex winced.

"Sorry," I said. I glanced sideways at Dex. "Are you laughing at me?"

He was, but he coughed to cover it up. "Remember, you have to step down on the clutch when you're starting the car," he said. "Just like when you're shifting gears."

"Oh, right. Sorry," I said again. I turned the key, this time pressing down on the clutch. The engine roared to life. Triumphant, I turned to grin at Dex. "Look! I did it!"

"Excellent. Now just try not to strip the gears while you shift into first," Dex cautioned.

"Right," I said. I drew in a deep breath and then pushed the clutch down while grappling with the gearshift. Amazingly, I managed to do it, and when I pressed my foot to the gas pedal, the car lurched forward.

"I'm doing it! I'm driving!" I said triumphantly. Maybe I wouldn't be an epic failure after all! My dad had promised to buy me a used car once I passed my driving test. I could just see myself cruising around town in a cute little Jetta convertible, wearing chic sunglasses, my frizzy brown hair tamed back into a ponytail. Maybe I could even get Hannah to teach me how to straighten my hair with her hot iron. Then I would be the girl with the cool car and the shiny hair—

Dex let out a sudden squawk, abruptly ending my daydream.

"Miranda! You're driving on the sidewalk!"

"Sorry!" I jerked the steering wheel to the left to avoid hitting a NO PARKING AT ANY TIME sign. Flustered, I forgot to keep my foot on the clutch, and the car lurched and stalled again.

"Why don't you try that one more time?" Dex said patiently. "And this time, try to stay on the road, okay?"

•

Dex dropped me off at the beach house after our driving lesson.

"I'm never going to pass my driving test," I groaned. "Never, ever, never."

"That's the spirit. Positive thinking will get you everywhere," Dex said.

"I just don't understand it. Why is driving so hard for me?" I asked. "Practically everyone in the world can do it."

Dex looked thoughtful and drummed his fingers against the steering wheel. "Maybe it's your brain." He glanced at me. "I mean, not that you're defective or anything."

"Thanks a lot!"

"I just mean that maybe your brain works differently. Look, you can solve really complex math problems in your head, the kind that ordinary people can barely do using a calculator, right?"

This was true. I'd had the bizarre ability to calculate sums in my head ever since I was little. My calculator-like brain had gotten me into the Notting Hill Independent School for Gifted Children, better known as Geek High, where I'd just completed my sophomore year. To enter Geek High, you have to have an IQ of at least 125. Most of the students that matriculated there also had some sort of a special talent. My best friend, Charlie, was an amazing painter. And our friend Finn created top-selling computer games.

Dex continued. "Maybe the part of your brain that solves math problems is so enormous, it saps power away from other areas of your brain. Like the part that controls how you drive a car."

I wondered if Dex was right. Maybe this math dominance of my brain also explained why I have absolutely no fashion sense and can't apply eye shadow without poking myself in the eye. Still, it wasn't exactly flattering. I wanted my boyfriend to think of me as beautiful and charming, not as some sort of weirdo with a malfunctioning brain. Besides, it wasn't like I wanted to be able to solve equations in my head. Math bored me. I much preferred writing short stories to solving theorems.

"You're starting your new job tomorrow, right?" Dex asked.

I nodded. My summer job as an au pair to a ten-year-old girl named Amelia Fisher had been a last-minute surprise. Amelia was a student at Geek Elementary, and reportedly, a virtuoso at the piano. Our school headmaster, Philip C. Hughes, had recommended me to Amelia's parents, or so Mrs. Fisher had told me when she called to offer me the job.

"I hope Amelia likes me," I said. "I don't have a lot of experience with kids. I babysat once, and it was a nightmare."

"Why? What happened?" Dex asked.

"The kids wanted to play pirates."

"What's wrong with that?" Dex asked.

"'Pirates' meant they tied me to a tree. The little sociopaths left me there for the rest of the afternoon, while they went inside and watched a horror movie that their mother had specifically forbidden them to see. It was one of those gory ones, where people get hacked up with axes and stuff like that."

Dex sputtered with laughter. "Did they ever let you go?"

"No! Their mother found me there when she got home. And she actually gave me a lecture about responsibility and said that if the kids had nightmares from the movie, it would be all my fault! Can you believe that?" I shook my head. "That was the beginning and end of my babysitting career."

"So why exactly have you signed up to spend your entire summer babysitting?" Dex asked.

"Well, it's not babysitting exactly. I think an au pair is more like being a companion."

I felt weird telling him what Mrs. Fisher had actually said when she called to offer me the job: "Amelia has trouble relating to kids her age. I think it would be good for her to spend time with some-one who's grown-up exceptionally gifted, and knows what it's like."

I didn't like talking about being gifted. It sounded too braggy.

"I'm sure you'll be great," Dex said.

"Are you excited about your first day of work?" I asked.

Dex had gotten his old job back as a lifeguard at the local community pool. I was trying to be supportive and not fixate on the fact that this basically meant he'd be spending his summer surrounded by girls in bikinis.

"I'm just glad that I'll be near the beach so I can fit in some parasurfing while I can."

"While you can? What do you mean?" I asked. Dex surfed year-round. It was one of the perks of living in Florida.

Dex opened his mouth, as though he were about to say some-thing. But then he seemed to reconsider. He shrugged and shook his head. "Just that the pool is across the street from the beach, so I'll have easy access. Maybe I'll even be able to go surfing on my breaks."

I felt a twinge of unease. Was there something Dex wasn't tell-ing me? Or maybe I was just feeling guilty, because there was something—something important, something that could change the course of my entire life—that I hadn't yet told him.

My mom—who insists that I call her by her first name, Sadie—writes steamy romance novels under the pen name Della De La Courte. She'd temporarily relocated to London the previous year while she researched and wrote her next book, leaving me behind in Orange Cove to live with my dad and evil stepmother. The book was taking longer to complete than Sadie had originally thought, so when she came home for a visit three weeks earlier, she'd an-nounced that she was going to stay in London for another year. Then she dropped a second bombshell: She asked me if I'd like to come live with her.

I'd gone to visit Sadie in London over Christmas break, and had loved it there. Orange Cove was a small town, where nothing much ever happened. Even worse, everyone in my hometown knew me as Miranda Bloom, the Human Calculator. Geek Girl Extraordinaire.

In London, I was anonymous. I could be anyone or anything. And the idea of actually living in such a huge international city was thrilling. Moving to London would also mean I wouldn't have to continue living with my evil stepmother, Peyton, for another school year.

But moving away would also mean leaving a lot of things behind. There was Dex, who, after months of confusion and misunderstandings, was officially my boyfriend. Just the idea of moving away, when we were finally a couple, made my stomach ache. And then there were my best friends, Finn and Charlie, and my new position as a writer for the Geek High magazine, *The Ampersand*.

I was so confused and conflicted about what I should do that I hadn't told anyone about Sadie's proposal that I move to London with her. I hadn't meant to keep it a secret—I just wanted a chance to think it through first. But the longer I went without telling anyone, the harder it seemed to be to bring it up.

"What are you doing after work tomorrow? Do you want to meet up?" Dex asked.

"I can't tomorrow. Charlie and I have plans," I said. "How about Wednesday?"

"Sounds good," Dex said. He leaned forward and rested his forehead against mine, so that his pale eyes loomed before mine. I could see the lighter golden flecks in his irises, and the scattering of freckles over his cheekbones. My breath caught in my chest, and all thoughts of moving to London and whatever it was Dex wasn't telling me flew out of my mind.

"See you later," he said, and then kissed me lightly.

"See you later," I said.

Chapter Two

The lingering zing from Dex's kiss continued to flutter in my stomach well after I'd let myself into the house and Dex had driven off. My brindle greyhound, Willow, greeted me at the front door, her long, lean body wriggling with happiness.

"Hi, girl," I said, patting her sleek head.

Willow followed me into the kitchen and looked on hopefully while I rifled through the fridge for a snack. I found some leftover pizza from the night before—basil and tomato, my favorite—and took the whole box out onto the back deck to eat. The view from the deck overlooked the ocean, so while I ate my pizza, I watched the tide roll in on whitecapped waves. Willow settled herself down at my feet and dozed in the sun.

But the peace and quiet was short-lived. I could suddenly hear voices raised in argument coming from inside the house. Even the roar of the ocean didn't stop me from hearing every word that was said. Or, more accurately, yelled.

"What were you *thinking*? You *knew* we had plans that night!"

"*Obviously*, I didn't, or I wouldn't have arranged the *business* trip for that weekend."

The cold female voice belonged to my stepmother, Peyton, whom I had not so affectionately nicknamed the Demon. The low-pitched growl belonged to my dad. It sounded like they were in the kitchen. I hunched down in my chair, hoping they wouldn't notice me. I'd learned from experience that when my dad and Peyton were fighting, it was best to stay out of their way.

"Is it really so hard to check with me *before* you make plans to be out of town?" Peyton asked.

"I didn't have a choice in the matter. It was the only weekend the client could meet with me," Dad replied. He was an architect, and frequently traveled to meet with clients or visit a building site. In fact, he and Peyton had met through his work, when she hired him to design the beach house. The Demon was the heiress to a mouthwash fortune.

"So your clients are more important to you than I am?" Peyton asked, her voice shrill with anger.

"Some of us have to work for a living," Dad replied in a cold, cutting tone.

The sliding glass door opened behind me, and I turned to see my stepsister, Hannah, walk out onto the deck. The voices of our fighting parents became momentarily louder—"Thoughtless!" "Selfish!"—before Hannah firmly slid the door shut behind her. She was holding her white Persian cat, Madonna. The cat took one look at Willow and hissed evilly.

"Hey," Hannah said.

"Hi," I said.

"Is it just me or are they getting worse?" Hannah asked.

"It's not just you," I said. Richard and Peyton had been fighting a lot lately. And I knew all too well what they were fighting about: *me*. Peyton hadn't wanted me to move into the beach house with them the previous year. My continued presence had been a source of conflict.

"I'm sick of it. And it's stressing Madonna out. She keeps getting hair balls," Hannah said, collapsing into the chair next to mine. Madonna didn't look particularly stressed out. Her flat, malevolent eyes were still fixed on Willow. Willow—who was terrified of the cat, despite being larger, equipped with fangs and bred for hunting—shrank back and skulked behind my chair.

"Coward," I said, patting Willow reassuringly. "Are you all packed and ready to go?"

Hannah's investment banker father and stepmother lived in Manhattan. She flew up to see them several times a year, and was leaving the next day for a weeklong visit.

"No, but I can finish tonight," Hannah said.

"I thought you were going out with Emmett," I said.

Emmett Dutch was Hannah's boyfriend, and a year ahead of me at Geek High. I'd had a crush on him for years, and was heartbroken when he and Hannah first started dating the previous year. Thankfully, I was over that now. I had Dex, and besides, Emmett and Hannah made a really cute couple.

"He canceled," Hannah said moodily. She crossed her arms and stared out at the ocean. "He has to work."

"Where's he working this summer?"

"At the Sno-Freeze," she said.

"That's where he worked last summer, too," I remarked, then flushed when Hannah looked at me, surprised. I'd never told her about my former feelings for Emmett, so she had no reason to know that I'd spent two years of my life gathering every nugget of information about him that I could find. "Geek High is small. Everyone knows everything about everyone," I said quickly.

Hannah nodded, accepting this explanation. "He was promoted to assistant manager. Emmett was really excited about it because he got a raise, but basically it means that when anyone calls in sick, he gets stuck working their shift. It's so incredibly lame. He's worked every night this week, and now I'm not going to get to see him before I leave on my trip."

"That's too bad," I commiserated. I pushed the pizza box in Hannah's direction. "Want some pizza?"

Hannah's nose wrinkled. "Do you know how many fat grams are in one slice of pizza?"

"No idea," I said.

"A lot," Hannah said ominously. "I have to lose ten pounds."

"Are you insane? You don't need to lose weight."

"I do if I'm going to be a model! Do you know how tiny those girls are?" Hannah said.

"I didn't know you wanted to model," I said. I thought my stepsister was certainly pretty enough to model. In fact, she was annoyingly pretty. While I was stuck with a tall and gangly body, frizzy hair and a too-big nose, Hannah looked like a princess straight from a Disney fairy tale. She had long, platinum blond hair, large blue eyes, a tiny button of a nose, and perfect rosebud lips. It was no wonder that Emmett Dutch, god of Geek High, had taken one look at Hannah and fallen madly in love with her. "I thought models were really tall, though."

"Kate Moss isn't," Hannah said defensively. "She's five-foot-six, my height exactly. Well, minus an inch or so."

"Oh. Well. Good for you," I said, trying to be supportive.

Hannah nodded. "Can you keep a secret?" she asked.

"That depends," I said. "How juicy is it?"

Hannah leaned forward, her blue eyes now bright with excitement. "Jackie has arranged for a photographer she knows to do a photo shoot with me. He's going to put together a portfolio for me so I can start auditioning for modeling jobs."

I'd never met Hannah's stepmother, but even so, I'd always been a bit jealous of her relationship with Hannah. Jackie seemed to truly adore Hannah, and treated her like the daughter she'd never had. It was a stark contrast to how the Demon barely tolerated my presence in the beach house.

"That's nice of her. Why is it a secret?" I asked.

"My mom." Hannah made a face. "She's totally against the idea of my modeling. Did you know that she changed the terms of my trust fund so that I only get the money if I go to college first? So lame. Although I guess if I'm a really famous model, I won't need a trust fund."

Surprisingly enough, I actually agreed with the Demon on this. What were the chances that Hannah would make it in modeling? I certainly wasn't an expert in the field, but I had to imagine there were thousands of girls competing for such a high-paying, glamorous job. It made a lot more sense for Hannah to go on to college. Even if she did pursue modeling, she'd have her education to fall back on if it didn't work out.

"What time is your flight out tomorrow?" I asked.

"Ten," Hannah said. She rolled her eyes. "It means I'm going to have to get up at, like, dawn in order to get to the airport in time."

"It'll be good practice for when you're a model and having to get up early for photo shoots," I said.

I was just teasing, but Hannah nodded seriously. "That's true. Although you know what Linda Evangelista said."

"Linda who?" I asked.

"You don't know who Linda Evangelista is?" Hannah asked, her mouth dropping open.

This happened a lot with Hannah. She and her friends studied fashion magazines the way archaeologists examine ancient ruins. I rarely knew what they were talking about when they started discussing designers and models.

"She's, like, only one of the most famous models ever. She was one of the original supermodels," Hannah said.

"Oh," I said, nodding. Even I had heard of supermodels.

"Anyway, Linda Evangelista once said that she wouldn't get out of bed for less than ten thousand dollars a day," Hannah said. She flipped her blond hair back over her shoulders. "I bet she didn't have to get up at dawn for photo shoots. They probably waited for her. That's the kind of model I want to be."

"You mean rich, phenomenally successful, and discourteous?" I asked.

"Exactly," Hannah said. She stood suddenly. "I think I'd better pack a few more outfits. Just in case."

"Just in case what?" Peyton asked, appearing at the back door.

Peyton was very pale and thin, and had very short, spiky blond hair. Her personality was so chilly, I could swear that whenever she walked into a room, the temperature would dip by fifteen degrees.

Hannah and I both looked up, startled. Neither one of us had heard the sliding glass door open. I wondered how much of our conversation she'd overheard. I glanced quickly at Hannah and could tell from her uneasy expression that she was wondering the same thing.

"I thought you were finished with your packing," Peyton continued.

"Mostly," Hannah said. "But I think I want to bring my Tocca dress. And maybe my high-heeled Mary Janes. Oh! And my white jeans." She stood. Madonna fell to the ground, hissing with displeasure, and stalked back into the house, fluffy white tail twitching. "Maybe I should just bring another suitcase."

Hannah hurried off to deal with her packing crisis. This, unfortunately, left Peyton and me alone. I tried very hard never to be alone with my stepmother. When she stared at me with her cold gray eyes, nostrils flaring and lips pressed into a thin line, it gave me the heebie-jeebies.

"Miranda," Peyton said. She extended one arm, pointing an accusatory finger in Willow's direction. "Your *dog*."

"What about her?" I asked, bracing myself for another anti-Willow tirade. Peyton hated Willow even more than she hated me. She was constantly making nasty comments about how Willow smelled—which she didn't at all—or how loudly she breathed. But then I glanced over at Willow and saw that she was busily wolfing down the rest of the pizza straight from the cardboard box. I yelped and lunged for her. "Willow! Don't eat that! Dairy always upsets your stomach."

Willow managed to suck down a few last bites of pizza before I could grab it away from her.

"If that dog can't behave itself, it can't be in the house," Peyton hissed.

Peyton had been on a one-woman mission to have Willow banned from the beach house ever since we moved in the previous year. So far, my dad had overruled her attempts. But the more Peyton and my dad fought, the more time he spent at his office. He hadn't been home in time for dinner in over a week. So without him around to run interference, I worried that it would only be a matter of time before Peyton succeeded in banishing Willow to the garage.

"She's not in the house," I pointed out. "We're on the back deck."

Peyton stared malevolently at me for a long moment, before turning on one four-inch stiletto heel and marching back into the house.

"Richard!" I heard her screech. "Where are you? Please come here right this instant, and do something about that animal."

I sighed and rubbed Willow's head. Every moment spent in Peyton's presence made the prospect of moving to London even more attractive.

Chapter Three

Until I passed my driving test, my ten-speed was the only form of independent transportation I had, so the next morning I biked over to the Fishers' house. They lived about two miles away, in a quiet neighborhood full of modest-sized homes set back from the road with well-tended lawns and flower beds. The Fishers' house, the third on the right, was yellow with white shutters and a glossy black door. Someone inside was playing the piano, a methodical recitation of scales. I rang the doorbell, feeling a flutter of nerves. This was it—my first day of work at my first real job.

The door opened almost immediately, and a woman smiled down at me. She was thin with dark curly hair cut in an angled bob. Black-framed glasses were perched on her nose, and she wore a long orange silk tunic with a mandarin collar over matching wide-legged pants.

"Hi, Miranda?"

I smiled back at her and nodded, feeling suddenly shy.

"I'm Elise Fisher. Please come in."

I stepped into the front foyer of the Fishers' house, and as I did, the sound of the piano scales grew louder. Through a pair of closed French doors just to the left of the hallway, I could see a girl with long dark hair seated at a black grand piano, her back to me. She sat erect on the bench, her posture perfect, and her hands traveled gracefully up and down the ivory keyboard. I could tell from the set of her shoulders that she was concentrating deeply.

"Why don't we go sit down and talk, and then I'll introduce you to Amelia?" Mrs. Fisher suggested.

I followed Mrs. Fisher back to the kitchen, which had gray walls and a slate gray countertop. It felt like I'd stepped into a rain cloud. Only the light blond wood of the cupboards and kitchen table broke up the gloomy darkness of the room.

"Go ahead and sit down," Mrs. Fisher said, gesturing toward the rectangular table. "Can I get you something to drink?"

"No, thank you," I said, sitting in one of the high-backed chairs. The sound of the scales continued to drone on in the background.

Mrs. Fisher poured herself a cup of coffee from the carafe on the countertop, and then sat across the table from me. She smiled warmly.

"You came highly recommended. Headmaster Hughes said that you are an excellent student and a valued member of the Notting Hill Independent School community."

I managed to suppress a snort of indignation. The previous school year, Headmaster Hughes had basically blackmailed me into organizing the annual Snowflake Gala. Then he coerced me into staying on the Mu Alpha Theta math competition team.

Mrs. Fisher continued. "I think this will be an excellent opportunity for Amelia. She's very gifted—not only does she have a genius-level IQ, but she's well on her way to becoming one of the top pianists of her generation. Spending time with you—someone who's grown up gifted and knows what it's like, what challenges gifted children face—will be enormously helpful for Amelia."

"You know I don't play the piano, right?" I said worriedly. "I'm not at all musical."

Mrs. Fisher smiled. "That's fine. Amelia already has a music teacher. She just needs to be exposed to what it's like to be a normal kid. Well. A normal *gifted* kid. You don't have to do anything special. Just spend some time with Amelia. Talk to her. Tell her about your experiences."

My experiences? I felt a twinge of apprehension. I wasn't sure what Mrs. Fisher wanted me to talk to Amelia about. Being gifted had caused me some problems, especially while I was still enrolled in a normal school. I learned the hard way that most teachers don't appreciate being corrected in front of the class, even when they're dead wrong. In fact, they tend to put you in detention for it.

But since Amelia was already attending Geek Middle, she would never have to face that particular problem. All of the faculty at Notting Hill was specially trained in how to teach high-IQ kids.

The same thing went for making friends. Genius kids tend to stand out at normal schools. And usually not in a good way. But when all of your classmates are just as geeky as you are, it's a lot easier to fit in.

The scales suddenly stopped.

"Amelia!" Mrs. Fisher called out. "Come here and meet Miranda."

Either Amelia didn't hear her mother, or she simply chose to ignore her, because a moment later, the music started up again. At least Amelia had moved on from the scales and was now playing something classical and complicated.

Mrs. Fisher didn't seem angry. She took another sip of her coffee.

"Amelia's a very dedicated musician. She practices for hours every day." She hesitated, setting her coffee mug on the table. "In fact, I should warn you: Amelia's not very pleased that I've hired you."

"She probably thinks she's too old for a babysitter," I said sympathetically. I remembered feeling the same way when I was her age.

"No, that's not it. I think she's more concerned that this arrangement will interfere with her practice time," Mrs. Fisher said. "I've assured her that you won't bother her while she's playing."

"Oh." I was momentarily taken aback. "When does she practice?"

"During the school year, she practices for an hour before school, an hour during school, and then two hours after. In the summer, she plays a bit more—usually for a few hours in the morning, and then a longer session in the afternoon."

I was stunned. Amelia was only ten years old. How could she be so dedicated at so young an age? And what could Mrs. Fisher possibly expect me to teach her? Sure, I could solve math theorems in my head, but that wasn't something I worked at. I'd never spent hours at a time studying math.

"I thought you could plan on coming every weekday from around nine to three or so. You can hang out while Amelia practices—feel free to bring a book or your laptop or whatever— and then the two of you can have lunch and spend some time together," Mrs. Fisher said. "I work nearby—I'm an interior designer, and my office is on Shoreline Avenue—so I'll be close if you need me."

The idea of spending all day, every day, just sitting at the Fishers' house and listening to Amelia play the piano didn't sound like much fun. On the other hand, Mrs. Fisher had already agreed to pay me ten dollars an hour. And sitting around reading while Amelia practiced certainly sounded a lot easier than a summer job bagging groceries.

And, on the bright side, I'd have plenty of time to write. I was currently working on a short story about a girl who no one ever notices, until one day she actually becomes invisible. I'd brought my notebook with me to the Fishers' house, tucked away in my backpack, just in case I had some time to work on it.

"Sounds great," I said. "What does Amelia like to do? Other than playing the piano, I mean."

My question seemed to confuse Mrs. Fisher. "What does she like to do?" she repeated. She shrugged. "I suppose what any other gifted ten-year-old likes to do. What did you do at her age?"

I tried to remember. "I liked arts and crafts. Biking. Going to the playground. The beach."

"Not the beach," Mrs. Fisher said. "Amelia doesn't swim."

"She doesn't?" I asked, surprised.

While my mother, Sadie, had never exactly been a role model of maternal responsibility, she had enrolled me in swimming lessons before I could walk. After all, we lived in Florida, and were never far away from the water. Besides the beach, there were swimming pools and rivers. When I was Amelia's age, I'd practically lived in the water. How could Amelia live here and never have learned how to swim?

Mrs. Fox stood and headed for the living room. "I'll go get Amelia," she called back over her shoulder to me. "It's time for her break anyway."

From the other room, I could hear the piano stop abruptly and then the sound of muffled voices. It sounded like they were arguing, although I couldn't hear what the source of the conflict was. Maybe Amelia didn't want to stop practicing. Or maybe she just didn't want to meet me.

Mrs. Fisher returned to the kitchen, this time trailed by a sullen young girl. Amelia was small for her age, with fine bones and angular features. She had long, straight, dark brown hair, a thin face that ended with a stubborn chin, and a snub nose that turned up at the end. Her brown eyes were round and large for her face.

"Hi," I said in my friendliest voice. "I'm Miranda."

Amelia stared at me, her gaze coolly appraising. It would have been unnerving to be looked at that way by anyone, but coming from such a small girl, it was even more disturbing. I stopped smiling and ran a tongue over my teeth, trying to see if there was something stuck there.

"Amelia, say hello to Miranda," Mrs. Fisher prompted.

"Hello," Amelia said with no enthusiasm.

Convinced that my teeth were clean, I smiled again. "We're going to hang out together this summer. I'm sure we'll have lots of fun," I said, sounding overly enthusiastic.

Amelia crossed her arms over her thin chest and gave me the hairy eyeball. "Thanks, but I'm not interested in having fun."

"Okay. Then I'll do my best to bore you," I joked. "I'll come up with math problems for you to solve."

Amelia didn't laugh. I looked to Mrs. Fisher for help.

"Amelia, we've talked about this," Mrs. Fisher said. "You're too young to stay here by yourself while I'm at work."

"Then why can't Maria stay with me?" Amelia asked.

"Because she has a new job with another family," Mrs. Fisher said. She turned to me. "Maria was Amelia's nanny. Amelia's been having a bit of separation anxiety."

"I am not," Amelia said, giving her mother a withering look. "Maria spent all day talking to her sister on her cell phone and pretty much ignored me. But at least she left me alone when I practiced."

"I've already talked to Miranda about your practice time," Mrs. Fisher said soothingly. "Now, I'm going to go to work for a few hours. You girls will have a chance to get to know each other." Mrs. Fisher began to gather up her car keys, sunglasses, and handbag, preparing to leave. She smiled encouragingly at me. "All of our contact numbers are posted on the bulletin board next to the phone and there's tuna salad in the fridge for lunch." She leaned over to kiss Amelia's scowling face, and then she turned and headed out, calling back over her shoulder, "Have fun, you two!"

When the door closed, leaving us alone, I smiled at Amelia. "What do you want to do?" I asked. "I brought my bike. We could ride down to that playground at the end of the street."

Amelia stared at me. "I don't have time for this. And I'm not going to pretend like we're friends or something."

This was getting ridiculous. I was not about to be put in my place by a ten-year-old girl.

"So that's a no to the park, huh?" I said. I crossed my arms, too, and did my best to return the icy glare. "We could play a board game. Do you have Monopoly?"

"No."

"Scrabble?"

"No."

"Candy Land?"

Amelia rolled her eyes. "I'm not a baby."

I had to stifle the urge to retort, "Could have fooled me." Taunting Amelia probably wasn't the best way to win her over.

"What would you like to do, then?" I asked, my patience eroding.

"Practice," Amelia said. And with that, she turned and marched back toward the living room. A moment later, I heard the music start again. This time, she'd chosen to play a dark and foreboding piece that thundered darkly. It was a musical temper tantrum.

I wondered if I should go after her. But then what? I couldn't force her to hang out with me. I unzipped my backpack, pulled out the spiral notebook I wrote my short stories in, and sat back down at the kitchen table. If I was going to be stuck here for hours, listening to Amelia practice, I might as well get some writing done.

Chapter Four

"She hates me," I said.

"I'm sure she doesn't hate you," Charlie said. "She was probably just mad at her mom and taking it out on you."

I considered this. "No. I'm pretty sure she hated me," I said.

After work, I'd met my best friend, Charlie Teague, at the bowling alley, where she'd gotten a summer job. Her shift was over, too, so we sat at one of the high tables, drinking sodas and watching the women's senior bowling league—the Pinkies, complete with matching neon pink bowling shirts—compete against a visiting team.

The bowling alley was dark and smelled like feet, but even so, I envied Charlie's job. I'd spent six long hours at the Fishers' house, during which time Amelia hadn't spoken another word to me. Instead, she spent the entire day playing the piano, breaking only to eat the tuna sandwiches I made for lunch. While she ate, she kept her eyes fixed on her plate and ignored all of my attempts to draw her out. The only bright spot of the day was that I'd finished my short story, and even thought up a title for it— *How to Get Noticed*. But now I was already dreading having to go back to the Fishers' tomorrow. Amelia's unrelenting hostility was getting to me.

"She refused to speak to me. She just practiced the piano the entire time I was there," I said.

"She sounds intense," Charlie remarked. Charlie was short and wiry, and had recently dyed her cropped hair a deep eggplant purple. She was wearing a short-sleeved blue-and-white-striped shirt emblazoned with BOWL-A-RAMA across the front. Charlie had managed to make the uniform look chic by wearing it over a white-ribbed tank top and tying the bowling shirt at the waist.

"She is," I agreed. "In fact, from what I saw today, I'd say she's obsessed."

"Hmm," Charlie said. "I suppose obsession isn't always a bad thing. I've done some of my best work when I've been in the middle of an intense all-nighter."

Charlie was an amazing artist. Lately, she'd been painting huge canvases that took up the whole wall of her garage (which her parents had converted into a studio for her). But Charlie was also manic-depressive, which meant that she went through phases where she didn't sleep much and tended to stay up all night, painting frenziedly, then go to bed for days at a time. Sure, she got amazing results, but it had never seemed very healthy to me.

"You're not ten," I said. "She's pretty young to be so single-minded."

"That's true," Charlie said, taking a sip of her soda.

"Anyway, I think I might quit. Is the bowling alley still hiring?" I said.

"Quit?" Charlie stared at me. "You can't quit. You have to help this girl. Teach her how to live a more balanced life. If she doesn't have something in it other than her music, she'll burn out before she's fifteen."

"How am I supposed to teach her anything? Didn't you hear the part about how she won't speak to me?" I asked.

"You'll just have to try harder. Find a way to break through to her," Charlie said.

"How exactly am I supposed to save her when Amelia won't even acknowledge my presence?"

"I don't know," Charlie admitted. "We'll have to think of something. Do you know anything about classical music?"

"No," I said. "Nothing."

"That's too bad. Maybe you could learn enough to be able to talk about it with her. That might get her to open up."

"I don't think I could possibly learn enough about the piano by tomorrow to convince her that I'm interested in it. I can't even play 'Chopsticks,'" I said gloomily.

"You have to think of something. This is a matter of life and death."

"No, it's not."

"Okay, it's not. But it is a matter of happiness and personal fulfillment versus years of loneliness and isolation," Charlie said.

"Hello, my little chickadees," Finn said, appearing at our table and sitting at one of the tall stools. "How's my posse doing on this fine afternoon?"

Finn Birnbaum was very tall and very pale, and had shaggy brown hair, mischievous blue eyes, and a scar over his mouth, now faded to a pale silver, that was left over from the surgery he had as a baby to correct a cleft lip.

"Miranda and I have been working all day," Charlie said pointedly. "What about you? Have you done anything remotely productive?"

Finn was, as usual, unperturbed by Charlie's needling. He smiled sweetly. "I was very productive. I slept until noon, thus making sure my growing body was properly rested. Then I ate three bowls of Lucky Charms and watched cartoons to stimulate my mind. Then I hacked into the Geek High server, just as a limbering exercise to make sure my mad computer skills don't atrophy. And then I took a nap, woke up, and headed over here."

"How is sleeping all day, watching cartoons, and eating cereal productive?" Charlie demanded.

"You're leaving out the part about my hacking into the school network," Finn said.

"Do you want to know what I did today?" Charlie continued.

"Not really," Finn said. "Harsh, yes, but I believe honesty is the best policy."

"You're a role model to us all," I said sarcastically.

Charlie, ignoring both of us, continued. "I got up really early, so I could paint for a few hours before I had to be at work here at eight thirty."

"Brutal," Finn said.

"And then I got here, and, as the newbie, I got stuck with shoe duty. Which basically means that I've spent the last eight hours taking people's stinky shoes from them and handing them even stinkier bowling shoes. And then, when they turned the bowling shoes back in, I had to spray them down with Lysol, in a futile attempt to eradicate the funk."

"Excellent. Now go get me a soda," Finn told her.

"Get it yourself," Charlie snarled.

"Don't you work here? Aren't you supposed to do whatever I say?" Finn looked puzzled. "What happened to the customer always being right?"

"Were you even listening to me?"

"Not really," Finn admitted. "I started to, but then you went off on one of your rants, and when you do that, I basically only hear this." He held up one hand, and opened and shut it, like a bird snapping its beak. "Wah, wah, wah. So, where's my soda?"

Charlie looked longingly at her soda, and I knew she was picturing herself dumping it over his head. The fact that her manager was still there, manning the cash register, was probably the only thing stopping her.

I decided to step in. "Charlie doesn't work at the snack bar."

"Really? I would have thought that would be preferable to touching people's shoes," Finn said.

"It would." Charlie sighed. "But apparently you have to work here for months before you climb up the ladder from shoe handling to the snack bar. One of the fry guys told me he was on shoes for six months before he got promoted. Still," she added, looking more hopeful, "he was only working part-time. I'm here full-time, at least for the summer. Maybe I'll move up faster."

"That's the ticket," Finn said. "Keep your eyes on the prize. Reach for the brass ring. Ouch!" He leaned forward to rub the shin Charlie had just kicked. "There's no need to get violent."

"The sad thing is that as bad as handling other people's shoes is, Charlie's summer job is better than mine," I said.

"Child care isn't all you dreamed it would be?" Finn asked. He reached for my soda, but I moved it before he could take a sip. Finn backwashed.

"No," I said.

"That sucks," Finn said cheerfully. "I'm glad I don't have to work a crap job."

Finn had become a self-made multimillionaire by creating a series of incredibly popular and incredibly violent video games, the most succesful of which was called Grunge Aliens. He'd never have to slog away at a minimum-wage job. For that matter, he'd never have to slog away at *any* job. Finn was set for life. I picked the straw up out of my Coke and flicked soda at him.

"Hey, now!" Finn said. "There's no need for that!"

"Yes, there is. You're being incredibly annoying," Charlie told him. But then she looked thoughtful and turned to me. "You know, he could be just what we need right now."

"He who?" Finn asked.

"You," Charlie said. "When you interrupted us, Miranda and I were discussing the girl she's watching this summer." Charlie filled Finn in on Amelia's musical gift and the moral imperative of my helping Amelia achieve a more balanced life. "We need to figure out a way to get Amelia to open up to Miranda. And you're the most devious person we know."

"Flattery will get you everywhere," Finn said. He bridged his hands and tapped his fingertips together. "But I have to admit, I'm intrigued. I've never attempted to turn anyone into a minion before."

"I don't want to turn her into my minion!" I said. "I just want to get her to talk to me."

Finn waved this away with a flick of one hand. "The question is, which comes first, establishing trust or establishing your supremacy?"

Charlie rolled her eyes. "Why did I think he would be helpful?"

"Just hear me out," Finn said. "On the one hand, you could win her over first—make her think you're sympathetic, a friend, an ally. The best way to go about it, really, is to target a common enemy. The most obvious person to fill this role would be her mother—which only makes sense, because it would also serve to undermine her mom's authority when you're ready to start asserting your own domination."

"Finn!" I said.

He ignored me. "Anyway, you make nice, you get her to trust you, you tell her that her mother will never understand her. You get the picture. And then once you get that bond established, *boom*." He sliced his hand down. "You start establishing your authority. Start off small—tell her things instead of asking, send her on errands, criticize her when she makes mistakes. Or there's the second option. Start off taking a position of unquestioned authority, and bend her to your will right away, like in the military," Finn continued.

"There's something wrong with you," Charlie told him. "Seriously wrong."

"I'm supposed to be helping this girl, not dominating and manipulating her," I added.

"I suppose we shouldn't be surprised," Charlie said. "After all, this is the mind who thought up Grunge Aliens, which—if I remember correctly—a reviewer called the most violent video game of all time."

But Finn wasn't listening. He was instead eyeing a tall, leggy girl bowling on lane four with a group of friends. She wore her strawberry blond hair tied back in two low pigtails, and had an expression of fierce concentration as she hooked the ball forward, sending it straight down the lane.

"Hello, hello. Who do we have here?" Finn said. "Do either of you know her?"

"No," I said, shaking my head.

"What is the point of having chicks as friends if you can't introduce me to cute girls?" Finn complained.

"I know her. Her name's Phoebe McLeod," Charlie said. "I went to elementary school with her, before my parents moved me to Geek Elementary. I think she goes to Orange Cove High now."

The redheaded girl turned, smiling, and slapped hands with her friends. She had a long, straight nose, a spattering of freckles, and pretty almond-shaped eyes.

"Love at first sight," Finn said in an odd, strangled voice.

Charlie gave him a sharp look. "What are you talking about?"

"That girl. I think I'm in love with her."

"You don't even know her. How can you be in love with someone you don't even know?" Charlie asked.

"Good point," Finn said. He hopped off his stool and strode decisively toward lane four.

"Finn, you idiot, what are you doing?" Charlie called after him. If Finn heard her, he didn't respond. "What is he doing?" she asked me.

"I think he's introducing himself," I said, watching as Finn walked up to the group of girls. Charlie and I both leaned forward, straining to hear him over the racket of balls knocking into pins.

"I heard you're the go-to girl for bowling lessons around here," Finn said to Phoebe.

"Oh, please," Charlie scoffed. "That's the lamest line I've ever heard."

Phoebe's friends seemed to agree with Charlie. They tittered and exchanged scornful looks. But Phoebe just gazed at Finn, her head tilted to one side, and smiled beatifically up at him. "I doubt it. This is my first time bowling."

Finn grinned back at her. "Then I guess you must be a natural. I'm Finn, by the way."

"Hi, Finn. I'm Phoebe."

"And I'm going to be sick," Charlie said, jumping off her stool. "I'd rather touch people's sweaty shoes than watch this."

I stood up and followed Charlie as she stomped out of the bowling alley and into the dazzling light outside. I'd had reason in the past to suspect that Charlie and Finn might have feelings for each other that went beyond friendship. In fact, Finn had been similarly annoyed when Charlie started going out with her now-ex-boyfriend, Mitch. But when Charlie and Mitch broke up, Finn didn't make any move to change the status of his relationship with Charlie. Instead, everything between Charlie and Finn went back to normal—Finn did his best to torment Charlie, and, in return, she insulted him at every possible opportunity.

But now, seeing Charlie's expression—her brow furrowed, her

lips pressed into a tight, white line—I thought that the feelings might still be there, at least on Charlie's side. But I knew better than to ask her. She'd just deny it, and worse, would get into a snit with me. And since Charlie and I had just made up from our last fight, which had lasted several months, I didn't want to stir the waters again so soon.

Charlie stopped abruptly in the parking lot, kicking a stone aside.

"I don't even think she's that pretty, do you?" Charlie asked me. "And I'm pretty sure her hair color isn't natural."

I decided not to point out the obvious—that Charlie's own hair hadn't been a natural shade since she bought her first box of hair coloring at the age of eleven—deciding that this observation would just irritate her further. So instead I shrugged and said, "I thought she was cute."

"I don't. Her nose is too thin," Charlie said. "And her nostrils are too large."

"Really? I didn't notice that," I said.

"How could you not notice? They're freakishly large. I've seen horses with smaller nostrils," Charlie said. She kicked another stone out of her way. "They're so big, you could park a car in there."

"Hmm," I said noncommittally. I didn't think that Phoebe had abnormally large nostrils. She was actually quite pretty. But I had a feeling Charlie wouldn't want to hear that just now.

"Do you need a ride home?" Charlie asked. Unlike me, Charlie already had her driver's license and an ancient Jeep, which she'd inherited from one of her older sisters.

"I biked over," I said, gesturing toward my silver ten-speed, which I'd chained to the bike stand outside the bowling alley.

"That's okay. We can throw your bike in the back of the Jeep."

On the drive back to the beach house, Charlie was silent. I didn't mind. I was turning the Amelia problem over in my head. I wondered if Charlie was right—maybe I did have a moral obligation to help Amelia. I had no intention of turning her into my minion, of course . . . but maybe, just maybe, I could teach her that it was possible to have an extraordinary talent and still live an ordinary life. Amelia could have friends, and be silly, and have interests outside of her music.

Yes, I decided, I should help her. Besides, I'd already accepted the job. I couldn't quit after one day. I'd go back tomorrow, and I'd figure out a way to get Amelia to open up to me.

The only question was, how exactly was I supposed to go about doing that?

•

Dex called me on my cell phone that night after dinner. I was in my room, stretched out on my bed, rereading *How to Get Noticed* and wondering if I should expand on the story, maybe even turn it into a short novel. I'd never taken on such a big project before, but the idea was exciting.

"Hey, you," Dex said. His voice was soft and warm in my ear, and I felt the familiar zing shoot through me. "How was your day?"

"Let me put it this way—it was so bad, I found myself hoping Amelia would ask me to play 'pirates' with her," I said.

Dex laughed. "It was worse than being tied to a tree?"

"Almost. Do you know anything about classical music?"

"Mozart. Beethoven. Bach."

"Can you teach me about them?" I asked eagerly.

"No. All I know is their names."

"Oh," I said, deflating. "That's not going to help much. I was hoping to bond with Amelia over music."

"I can teach you how to pull a quarter out of her ear," Dex suggested.

"Thanks, but I don't think she's the kind of kid who will be impressed by magic tricks. Any other ideas?"

Dex thought for a few moments. "I make excellent paper airplanes. Would she like that?"

"Doubtful."

"Other than surfing and playing lacrosse, that pretty much exhausts my list of talents," Dex said.

"Thanks anyway. I'll figure something out. How was your first day of work?"

"Excellent. No one drowned, which is always a big plus when you're a lifeguard."

"Did you get to save anyone?"

"No. I did break up a cutthroat game of Marco Polo," Dex said.

"How can Marco Polo be cutthroat?"

"Let's just say it involved DP-ing," Dex said ominously.

"What's that?"

"It stands for Down Pants-ing."

"Oh," I said. "Yeah. That doesn't sound good."

"Let's just say that I saw more of Jacob Maddigan and Robby Rios than I ever wanted to see."

I laughed. Right now, talking to Dex, was the happiest I'd felt all day.

"Are we still on for tomorrow night?" Dex asked.

"Absolutely," I said.

Chapter Five

"Hi, Miranda," Mrs. Fisher said as she opened the front door to me on my second day of work. "How are you this morning?"

"Hi, Mrs. Fisher. I'm fine, thanks," I said. I shouldered my knapsack. Along with my writing notebook, it contained everything I could think of to bring that would interest a ten-year-old girl: art supplies, including construction paper, craft felt, glue, glitter and feathers, board games, and a selection of makeup pinched from Hannah's bathroom drawer. She'd left for her trip to New York the day before, and so wouldn't notice the missing candy-hued lip glosses and sparkly eye shadows.

"Amelia's practicing," Mrs. Fisher said, stepping aside to let me in.

I'd already figured this out, as I could hear the repetitive rise and fall of piano scales coming from the living room.

"She said that you two got along well yesterday," Mrs. Fisher said, striding away down the hall.

"She did?" I asked, trailing behind her.

If Mrs. Fisher heard the surprise in my voice, she didn't comment on it. She seemed to be in a hurry this morning, simultaneously sorting through the mail, drinking coffee, and fastening a chunky beaded bracelet onto her wrist.

"I'm sorry to rush off on you, but I have a client meeting I have to get to. I didn't get a chance to make you girls lunch, but there's some leftover pasta in the fridge. You can reheat that in the microwave," Mrs. Fisher said, gathering up her belongings.

"Sure, no problem," I said in a tone that I hoped inspired confidence.

"Bye, Miranda. Have a good day."

"Bye," I said.

"Good-bye, Amelia," Mrs. Fisher called out, raising her voice to be heard over the droning scales.

Amelia didn't answer her, but Mrs. Fisher didn't seem to notice. Her cell phone rang, and she clicked it on and lifted it to her ear.

"Hello," she said, leaving the house in a cloud of perfume, click-clacking heels, and animated conversation directed into the small, silver phone. When the door closed behind her, cutting her off midlaugh, the house suddenly seemed very still and quiet, save for the sound of Amelia's piano.

"Here goes nothing," I muttered to myself. I turned and headed toward the living room.

•

The Fishers' living room was large, but still cozy and full of comfortable furniture—chairs, two couches, tables, bookshelves, and, of course, Amelia's large piano.

Amelia sat at the piano, her back perfectly straight, and her small hands gliding easily over the keys. Her long dark hair was fastened back in a ponytail.

"Hi, Amelia," I said as I walked up behind her.

She ignored me. I had expected this, and had already planned my line of attack. I was going to annoy Amelia into talking to me. Finn had inspired the idea by example.

I leaned on her piano and watched her play. I could tell from the slight stiffening in her back and the tight line of her lips that my presence was already having an effect.

"What are you playing?" I asked. "Are those scales?"

Amelia didn't answer, but she immediately stopped playing the scales and instead began to play something quick and jaunty. I thought it sounded vaguely familiar.

"Wasn't that on a commercial or something?" I hummed it. "I'm pretty sure it was, although I can't remember what for. Was it for an airline? Or maybe it was a cat food commercial?"

Amelia immediately stopped playing and glared up at me.

"It's a sonata written by Joseph Haydn, if you must know," she said, her voice round with contempt.

I kept my expression pleasantly neutral. "Was he a famous composer?"

Amelia's lip curled. "You don't know who Haydn was?" she asked.

I shook my head. "Nope."

"Haydn was an illustrious eighteenth-century Austrian composer. He was a contemporary of Mozart and he taught Beethoven." Amelia tossed her hair and sneered at me. "I can't believe you've never heard of him. I thought you were supposed to be a genius."

What sort of a ten-year-old used the word *illustrious*? I wondered. And why did people keep saying *I thought you were supposed to be a genius* to me? First Dex, now Amelia. But I couldn't lose my temper now.

"Just in math. I don't know anything about music. Maybe you could teach me," I suggested cheerfully.

Amelia folded her arms across her chest and looked at me as

though I were a cockroach skittering across the floor. "And why would I want to that?" she asked.

I felt my patience slipping away. "Look," I said. "Your mom hired me to hang out with you, and I fully intend to do my job. So I'll make you a deal—once a day, you do some sort of extracurricular activity with me. It doesn't have to be anything big. We could just go for a walk, or go bike riding, or just sit and color. If you do that, I'll let you practice in peace."

"And if I don't?" Amelia asked.

"I'll bug you," I said promptly. "Every time you sit down to practice, I'll stand right here and do everything in my power to annoy you."

"You can't do that!" Amelia said, outraged.

I shrugged. "Sure I can. So there's really no point in fighting me. Do you like arts and crafts? I brought glitter glue with me. And I brought Monopoly, too, if you'd rather play a game."

Amelia's eyes narrowed to angry slits. She turned abruptly away, lifted her hands, and began to play again.

"Ignoring me isn't going to work," I cautioned her.

Amelia continued to play. I sighed. She wasn't giving me any choice. I cleared my throat and began to sing.

"Baa, baa, black sheep, have you any wool?" I sang enthusiastically, but off-key. I never could carry a tune. *"Yes, sir, yes, sir, three bags full."*

Amelia thumped her hands down on the piano keys in a crash of frustration. "Stop that!" she cried. "I can't concentrate!"

"One for my master, one for my dame, and one for the little boy who lives down the lane," I continued.

"What do I have to do to make you stop?" Amelia asked.

I stopped singing. "Play Monopoly with me," I said.

"Just one game?"

"One game," I agreed.

"And if I do, then you'll let me practice?"

"Yes," I said, adding, "At least for today."

"Fine," Amelia said, spitting the word out. "I'll play one stupid game of stupid Monopoly with you."

"Good," I said sweetly. "I'll set the board up on the kitchen table."

•

Thirty minutes later, I owned most of the real estate on the board, and had built at least one hotel on each property. Amelia was playing, but without any enthusiasm or effort. She rolled the dice and paid whatever fines she accrued, but didn't buy a single property. It was pretty obvious that her goal was to go bankrupt as quickly as possible in order to end the game.

"Passive-aggressive Monopoly," I said as she handed over the rent on the luxury property I'd built on Park Place. "This is fun. Is it my turn?"

Amelia didn't reply. She'd stayed mute throughout the game, keeping her lips pressed together in a tight, white line.

I rolled the die. "One, two, three . . . oh, look, I landed on Community Chest."

The game was over in a record forty-two minutes. Amelia paid over the last of her rent money to me, and then, still not saying a word, she stood, turned, and marched back to the living room. A moment later, the sound of piano music drifted back into the kitchen.

As I stared down at my Monopoly empire, I couldn't help thinking the whole exercise had been pointless. True, I had gotten Amelia away from her piano for a while. But it hadn't been the bonding experience I'd hoped for. In fact, if anything, I'd just alienated her even further. With a frustrated sigh, I swept the pieces of the Monopoly game back in the box.

•

After that, the rest of the day passed much as the day before had. Amelia spent all morning and afternoon practicing, breaking only for lunch, which she ate in silence. We ate lunch together, but Amelia refused to speak to me.

No matter how hard I tried to concentrate on my writing, my thoughts kept drifting away like puffy clouds in a blue summer sky. I wondered what would happen between Dex and me if I decided to move to London to live with Sadie. Would we stay together, or break up? We hadn't been dating all that long, and I'd heard long-distance relationships were hard to sustain even between people who'd been together for a while. Then I thought of Charlie, and how she'd lost herself when she was dating Mitch, and that I didn't ever want to be that sort of person—the kind who puts her boyfriend ahead of everything else in her life.

I shook my head, trying to dislodge all thoughts of this dilemma. I had to make a decision soon, but I didn't have to figure it out today. I redoubled my efforts with my story, but no matter how hard I tried to concentrate, I found myself instead listening to Amelia's music. The song she was playing was absolutely beautiful, slow and soothing. I wondered what it was. Another Haydn piece? I tried to figure out if it sounded like what she'd been playing earlier, but quickly gave up—I just didn't know enough about music to distinguish one classical piece from another.

I stood, abandoning my writing, and walked back to the living room, irresistibly drawn to the music. I didn't think Amelia had noticed my arrival. I stood behind a wing chair and out of her line of sight, and listened to her play. The song grew in intensity, unfolding as she coaxed the melody out of the keys. I'd always thought that classical music was boring. But this certainly wasn't. As I listened, the fine hairs on my arms stood on end. Amelia finished the piece and sat so still for a moment that I wondered if she'd fallen under her own spell.

I clapped. "That was amazing," I said.

Amelia started, and turned around. Her expression was wary, suspicious that I was here to coerce her into participating in another nonmusical activity.

"What's the name of it?" I asked.

"It's Beethoven's *Moonlight Sonata,*" Amelia said. "It's a really famous piece."

"I can see why. Look at my arm." I held it up. "I have goose bumps. But I think that might have more to do with your playing than anything else."

I wasn't humoring her. Amelia was an extraordinarily gifted musician. She played with such grace and feeling, the music soared inside me in a way I'd never experienced before, and especially not with classical music.

Amelia bowed her head. "Thanks," she said, almost begrudgingly.

"Play me something else," I suggested.

Amelia looked up. "Really?"

"Yes."

"What do you want to hear?"

"You pick. Anything," I said. I sat down on the white wing chair and folded my hands on my lap.

Amelia considered my request, and for a moment, I thought she was going to refuse. But then she shrugged one shoulder, lifted her fingers to the keyboard, and began to play. This piece was quite different from the last. Her fingers danced over the keyboard, teasing the song out, while I leaned back in my chair and let the music wash over me.

Chapter Six

"I'm impressed. I had no idea you were so devious, Miranda," Dex said that evening.

We were sitting in the theater while we waited for our movie to start, sharing a large popcorn with extra butter. One of the many things I liked about Dex was that his appetite was as large as mine. I could never be one of those girls who claim to get full grazing on lettuce leaves and carrot sticks.

"What do you mean?" I asked, reaching for a handful of popcorn.

"You totally played Amelia," Dex said.

"No, I didn't," I said.

"Sure you did," Dex said. "She wasn't talking to you before, right? But then you complimented her, schmoozed her up, and *ta-da*—now you're best buddies."

"Ta-da? There was no ta-da," I said. "First of all, we're not best buddies. We've only just gotten to the point where she'll stay in the same room with me. And second, I wasn't trying to manipulate her into liking me."

"Deny it all you want," Dex said. "But it's hard to argue with results. Didn't you say she agreed to go to that pottery painting place with you tomorrow?" He smiled at me in a way that made my stomach flutter. "That's definite progress."

Amelia had agreed to go to the pottery studio with me, which I considered a minor victory. I hadn't expected her to go along with the idea when I proposed it, but she surprised me.

"Sure," Amelia had said, shrugging. "It's better than stupid Monopoly."

I now reached for another handful of popcorn, tossing the buttery kernels into my mouth one at a time. "I was going to suggest we go to the pool, but Amelia can't swim."

"Really?" Dex frowned. "That's not very safe, especially when you live in a town surrounded by water."

"That's what I thought," I said. "You're a lifeguard. Do you ever give swimming lessons?"

"I could. Does she want to learn how to swim?" Dex asked.

I shrugged. "Probably not, but I'll ask her. Although considering how contrary Amelia is, I'd probably have better luck if I use reverse psychology. I'll tell her that under no circumstances is she ever allowed near a pool. She'll be swimming laps within a week just to prove me wrong."

"See? You *are* devious," Dex said.

"Dex?"

Dex and I both looked up at the sound of his name. The girl standing there in the aisle, beaming down at my boyfriend, was gorgeous. She was tall and slender, with thick golden blond hair that fell in waves down around her shoulders. She had large brown eyes, a perfectly straight nose, and full lips that were curled up in a devastating smile. She was probably the prettiest girl I'd ever seen outside of movies and magazines. She was even prettier than Hannah.

I hated her on sight.

"Wendy!" Dex said.

He stood and, to my horror, *hugged* her. Wendy? Had Dex ever mentioned a Wendy? And then, with dawning dread, I realized who she was.

Wendy Erikson. Dex's ex-girlfriend.

Hannah once told me Dex and Hannah had broken up when Wendy transferred from Orange Cove High to a prep school somewhere up north, so she'd be closer to New York City, where she was pursuing a modeling career. Hannah had been incredibly envious of Wendy's success there. I think it was part of what had gotten Hannah so gung ho about launching her own modeling career.

But knowing that Wendy was somewhere out there—perfect and pretty, but also far, far away—was another thing entirely to being confronted with her gorgeousness in the middle of the Orange Cove Cineplex.

"How have you been?" Dex asked Wendy, his voice warmly affectionate.

"Great," she said, touching his arm. "How about you?"

"Good," Dex said. Then, as if just remembering that I was sitting there, he turned to me. "This is my girlfriend, Miranda."

Dex grabbed my hand, gently pulling me to my feet. I felt a teeny-tiny bit better. He had told her I was his girlfriend. This meeting would have been ten thousand times more hideous if Dex had introduced me as just a friend. And he was holding hands with me in front of her. That was a good sign, too.

Wendy beamed at me. "Hi, it's nice to meet you. I'm Wendy," she said. She was dressed simply in a white tank top, khaki shorts, and silver leather sandals, but somehow managed to make the ensemble look effortlessly chic. A gold pendant in the shape of a W hung at her throat, and she hooked one finger over it, sliding it absently up and down its gold chain.

I forced my mouth into a smile. "Hi. It's nice to meet you, too," I said.

Wendy turned her attention back to Dex. "So, what've you been up to, Dex?"

"Same old. Surfing, lacrosse, you know. How about you? How was boarding school?" he asked.

"Good, but crazy busy between school and work. It doesn't leave a lot of room for downtime." She laughed, and stroked a stray lock of blond hair from her cheek. "It's actually a relief to be home for the summer."

"You're here for the whole summer?" Dex asked interestedly.

I'd actually been wondering the same thing. Only in my head, it was more of a high-pitched, panic-stricken scream: *You're here for the whole summer? NO!!!!!!*

"Most of it," Wendy said. She touched Dex's arm again. I really, really wished she would stop doing that. "How about you? How's old Orange Cove High?"

"No complaints. Our lacrosse team made it to sectionals, which was cool, although we lost in the semifinals."

"What are you doing this summer? Are you lifeguarding again?" she asked.

"Sure am," he said. He grinned. "It's the only job I know of where you get to go for a swim whenever you need to cool off."

"That's great. We had so much fun at the pool last summer, didn't we?" Wendy said. "And I had the best tan of my life. I guess that's the perk of being the lifeguard's girlfriend." Wendy grinned at me, including me in the joke.

I wanted to smile confidently, but my face had gone numb. She had spent all last summer hanging out at the pool? Why hadn't Dex told me that? And what other pertinent nuggets of information was he holding back?

"Miranda hasn't been by the pool yet," Dex said. He squeezed my hand. "She's been too busy working to come by and worship at my lifeguard chair."

Wendy and I both rolled our eyes at this, and Dex laughed.

"You should keep an eye on him, Miranda. The girls at the pool are always all over the lifeguards." Wendy smiled and winked at Dex. "That's why I spent so much time hanging out there last year."

What? *What!* I felt like screaming, but managed to swallow it back. Even though we went to different schools, I knew all too well how popular Dex was. One of Hannah's friends, Avery, had had a huge crush on him last year. She was furious when he and I started dating, and from what Hannah told me, Avery wasn't the only one. But something about Dex had always made me feel safe trusting him with my heart.

But that was before I'd seen firsthand how gorgeous Wendy was. And before I'd heard about the hordes of bikini-clad girls who were apparently lying in wait for my boyfriend.

Wendy looked up and waved at someone in the back of the theater.

"I have to go. Jody's waiting for me," she said. She smiled at Dex and gave his arm one last squeeze. "It was great to see you. Maybe we can get together sometime for a coffee and catch up more."

"Sure," Dex said easily. "Good to see you, Wends."

Wends? He was using a special, cutesy nickname for her? Could I just die now?

We sat back down. I wanted him to say something reassuring—something like *Blond models are seriously overrated* or *She may seem like a nice girl on the surface, but underneath it she has a small, charred piece of coal in place of a heart*—but Dex just smiled to himself and shook his head.

"Wendy Erikson," he said. "It's been a long time since I've seen her."

There were so many things I wanted to ask. *Were you ever in love with her? Are you still in love with her? And if so, where does that leave me?*

But the words stuck in my throat like a piece of dry toast. I wasn't at all sure I wanted to hear his answers.

The lights dimmed, and the previews began. I huddled back in my seat, wrapping my arms around my body while I tried to swallow back my anxiety.

Dex leaned toward me. "Want some popcorn?" he whispered, his warm breath tickling my ear.

"No, thanks. I'm good," I said.

"Are you sure?" he asked, jostling the bag to tempt me. "I've never known you to turn down popcorn. Especially greasy movie theater popcorn with the fake butter flavoring on it. Your favorite."

"I'm sure," I said dully. My stomach felt so pinched and sour, the last thing I wanted was food.

"More for me," Dex said. He leaned back in his seat, but he reached over and took my hand in his, entwining our fingers together. My heart lightened a bit. If Dex still liked Wendy, he'd be sitting with *her*, holding *her* hand, I reminded myself. There was no reason to be so paranoid.

"I think I will have some popcorn after all," I said, reaching for the bag with my free hand.

An older woman with short frosted-blond hair who was sitting directly in front of us twisted around in her seat and shot me a dirty look.

"Shh!" she said. "The movie is starting."

I could feel a hot flush blooming on my face. "Sorry," I said, even though I thought she was being a bit sensitive. The movie hadn't even started yet; they were just at the part of the previews where they ask everyone to turn off their cell phones.

The woman turned back around, and I cringed down in my seat. A moment later, I felt an elbow pushing softly against me. I turned to find Dex grinning at me.

"You're in trouble now," he said softly in my ear.

I couldn't help giggling, but I put my hand over my mouth to muffle the sound.

Dex nodded at the woman sitting in front of me, and lifted one finger to his lips. "Shhhh!" he said.

I opened my eyes wide and mouthed, "Stop it!"

Dex grinned at me. I felt the familiar zing. The movie began, and all worries of Wendy Erikson faded away.

Chapter Seven

Amelia and I sat quietly at our table, dabbing paint on white ceramic. She was painting pink and purple flowers on a giant coffee mug, while I was doing a poor job of adding polka dots to a rectangular platter. I'd had a vague idea of sending it to Sadie as a birthday present when I began the project, but it was turning out to look like something a three-year-old would paint.

Amelia hadn't said much since we biked over to the ceramic studio. Even so, I had the definite feeling that there had been a significant decrease in her hostility level. Was this the result of my having expressed an interest in her music? I wondered. Or was something else going on?

"Have you done this before?" I asked Amelia.

"No," she said. "I mean, I've painted before. In art class at school."

"I'm not much of an artist, either. Obviously." I scrutinized my platter. I'd painted too many polka dots on one half of the platter, and then overcorrected by not painting nearly enough on the other side. I sighed and dipped my paintbrush into the paint pot. Maybe I should just forget the polka dots and paint the whole thing purple instead. "What do you like to do? Other than playing the piano, I mean."

Amelia shrugged. "Nothing really."

"Come on. There must be something."

Amelia shook her head.

"Do you like reading?"

"You mean for school? I guess."

"No, I mean for fun," I said. "I was about your age when I discovered all of my favorites. *Secret Garden*. *The Little Princess*. Oh, and *Anne of Green Gables*. That's my absolute favorite book of all time."

"I've never heard of it," Amelia said.

"I'll loan you my copy, if you want," I said.

She shrugged—clearly, reading was not a passion—but I pushed on.

"Do you play any sports?" I asked.

"No," Amelia said, this time more definite. "I'm not allowed to. I could injure my hands."

"Really?" I asked. I wasn't the most athletic girl in the world, but even so, that sounded over-the-top. Shouldn't a ten-year-old be allowed to dribble a basketball or swing a tennis racquet without worrying about career-ending injuries? "How about soccer? That's a hands-free game."

"My mom said I could still get hurt."

"Track and field?" I pressed on.

Amelia shook her head. "I don't like to run."

"Do you like movies? Or music? Pop music, I mean. You must like doing something other than just playing the piano," I persisted. "No matter how good you are or how much you love it. No one does just one thing."

"You do stuff other than math?" Amelia asked.

"Absolutely!" I said. I swirled my paintbrush over the platter. "To be honest, I don't even really do that much math. Pretty much only what I have to do for school. And for some reason, adults at parties love asking me to multiply numbers. I have no idea why. I could give them any response at all, and they wouldn't know the difference."

"You don't like math?" Amelia looked up from her coffee mug—which was looking far better than my platter—and stared at me, her mouth gaping open. "But I thought you were supposed to be gifted."

"I am. But that doesn't mean I want to spend all of my free time solving math theorems."

"My mom says that if you're given a great gift, you have a responsibility to develop it," Amelia said. She said this in a rather flat, mechanical way that made me suspect she'd heard it more than once.

"Hmm," I said. "I get what she means. But at the same time, what if you don't enjoy what you're gifted at? I think a person should be able to decide what she wants to do with her life, and not have a random talent decide it for her. It's free will."

I could tell Amelia was absorbing this. Her brow furrowed, and she chewed on her lower lip. I wondered if it had ever occurred to her that she could have a life beyond the piano. But, not wanting to stress her out, I decided to change the subject.

"Have you ever been bowling?" I asked.

Amelia shook her head. "No. Never."

"I know what we're doing tomorrow, then," I said, pulling a pot of pink paint closer. I decided to scrap the idea of polka dots altogether and try stripes instead. "And don't worry—you can't hurt your hands bowling."

•

As I biked back to the beach house in the late afternoon, I thought back on the day and decided it had been a definite improvement. After our outing to the ceramic painting studio, Amelia had spent most of the rest of the day practicing. I thought that for the first time, I'd managed to draw her out, at least for the hour or so that we painted. That was progress. And it seemed as though Amelia had a pretty good time. She'd been excited about giving the mug she painted to her mom.

As always, I could taste the salt from the sea breeze as soon as I turned onto our street. The beach house was a large, modern building designed by my architect father and paid for by my millionaire stepmother. It had seemed even larger—and lonelier—since Hannah had left for New York City. When I first moved into the beach house, I hadn't liked Hannah very much. But I'd gained an appreciation for my stepsister over the past year. True, she was selfish and spoiled, but under her glossy, excessively groomed exterior, she had a good heart.

I rode into the driveway, hopped off my bike, and wheeled it into the garage. Peyton's enormous SUV and my dad's silver sedan were both parked there, along with the shiny new Lexus Hannah had received for her sweet sixteen-birthday present.

I sighed. Great. If Dad and Peyton were both home, I was probably about to walk in on yet another fight.

I let myself in through the garage door, which opened onto a small hallway just off the kitchen. I waited there for a beat, listening for the sound of raised voices or crashing plates—sometimes Peyton liked to throw things when she was in a temper—but it was amazingly silent. I walked through the silent kitchen to the front foyer, and then made a right, heading toward my room. Or, as Peyton still liked to call it, the guest room.

Willow was asleep on her plush, round bed. She lifted her head, yawned hugely, and wagged her long, thin tail.

"Hi, Willow," I greeted her. "Do you want to go for a walk?"

She did, although it took her a few long minutes of stretching and arching her back like a cat before she'd allow me to slip on her red martingale leash and lead her out the sliding glass doors off the kitchen. My dad was sitting on the back deck, his back to me and his feet propped up on the railing, as he gazed out at the ocean.

"Hey," I said. "I was wondering where everyone was."

He twisted around in his seat, turning to see me. "Hi, sweetheart. I didn't hear you come in."

"It's windy out here," I said as my wavy brown hair whipped into my face, momentarily blinding me. "You probably can't hear much of anything."

But my father wasn't listening. He'd turned back to stare broodingly out at the ocean. His shoulders were hunched and his hands were braced against his legs.

"Is everything okay?" I asked, raising my voice a fraction to be heard over the surf and gusting wind.

"Fine, fine," Dad said, waving his hand. "Things are just . . ." He trailed off and glanced at me. "I'm sure you've noticed some tension around the house lately."

"Yeah," I said. "Maybe a little." I glanced around. "Where's Peyton?"

"She's lying down. She said she has a migraine," Dad said. From his tone, I got the distinct impression that Peyton wasn't suffering from a headache, but retreating after yet another of their frequent fights.

"It's my fault, isn't it?" I said, wrapping Willow's leash around my hand.

Dad looked up, surprised. "That Peyton has a migraine?"

"No. That you two are fighting so much. It's because I'm living here."

"Of course not! Why would you think that, honey?"

"Come on, Dad," I said. "Peyton's been furious ever since I moved in. I know it's true. I'm not blind. Or deaf, for that matter."

My father's face tightened. "You're my daughter. You'll always be welcome where I live. No one should ever make you feel otherwise."

I probably should have felt gratified that my dad was sticking up for me. For the first few years after he and my mom divorced—during which time he met and married Peyton—my dad hadn't had a lot of time for me. And then, when I first moved into the beach house the year before, he'd seemed oblivious of how Peyton treated me. He preferred to pretend that we were all one happy family, despite all evidence to the contrary. But over time, Dad slowly caught on that Peyton truly didn't want me there. And that's when the fights began.

But instead of being glad my dad was finally taking my side, knowing that I was the cause of their fights made me incredibly uncomfortable. I didn't want to be the source of so much strife.

"Every married couple has problems they work through. Peyton and I just need to improve our communication skills. That has nothing to do with you," Dad continued.

It was a nice thing to say, I thought. Even if it was a lie.

"I guess I should tell you—Sadie has asked me to move to London to live with her there," I said carefully.

My dad looked at me sharply. "Is that what you want to do?"

I shrugged. "I have mixed feelings," I said. "I keep pro-conning it. You know: coming up with all the reasons why I should go, and all the reasons why I shouldn't."

"You'd have to leave your friends. And Willow," Dad said.

"No, I can bring Willow with me. Although she'd have to travel in the cargo hold on the plane, which would probably freak her out," I said. "But yeah, there are my friends. And my school."

"You'd go to school there," Dad pointed out.

"I know. But I'm going to be writing for Geek High's literary magazine next year. That's something I've wanted to do for a long time," I said.

Dad nodded. "It sounds like you have a lot of thinking to do."

"Yes," I said. Willow whined and looked longingly out at the beach. "I'd better take her for her walk."

"Okay," Dad said. He hesitated. "Honey?"

"Yeah?"

"I'll understand if you decide to go to London. It would be a great experience and I know you miss your mom. But please don't go because you think you're not wanted here," Dad said earnestly. "I've loved having you live with us."

I smiled at him. "Thanks, Dad."

"And Peyton . . . well, I know she hasn't been entirely welcoming to you."

That was the understatement of the year, I thought. Peyton's nostrils flared with dislike every time she saw me.

"But it's not personal. I know that might not make sense to you, but it's really not about you. It has more to do with her relationship with me. I don't think she ever envisioned sharing her house with a stepchild," Dad continued. "She has a hard time adjusting to new situations."

I nodded. "I understand," I said, although I really didn't. Peyton had everything in the world—money, status, a beautiful house, a nice husband, a gorgeous daughter. She spent her days getting facials and having lunch with her friends. What did she have to be bitter about? But I appreciated that for once my dad hadn't lied to me by insisting that Peyton loved having me live with them.

Willow whined again as she caught sight of a flock of seagulls foraging on the beach. In Willow's mind, she was a great hunter. I decided not to point out to her that she'd never actually managed to catch anything. It wouldn't be good for her self-esteem.

"Come on, girl," I said, giving her leash a gentle tug. "Let's go for our walk and see if today is the day you finally catch a seagull."

Chapter Eight

When we got to the bowling alley the next afternoon, Amelia seemed nervous. She hesitated just inside the front door, standing with one leg twisted around the other, and her arms folded over her thin chest. Her eyes, normally large, seemed huge and dark in her small, angular face.

"There's nothing to be worried about," I said encouragingly.

Amelia shot me a scathing look. "I'm *not* worried," she said.

She'd been touchy all morning, ever since I first got to the Fishers' house. Any progress we'd made the day before seemed to have vanished. Amelia had barely acknowledged me when I greeted her—although she was practicing her scales at the time—and then became positively mulish when I'd reminded her we were going bowling.

"I can't," Amelia had said flatly. "I have to practice extra today to make up for the time I took off yesterday to go paint pottery."

"We were only at the ceramics studio for an hour," I'd said.

"I know! A whole hour!"

I'd tried to sweet-talk her into going with me, then tried to bribe her—promising that we'd cut tomorrow's activity short to allow her more practice time—and when that failed, I resorted to threats.

"Bowling," I said firmly. "Or else, I won't give you a moment of peace for the rest of the day."

Amelia had not given in gracefully. She scowled, and huffed, and dragged her feet getting ready to leave, until I finally pointed out that the longer it took us to get there, the less time she'd have to practice later. She finally came along, silent but seething with resentment. Amelia hadn't said a single word to me during our bike ride to the bowling alley. I decided it was time to make peace.

"Come on, this will be fun," I said encouragingly.

Amelia just looked at me, disbelief stamped on her face.

"The first thing we have to do is get bowling shoes," I said. "Look, my friend Charlie is working. Let's go say hi."

Amelia and I stood in the shoe rental line behind a family of four. Charlie smiled and waved when she saw us.

"Who's that?" Amelia asked.

"That's Charlie," I said.

"But Charlie's a boy's name," Amelia said.

"Not always. It's short for Charlotte," I explained.

Amelia's mouth twisted. "That's stupid. Girls should have girls' names. And her purple hair looks dumb."

I bit back the impulse to say something equally immature—something along the lines of *Oh yeah? Well, I'm rubber and you're glue, so anything you say bounces off me and sticks to you!* But then I remembered that I was supposed to be the mature, responsible one in our relationship, so I just smiled serenely. The family in front of us finished collecting their bowling shoes, and Charlie waved Amelia and me forward.

"Hi!" Charlie said brightly. She smiled at Amelia. "You must be Amelia. I've heard a lot about you."

Amelia shot me a deeply suspicious look, clearly not believing that I could have said anything nice about her, but finally muttered, "Hi."

Charlie raised her eyebrows at me. I rolled my eyes heavenward.

"I take it you two are here to bowl?" Charlie said.

"That's right," I said. I took off my shoes and handed them to Charlie. "I'm a size nine."

Charlie took my shoes, holding them gingerly with two fingers.

"My shoes aren't stinky," I said indignantly.

"That's what you think," Charlie said, sliding them into a cubby and handing me back a pair of ugly red-and-black bowling shoes. "But handling people's footwear is what gets me the big bucks." Charlie smiled at Amelia. "Hand over your shoes, and I'll get you set up with a pair of lovely bowling shoes, too. What size do you wear?"

"Um, no, thanks. I'm good," Amelia said.

"Aren't you going to bowl?" Charlie asked.

"Yes, she is," I said firmly.

"I want to wear my sneakers," Amelia said.

"You have to wear bowling shoes on the lanes. It's the rule," Charlie explained.

"But I don't want to wear someone else's shoes," Amelia said, looking appalled. "That's so gross."

"I know, isn't it?" Charlie agreed. "But we clean them out after every use." She demonstrated this by picking up a shoe, and spraying a perfumed cloud of Lysol into it. "See? Ninety-nine point nine percent germ free."

Amelia reluctantly kicked off her sneakers and handed them over. Charlie pushed a pair of baby blue bowling shoes with Velcro fasteners over the counter.

"I call this pair the Lucky Blues," Charlie said, with a wink in Amelia's direction. "Everyone who wears them bowls nothing but strikes." She handed me a flyer with instructions on how to log on to the computer for our assigned lane. "You're on lane three. There are instructions on how to use the bumpers—you know, those things that keep the balls from going into the gutters—on there. People like to use them for kids."

"Do I get to use the bumpers, too?" I asked.

"No," Charlie said. "You'll have to rely on your skill."

"I think I'm in trouble," I said, and we both laughed. Amelia didn't join in. She just stood there, blue shoes clutched in her hands, looking miserable.

•

Amelia was not a natural bowler. At first, she was too tentative, pushing the ball so gently, I wondered if it would come to a complete stop before it reached the pins. I tried coaching her—I wasn't a great bowler myself, but I knew the basics—but Amelia ignored me. Clearly she had decided that if I was going to make her participate in nonmusical activities, she would do her best to make the outings as unpleasant for me as possible. So far, her plan was working splendidly.

"Good job," I said when Amelia had finally put a bit of heft in her toss and managed to knock down five pins.

"Whatever."

I could feel my temper reach its breaking point. "This isn't supposed to be torture."

"You could have fooled me. You're the one who made me come here," Amelia retorted.

"I thought it would be fun," I said.

"I didn't," Amelia said. She shrugged her thin shoulders. "You can make me bowl, but you can't make me enjoy it."

"There's the spirit," I muttered.

"Hey, foxy ladies," a familiar voice said.

I turned, and saw Finn slouching over, his hands stuck in his pockets. He looked pleased with himself. I hoped he hadn't finally realized his life's ambition of successfully hacking into the CIA's computer system.

"Hey," I said, holding up my borrowed purple bowling ball. "What are you doing here?"

"I have a hot date," Finn said.

"Does anyone ever say they have a cold date? Or a lukewarm date?" I asked.

"Not me," Finn said. "I only go for the hotties."

"Lovely," I said. "Who's your date? That girl you met here the other day?"

"Yep," Finn said smugly. He regarded Amelia. "Hello. You must be Miranda's underling."

"Finn," I said warningly. Then, turning to Amelia, I said, "Amelia, this is my friend Finn. Finn, this is Amelia."

"Hi," Amelia said so softly, I wasn't sure she'd spoken at first. I glanced at her, and saw that her eyes had gone very large and very round, and she was staring at Finn as though he had personally invented the piano.

Uh-oh, I thought. I hoped Amelia wasn't developing a crush on Finn. Crushes are never easy. And crushing on an older teenage computer genius who lacks a moral compass is an especially bad idea.

"We should probably get back to our game," I said, holding up my bowling ball.

But Finn—who has never grasped a subtle hint in his life—sat down on one of our lane seats. "I have some time to kill before Phoebe gets here. I'll hang with you while I wait."

"Lucky us," I said, without enthusiasm.

While I bowled a spare, I could hear Finn chatting with Amelia.

"I hear you're a musical prodigy," he said.

"I don't know about that," Amelia said modestly.

"Are you one of those people who can hear a song once and play it perfectly?" Finn asked.

"No," Amelia said.

"That's too bad. That would be a cool thing to be able to do. Almost like a superpower," he said. Then, reconsidering, he said, "Or maybe a minor superpower. I mean, it's not like being able to morph into an animal or run faster than the speed of light."

"I can play Rachmaninoff's Piano Concerto Number Three," Amelia said. "It's one of the most difficult pieces a pianist can attempt."

"That's pretty cool," Finn said.

"Your turn," I said to Amelia. She reluctantly got up and retrieved her bowling ball from the return. I noticed that she had dropped the sullen attitude for the first time all day. I guessed it was for Finn's benefit.

I sat down next to Finn. "You're meeting Phoebe here?" I said.

"Yep," Finn said.

"You couldn't think of a better place for a first date?"

"What's better than bowling?"

"I don't know. A nice dinner out. A walk on the beach. A surprise trip to Paris," I suggested.

Finn wrinkled his nose. "That's a bit obvious, don't you think?"

"But bowling is subtle?" I asked.

"Exactly," Finn said. "Subtle and cool in a retro, old-school sort of way. Plus, I'm an excellent bowler, so it will give me a chance to show off my talents."

"You're a terrible bowler," I reminded him. "You always do that weird shimmy thing with your hips, and end up throwing it straight in the gutter."

Finn looked affronted. "I do not," he said.

"Yes, you do."

"Do not."

"Do too."

"Did you see me?" Amelia asked, appearing in front of us, her face pink with pleasure. "Did you see how many pins I knocked down?"

I glanced up at the overhead computer screen, where the ongoing score was kept. "You knocked down eight pins! Good job."

"Not bad, kid," Finn said. "But next time you should try it without the bumpers. Those are for losers."

"Finn," I said warningly.

"What?" he asked. He placed one hand, palm down, over his heart. "I always speak the truth."

I was about to tell him where he could stick his truth, but Amelia surprised me by smiling broadly. "It's okay. I should try it without the bumpers," she said.

Amazing. I spent hours and hours with Amelia, trying to break down her defenses, without any success. And then Finn swanned in, make a few smart-alecky comments, and Amelia was suddenly all smiles.

"I'm getting a soda," I said. "Amelia, do you want one?"

Amelia shook her head, but Finn perked up. "I'll take one if you're buying," he said.

"You can get your own," I said, and stomped off to the snack bar. On my way back to the lanes, I saw that there wasn't anyone waiting at the shoe rental counter, so I stopped by to chat with Charlie. She was leaning forward, elbows propped on the counter, staring vacantly out at the lanes.

"I'm so bored," she complained. "I can't believe I'm going to be stuck in here for the rest of the summer. There aren't even any windows. It's like being stuck in a really loud cave."

"At least it's cool in here," I said. "I feel sorry for Dex. He has to sit out in the sun all day." *Where he's surrounded by cute girls in tiny bikinis*, I added silently, before willing this unproductive picture out of my head.

"How is Dex?" Charlie asked.

I shrugged. "He's fine."

"Just fine?" Charlie shot me a shrewd look.

I sighed and tucked my hair behind my ears. "I met Dex's exgirlfriend the other night."

"So?"

"She's gorgeous. She's actually a model, if you can believe that. And I'm pretty sure she's still in love with him," I said.

"Why? Did she tell him that?" Charlie asked.

"No, of course not. What was she going to do? Announce, *Dex, I'm still in love with you*, right in the middle of our date?"

"Probably not," Charlie conceded. "But you have to admit, it would be a seriously gutsy move. You'd have to admire a girl who's willing to put it all out there, damn the consequences."

"Charlie!"

"Sorry. Why do you think she's still in love with him?"

"Just from the way she kept finding excuses to touch his arm. Oh, and she kept stroking her hair. Aren't those obvious signs of flirtation?" I asked.

"Hmm, I'm not sure. The arm touching, yes, definitely. But the hair stroking could just be a nervous tic. Did she expose her neck?" Charlie asked.

"What do you mean?"

"Like this." Charlie lifted her chin and tipped her head to one side. This made her look like an inquisitive, purple-haired bird. "When you see a girl doing that around a guy, it's a definite sign that she's interested in him."

"I can't remember if she did that," I said miserably. "But trust me, she's interested. I could tell. And they have this whole history together. It just makes me . . ." Insanely jealous. Absolutely miserable. Engage in wild fantasies about Wendy's perfect complexion breaking out in huge, pus-filled pimples. "Uncomfortable."

"What did Dex say about her?" Charlie asked. "Has he given you a reason to think there's something to be concerned about?"

"No, not really. But . . ."

"But what?" Charlie was starting to look impatient. She crossed her arms and pinned me with a sharp stare.

"It's probably nothing. But I keep having the feeling that there's something he's not telling me," I said.

"What about?"

"That's just it. I have no idea," I said. My stomach clenched nervously. Maybe Dex wanted to break up with me and wasn't sure how to tell me. But no, that didn't sound like him. After Charlie, he was the most honest person I knew. And when he called me last night, his voice had been warmly affectionate, and he'd been really supportive when I told him how well things had gone with Amelia at the pottery studio. But I couldn't shake the lingering worry that there was something he wasn't telling me. I just hoped that the something wasn't five-foot-nine with golden blond hair, chocolate brown eyes, and a crazy-good body.

"What's she doing back here again?" Charlie muttered, eyes narrowing. I followed her gaze and saw Phoebe McLeod walking through the front door of the bowling alley. Today, she was wearing her strawberry blond hair loose around her shoulders, and she looked bright-eyed and expectant.

"She's meeting Finn," I said.

"*What?*" Charlie asked, with such ferocity, I almost took a step back.

"They have a date. Although I told him it was totally lame of him to take her bowling on a first date. He has this delusional idea that he's going to impress her with his bowling prowess," I said.

"But Finn can't bowl. He does that weird thing where he shakes his hips right before he throws the ball," Charlie said.

"That's exactly what I told him."

We watched Phoebe's progress as she passed by the shoe rental and walked toward the lanes. She paused, glancing around until she saw Finn, who was still chatting with Amelia. Finn looked up, saw Phoebe, and stood to wave at her. Phoebe grinned back, tossed her hair over her shoulders, and waited for Finn to walk over to meet her.

"Hey, you," I heard Finn say when he reached her. "Are you ready to get beaten by the God of Bowling?"

"You wish," Phoebe replied, giggling. She punched him lightly on the shoulder. "I'm going to crush you."

"Hey, you're right about that neck thing," I said to Charlie as we watched Phoebe tip her head back, exposing a creamy expanse of neck.

"What does he see in her?" Charlie hissed.

I didn't think Charlie really wanted to hear the answer—that Phoebe was pretty, and flirty, and obviously liked Finn. I looked over at Amelia, who now stood alone at our lane, one arm wrapped around her body. I felt a surge of pity for her, as well as a flash of anger at Finn for deserting her. He might not think there was any harm in chatting Amelia up, but I knew only too well how painful it was to have an unrequited crush. It was especially hard at Amelia's age, when you wanted so badly for everyone to stop seeing you as a little kid.

"I have to go," I said.

Charlie didn't answer, and I wasn't even sure if she heard me. She was too busy staring at Finn and Phoebe, who were now walking toward the shoe rental counter.

"I wonder what size shoe she wears," Charlie muttered. "I'm going to give her the ugliest pair of bowling shoes we have."

I left Charlie to her date sabotage and headed back to Amelia. I could see her eyes shining, and wondered if it was just reflected light from the overhead halogens, or if she was holding back tears. I hesitated, wondering what to say. I didn't want to embarrass her.

"Do you think you've gotten the hang of bowling?" I asked. "Do you want to take down the bumpers and see if you can beat me?"

Amelia didn't say anything for a minute, and I wondered if she was going to return to the hostile silence she'd been treating me to all day. But then she surprised me by giving me a shy half smile, shrugged, and said, "Okay. Why not?"

Chapter Nine

TO: mirandajbloom@gmail.com
FROM: Della@DellaDeLaCourte.com
RE: A Foggy Day in London Town

Darling,

What do you mean you haven't decided where you're going to live next year!?! London is *so* much more fabulous than boring old Orange Cove!

I know that you were looking forward to writing for your school magazine, but trust me, darling—you'll have many, many more opportunities to write. But how many chances will you get to live in a dazzling international city?

I hope this reluctance doesn't have anything to do with a certain red-haired young gentleman! I know he's adorable, but really—there are plenty of cute ones over here, too. In fact, Henry was just asking about you the other day . . .

Please don't keep me in suspense for much longer . . . let me know as soon as you decide you're coming, and I'll book your plane ticket.

XXXOOO,
Sadie

I shut my laptop without replying to Sadie's e-mail. Was my mother right? *Was* I reluctant to go to London because of Dex?

I was also distracted by Sadie's mention of Henry. I'd met Henry Wentworth when I visited Sadie over the Christmas holidays, and we'd hit it off. Because of a misunderstanding with Dex—I'd accidentally given him the wrong e-mail address, and then when I didn't hear from him while I was in London, I thought he was blowing me off—I'd allowed my friendship with Henry to blossom into a brief romance. I'd put that all behind me once Dex and I sorted out our relationship, but Henry and I were still friends, e-mailing each other on occasion.

I shook off these thoughts. I was going to have to make a decision about London—and soon—but I really didn't want thoughts of Dex, Wendy, or even Henry to come into it. I needed to think about what was best for *my* future—my education, college prospects, career path. That, I reasoned, was what I would tell a friend who was in a similar situation.

I glanced at the clock and wondered what time the pool opened. I had weekends off from my job at the Fishers', but Dex had a more erratic work schedule. Sometimes he was on the early shift at the pool, sometimes the evening, and he rarely got two days off in a row, unless he specifically requested them. He'd told me the night before that he'd be on duty at the pool that morning.

I put on my boring navy blue tank suit, wishing, not for the first time, that I had enough style sense to pick out a trendy little bikini. The problem was, I had no idea what would look good on me. I made a mental note to ask Hannah for help when she returned from her trip to New York City. I might attend a school full of geniuses, but none of them matched Hannah's brilliance when it came to clothes and shopping.

It was ten past nine when I biked into the parking lot at the public pool. The temperature was just starting to heat up, the sun blasting down through a cloudless sky. By two, it would be painful to be anywhere near the blacktop parking lot. I dismounted my bike, locked it to the bike rack, and headed through the gate in the chain-link fence to the pool inside.

The pool was a large rectangle with half of the space roped off into lanes and the other half left open for the kids to noodle around in. There were already a few dozen people in the water—some serious-looking swimmers cutting easily through the water as they did their laps and a bunch of kids paddling and splashing around one another like a family of playful otters.

There was a cement deck surrounding the pool, and a number of chaises lined up on either of the long sides. On the short side closest to the parking lot, there was a snack bar, changing rooms, and an office where the lifeguards hung out when they weren't on duty.

I immediately looked up at the guard chair to see if Dex was there. He wasn't. Instead, there was an athletic-looking girl with short brown hair and wearing an orange tank suit, sitting in the guard chair. She had a whistle on a cord around her neck, and looked very capable and professional. I gave her a smile—she didn't return it, but then again, maybe she didn't see me—and then headed over to one of the empty chaise longues. I spread my towel over the chaise, took off my T-shirt and shorts, and lay down, feeling incredibly self-conscious. I glanced around.

Dex was nowhere to be seen. He'd told me that the guards only spent a half hour at a time in the chair. It was hard to keep up the constant vigilance needed while sitting out in the hot sun for longer than that. Once a shift was over, the lifeguard coming off duty would head into the air-conditioned office, to cool off, rehydrate, and wait for his or her next shift.

I could already see that Wendy had been right about the bikini girls. There were already quite a few of them at the pool, despite the earlyish hour. They were stretched out on chaises, their hair fanned out behind them and golden tanned skin on display. How many of them were there just to flirt with my boyfriend? I worried.

And then, as though I'd conjured her out of my thoughts, I saw her. Wendy Erickson. She and a friend were occupying two chaise longues on the side of the pool opposite from where I was. She was sitting up on her chaise, talking animatedly to her friend, but occasionally glancing around, as though checking to see if anyone was admiring her. And, as much I hated to admit it, there was a lot to admire. Wendy was wearing a tiny white-and-pink-striped bikini and large round sunglasses that made her look like a movie star. Her long blond hair was tied back with a brown tortoiseshell hair clip. Her friend was pretty, too—she had long, straight brown hair, a heart-shaped face, and a cute figure—but she wasn't nearly as glamorous as Wendy. Wendy's head swiveled in my direction, and before I had a chance to look away, she caught me watching her. She smiled and raised a hand in greeting. I gritted my teeth and waved back.

A wave of sickly hot insecurity washed over me. Why was she here? I wondered. How much time did she spend at the pool? Was she here to see Dex? And, if so, why hadn't he told me he'd seen her here?

"Miranda? Is that you?"

I looked up at the familiar voice, and my heart fell even further. Felicity Glen and Morgan Simpson were towering over me, both wearing unpleasant smirks on their faces. I'd been so busy worrying about Wendy, I hadn't seen them approach.

Felicity and Morgan went to school with me at Geek High. Felicity was petite with thick dark hair, catlike green eyes, a button nose, and Angelina Jolie lips. Morgan was short and square, with a round face and an unflattering dirty blond bob. They'd never liked me, which was fine by me, because I'd never cared for them much, either.

"Hey," I said without enthusiasm.

"What are you wearing? That bathing suit looks like something a seventh grader would wear," Felicity said. She smirked. "I guess if you don't have anything up top, it limits your options."

Was it any wonder my nickname for Felicity was the Felimonster? To make matters worse, Felicity was wearing a chocolate brown bikini edged with a thick band of turquoise that showed off her figure perfectly, including her more than adequately endowed top half. Even Morgan was wearing a bikini, although hers had a red tank top that came down over her belly button, exposing only a few inches of pasty white belly flesh.

My bathing suit—a boring navy Speedo—was so old I might well have had it since seventh grade. A hot flush spread over my face.

"Don't get too close to the pool, Felicity," I said.

"Why's that?" she asked.

"Haven't you seen *The Wizard of Oz*?" I asked.

"Of course I have," she snapped. "Duh, who hasn't?"

"Well, then you know what water does to witches," I said sweetly, enjoying the flash of rage that contorted Felicity's pretty face.

"Whatever," Felicity said. She tossed her dark highlighted hair back, turned on one perfectly pedicured pink toe, and stalked off, Morgan hurrying behind her.

I lay back in my chaise, trying to relax. It was hard to do. Between Felicity's and Morgan's hostile glares, and Wendy looking golden and gorgeous as she sunned herself on her chaise, my entire body was stiff with tension.

Maybe I should just go, I thought. I could slink back to the beach house and set fire to my horrible bathing suit. Could you burn bathing suits? I wondered. Or would the resulting smoke be too toxic? Maybe I should just throw it out instead. Less dramatic, but probably safer.

Yet at the same time, I didn't want to leave. Despite my ugly bathing suit and general insecurity about how I would fare in a direct comparison to the gorgeous Wendy, I knew I had to see Dex's reaction to Wendy and all of the other sunbathing girls. I needed to know if there really was something to worry about, or if I was just blowing it all out of proportion.

Then suddenly I saw a flash of red in the corner of my eye. It was Dex, emerging from the lifeguard office, his copper red hair gleaming in the sun. He was wearing a loose white T-shirt that had the word LIFEGUARD printed on both front and back, orange swim trunks, a black butt-pack that all of the lifeguards seemed to wear, and sunglasses to shade his pale blue eyes from the intense sun. I wasn't sure if I was just imagining it, but it seemed to me that as he began to walk around the perimeter of the pool, there was a general stirring of interest among the girls.

"Hi, Dex," I heard one of them call out.

"Are you here to save us?" another asked flirtatiously.

Dex smiled and waved, but didn't stop, not even when he passed by Wendy, despite the fact that she propped herself up on her elbows, shook back her long golden blond locks, and gave Dex a dazzling smile. Dex just continued his walk, turning and then turning again, until he was headed in my direction. And then, when he saw me, he did stop.

"Hey," he said, his voice full of pleasure. "I didn't know you were going to be here today."

"Surprise," I said, grinning back at him. "It's my day off, so I thought I'd come by to see you in action."

Dex leaned over and kissed me lightly. I couldn't help feeling a surge of victory amidst the familiar zing his kisses always set off inside me. *Take that, bikini girls,* I thought.

"Nice butt-pack," I said.

"Isn't it, though? I think it makes me look extra-tough," Dex said, flexing his biceps.

"Definitely," I said.

Dex glanced behind him, where the brunette lifeguard was watching us from her perch. "I have to go get on the chair. We're still on for tonight, right?"

I nodded happily. "What do you want to do?"

"My friends are having a cookout over by the beach. Do you want to go?"

"Sure," I said. Since Dex and I went to different schools, I hadn't met many of his friends. I felt a fluttering mixture of pleasure that he wanted me to meet them and nervousness over what they would think of me. "Should I bring anything?"

"Just yourself." Dex smiled. "I'll pick you up at seven, okay?"

"Great," I said.

He kissed me again, his lips light against mine in a way that made everything go blurry around the edges. "I'll see you later."

Dex turned away and walked over to the chair.

The athletic female lifeguard climbed down, and Dex took her place. He sat with his back erect, his expression unusually serious, as he scanned the swimmers. A group of kids was taking turns cannonballing into the pool, aiming their jumps so that they'd land on one another. Dex blew on his whistle and told them to cut it out.

The female lifeguard turned and walked back around the perimeter of the pool, in the opposite direction Dex had just come from. I guessed that this walk around the pool was required of both the incoming and outgoing lifeguards on each shift change. As she passed by me, the female lifeguard—who had ignored me when I came in—glanced curiously at me. Now that she knew I was Dex's girlfriend, I clearly rated extra interest. I could also see, out of the corner of my eye, Felicity and Morgan gawking at me. A quick glance in Wendy's direction let me know she wasn't staring, but I was sure she'd taken note of how Dex had greeted me.

Smiling to myself, I settled back on the chaise. But as the lingering effects of Dex's kiss wore off, an entirely unwanted thought popped into my head: If I was this insecure about how girls were throwing themselves at Dex when we lived in the same town, what would it be like if I lived on an entirely different continent?

Chapter Ten

"**I** need your help," I said to Hannah over the phone.

"What?" she yelled so loudly, I had to hold the phone away from my ear. I could hear music blaring in the background on her end.

"Where are you?"

"A club," Hannah said.

I glanced at the clock. "But it's only five. And anyway, I didn't think you were old enough to get into clubs," I said.

"Fashion people don't care about things like that here," Hannah said, in a tone of bored indifference. "And it's not like I'm drinking or anything."

"That's good," I said. "I need your help."

"Okay, but make it quick," Hannah said.

"I'm going to a party at the beach with Dex this evening, and I have no idea what to wear," I said.

Hannah's tone became brisk and businesslike. "Okay, here's what you need to do. Are you listening?"

"Yes," I said.

"Go into my room," Hannah said.

"Okay." I headed to Hannah's room, the portable phone tucked under one ear. Her room was very girly—it had lilac-colored walls, a big canopy bed swathed with white tulle, and a vintage vanity table covered in makeup and perfume. "Now what?"

"Go into my closet," Hannah directed.

I obligingly stepped into her enormous walk-in closet, which was crammed full of clothes, shoes, and handbags.

"Do you see the rack with the dresses on it?" Hannah continued.

"No," I said, overwhelmed by the sheer amount of stuff she owned. I turned around slowly in place. "Oh, wait, yes. It's right here."

"Okay. In the very middle of that rack, there's a red strapless Juicy Couture sundress. Do you see it?"

I looked for the color red. It took me a few moments, but I finally saw a glimpse of it wedged between a Lilly Pulitzer pink sundress and a long green knit dress.

"Are you still there?" Hannah asked in my ear.

"Yes. I think I found it." I pulled the hanger with the dress out and looked at the label. "Juicy Couture, right?"

"That's right. Wear that. It'll be perfect," Hannah said.

I looked at the red dress uncertainly. It was definitely cute—strapless with a smocked bodice and a tiered ruffle skirt. I just wasn't sure if it was the sort of dress a nonfashion girl like me could carry off. I lived in T-shirts and shorts.

"Do you like it?" Hannah asked.

"Isn't it sort of bare?"

"What do you mean?"

"It's just so short. And so strapless."

"That's why it's so perfect."

"I don't know," I said dubiously.

"Trust me," Hannah said. "You'll look gorgeous. Look, I have to go."

"Wait! What shoes should I wear with it?"

Hannah considered this. "Well, if you're going to be at the beach, you don't want to wear heels."

Since I didn't own any high heels, this wasn't really a problem.

"You have flip-flops, right?" Hannah said.

"Yeah," I said. "But they're not nice. They're just plain black plastic ones from Target."

"Those will be fine," Hannah said confidently. "Once you're on the beach, you can kick them off and go barefoot."

"Okay," I said, feeling a bit better. I still wasn't sure if I could pull off the dress, but Hannah knew more about these things than I could ever hope to. If she said this was the right thing to wear, I had to trust her judgment.

"I really have to go," Hannah said. "See you Sunday!"

"Bye. And, Hannah?"

"Yeah?"

"Thanks," I said, meaning it.

"No problem," Hannah said.

I smiled and turned off the phone. Maybe it wasn't so terrible having a stepsister after all.

·

When Dex pulled into the beach parking lot, it felt like the butterflies in my stomach had started to dive-bomb one another. What if Dex's friends didn't like me? What if I wasn't the sort of girl they expected him to date?

There were already a bunch of cars parked in the sandy lot, and as I climbed out of Dex's car, I could see a knot of people gathered near the barbecues. The beach wasn't visible—you had to walk up the boardwalk, which rose over a grass-covered dune—but there was a recreational area back by the parking lot, complete with a playground, basketball courts, a volleyball net, and picnic tables.

"Ready to meet everyone?" Dex asked, extending a hand to me. He didn't seem to have any clue how nervous I was.

I took his hand in mine, and instantly felt better. "Sure," I said, trying to sound confident.

We walked over toward the group. They had one of the barbecues fired up and were cooking hot dogs over smoking coals.

"Hey, Dex!" a few people called out. "Hey, man!"

Dex bumped fists with a few of the guys—all of whom looked athletic and vaguely familiar—and introduced me, although their names almost instantly slipped from my memory. I guessed some of the guys were on Dex's lacrosse team, and were vaguely familiar from the few games I'd watched at the end of the school year. They all smiled and said hello to me, and I began to feel my nerves loosen. I even saw a few people I knew, like Hannah's friends Tiffany and Britt. They were pretty identical twins, who both had their long hair in braids.

And then I saw Avery Tallis.

Avery was a thin-faced girl with narrow brown eyes flecked with gold and a very pointed chin. She wore her dark hair very short, and was already sporting a tan, shown off to great effect in a short lemon yellow sundress.

At one time, Avery had been Hannah's best friend, and was a semipermanent feature at the beach house. But then Avery stole a cashmere sweater out of Peyton's closet. Peyton had blamed me at first—naturally—until Hannah found out that Avery was the culprit. Ever since then, Avery hadn't been over and I'd gotten the definite feeling that her friendship with Hannah had cooled off.

I knew Avery didn't like me. When we'd first met, and she learned I was a student at Geek High, she had tried to manipulate me into doing her homework for her. I'd refused, of course, and from her annoyed reaction, I'd gotten the definite impression that

Avery wasn't used to people saying no to her. And then there was Dex. Avery had a huge crush on Dex, and after he broke up with Wendy, she'd launched a full-scale campaign to become his next girlfriend. Instead, Dex had started dating me.

Avery was now talking animatedly to Tiff and Brit, her eyes sparkling and her teeth flashing white in her tanned face. I had to admit, she was very striking. She wasn't as classically beautiful as Wendy Erickson or Hannah, but she was the sort of person who always stood out from the crowd, as though she'd been drawn with bolder strokes than everyone else.

She turned suddenly and met my gaze. Her golden brown eyes narrowed, and the smile left her face. Her gaze moved downward, taking in Dex's and my linked hands.

Uh-oh, I thought, with a sense of impending doom.

Avery walked purposely toward us, with a calculating smile on her catlike face. I braced myself.

"Hi, Dex," Avery said, giving him a huge smile. Her eyes flicked toward me. "Hello, Miranda. It's strange to see you here. Without Hannah, I mean."

Step one of the attack: Let me know that I'm the outsider.

As if I needed reminding, I thought.

"She came with me," Dex said. I looked up at him, and he gave me a quick wink. He knew exactly what Avery was up to. I wasn't surprised. One of the things I loved about Dex was how perceptive he was about people. It would have been incredibly annoying if he were taken in by Avery's superficial friendliness.

"Hannah's still in New York," I added.

"Isn't that Hannah's dress?" Avery asked, her thin dark eyebrows arching up as she looked me over.

Step two: Put me on the defensive.

"She said I could borrow it," I said, and was then instantly annoyed with myself for feeling like I had to explain. What I was wearing wasn't any of Avery's business. She and Hannah weren't even friends anymore.

"Oh," Hannah said, as though she didn't quite believe this. "It looks really"—she paused to look me up and down again— "*different* on you."

Step three: Make me feel as uncomfortable as possible about my physical appearance.

And the worst of it was, her ploy was working. I was incredibly aware of just how much I didn't fit with Dex's crowd. I was the outsider. A stranger. Sure, the guys had all been nice enough to me, although that was probably for Dex's sake. But I wasn't at all like the pretty, polished girls his friends dated. Like the girl he used to date, for that matter. The sort of girls who knew how to tweeze their eyebrows, and what conditioner would make their hair shiny, and where to buy trendy clothes. In fact, I felt like a fraud standing there in Hannah's dress, acting as though I belonged there, when I so very clearly didn't.

"Avery!" Britt called. "Come back here. We totally need your opinion on whether Tiff should get these shoes." She waved the glossy magazine the twins had apparently been studying for inspiration.

"Coming," Avery said. She gave Dex a wide, flirtatious smile. "Cute top, Dex," she said, plucking at the sleeve of his aqua blue polo shirt. "It really brings out your eyes."

"Thanks, Avery," Dex said politely, although I could hear amusement in his voice.

Avery smiled at him, and then, without saying another word to me, she turned and headed back to where her friends were poring over the magazine.

"Something tells me you're not Avery's favorite person," Dex said.

"Whatever gave you that idea?" I muttered, crossing my arms.

Dex glanced down at me, as first surprise and then concern

registering in his pale blue eyes. He took my hand and led me a few steps away from the crowd of his friends.

"What's wrong?" he asked, taking care to keep his voice soft.

"Nothing," I said, shaking my head.

"You're not letting Avery get to you, are you?" Dex asked. "You know what she's like."

I smiled faintly. "I know what she's like," I said.

"So why are you letting her get to you?"

"I'm not."

Dex raised his eyebrows. I knew he knew I wasn't being entirely truthful, but what was I supposed to say? *I don't think I fit in with your friends? After years of geekdom, I feel uncomfortable around the shiny, popular people?*

"Come on, let's go get some hot dogs," Dex said. "And then I'll challenge you to a game of hoops. One-on-one, you against me."

"I can't play basketball."

"Good, then we should definitely place a bet. Let's see—if I win, you have to wash my car—"

"No way!" I said.

"—and if you win, I'll give you another driving lesson," Dex finished.

"Absolutely not!" I said. "First of all, there's no way I'd win, and I don't want to wash your car. And second, I don't really want another driving lesson, either."

"Why not?" Dex asked, look affronted. "I'm a great driving teacher."

I glanced over at the crowd of his friends. A few of the guys had gotten out a soccer ball, and were kicking it back and forth. Two girls joined them, and surprised me by being fairly good players, despite the fact that they were wearing miniskirts and flip-flops. Meanwhile, Tiffany's boyfriend, Roy, was holding up a creation of three hot dogs, stacked vertically.

"It's a triple-decker dog!" Roy announced triumphantly, and then stuffed the whole thing into his mouth, to the cheers of the crowd.

"Don't you want to hang out with your friends? I don't want to get in your way," I said. I glanced over at the girls who were sitting at the picnic table, drinking Diet Cokes and talking animatedly. Avery sat in the middle of the group, holding court. When she saw me glance over, she smirked at me. Clearly, I would not be welcome there.

Great, I thought. So much for the social triumph of the geek girl.

Dex's hand encircled my wrist, and he tugged on it gently.

"I want to hang out with you," he said. "Now come on. Let's go shoot some hoops."

Chapter Eleven

I was sitting on my bed, reading, when I heard Hannah's voice echo in the hallway.

"I'm home!"

Willow was reclining on her bed, but at the noise she lifted her head and her ears perked up.

"It's okay, girl. It's just Hannah," I told her. Willow lay back down with a grunt and promptly fell back asleep.

I stood up, stretching, and padded out to meet my stepsister. I was surprised by how much I'd missed her and how empty the house had seemed in her absence.

By the time I got to the foyer, Hannah wasn't there, although her hot pink luggage was piled by the front door. I heard voices from the kitchen, and headed back there. Hannah was standing at the island, drinking Diet Coke from a can, while Peyton fussed around her.

"Hey," I said. "You cut your hair!"

Hannah beamed at me, turning her head from one side to the other, so I could admire her new look. She'd cut her long hair to a shoulder-length shaggy bob with bangs. It made her look so much older and more sophisticated, all traces of the Disney princess gone.

"What do you think?" she asked.

"I love it!" I said honestly. "You look amazing."

"Thanks," Hannah said happily. "Jackie took me to her stylist to get it cut. He's really famous. He does the hair for all kinds of celebrities and movie stars."

I was about to ask whose hair he cut, but Peyton's expression stopped me. Her nose was flaring, which was always a danger sign. Hannah didn't seem to notice.

"Do you want to see my portfolio?" Hannah asked.

Peyton frowned. "Your portfolio?" she repeated.

"Hold on," Hannah said, and practically skipped out of the room. Apparently, Hannah no longer planned to keep her modeling plans a secret from her mother. I glanced at Peyton—her face was pinched with displeasure—but I looked away before she felt the weight of my stare.

Hannah reappeared, with a black leather-bound book in her arms. She looked radiantly happy. "Wait until you see these photographs. They're amazing," she said, setting it down on the counter.

"So this is where everyone is," Dad said, appearing in the kitchen door. He hadn't shaved that morning, and he looked tired and rumpled. A few nights earlier, I'd found him sleeping on the couch in the living room. I wondered if he'd spent last night there, too.

"Hi, Richard! I'm back!" Hannah said.

"Hi, Hannah," Dad said, giving my stepsister a smile and a pat on the back. "How was your trip?"

"Fab-u-lous," Hannah said, drawing the word out into three syllables. "I was just about to show Mom and Miranda my new portfolio."

"Portfolio?" Dad asked. He looked at Peyton, who raised her eyebrows and shrugged.

We all stepped closer to look, while Hannah slowly turned the pages.

"Wow," I said, impressed.

The book was filled with page after page of professionally shot photographs, close-ups, and full-body shots, all featuring Hannah. She was right—they were amazing. Hannah looked absolutely beautiful in each and every picture. In fact, she looked like a real model out of a magazine.

For the first time, I appreciated my stepsister's obvious talent. Maybe her aspirations to become a model weren't as frivolous as I'd first thought. In fact, I felt a little ashamed of myself that I hadn't believed in her, and resolved to be more supportive from here on out.

"You look beautiful, sweetheart," Dad said.

"Thanks," Hannah said. She looked up at her mother, who had remained silent. "What do you think?"

Peyton drew in a deep breath. "They're very good," she finally said.

"Really?" Hannah was delighted. "You like them?"

"Yes, of course. But we've already talked about this," Peyton said. She folded her arms over her bony chest, clearly bracing herself for battle. "You're not running off to New York to model. You're going to get your education first."

"Peyton, you should hear her out," Dad said.

"She's my daughter, Richard," Peyton said sharply.

"Don't worry," Hannah said quickly. "I'm not dropping out of school, Mom. And I'm not moving to New York."

"See? That's good. Nothing to worry about," Dad said.

Peyton shot him the sort of look that would have turned my blood to ice. She was clearly not pleased with my dad's input. "Then what exactly are you proposing to do with this portfolio?" she asked.

Hannah drew in a deep breath, squared her shoulders, and said, "I want to audition for some local modeling jobs. Jackie talked to an agency in Miami that's agreed to represent me, and they said there are lots of opportunities for models in South Florida. I want to try it, just for the summer. You know—see if I get any work, see if I'm any good at it, see if I like it." Hannah spoke quickly and earnestly, looking hopefully at Peyton. "I promise I won't miss any school, once it starts," she added.

When Hannah finally finished, there was a long silence. Dad, Hannah, and I all looked at Peyton. She stood perfectly still, arms still folded across her chest, and stared at her daughter.

Finally, Dad spoke. "That sounds like a reasonable plan. Don't you think, Peyton?"

"You're not going to Miami by yourself," Peyton said. "It's not safe."

"You can come with me on every job," Hannah said. "In fact, you sort of have to. The agency requires I have a chaperone because of my age."

"And you'll check with me first before you accept any jobs?" Peyton said, hedging.

Hannah beamed, sensing that she had already won the battle. "Of course!"

Peyton sighed. "Okay. You can try it for the summer."

Hannah let out a high-pitched squeal and threw her arms around her mother. Peyton hugged her daughter back, and her face relaxed in a rare smile.

"Thank you, thank you, thank you!" Hannah said, hopping up and down in place.

"But only for the summer!" Peyton cautioned. "When school starts back up, you're going to focus on your studies. This year is your last chance to get your grades up before you start applying to colleges next year. Deal?"

"Deal!" Hannah said. She gave her mother one last hug. "I have to go call Jackie and tell her!"

Hannah dashed from the room before she saw her mother's expression sour at the mention of Jackie's name.

"I don't like the influence that woman has over Hannah," Peyton complained. "She's the one who's putting all of these modeling ideas into Hannah's head."

"Don't worry," Dad said. "I think you're doing the right thing."

Peyton let out a bark of humorless laughter, and turned on him. "Don't worry? Why would I worry? My daughter wants to pursue a mindless career that chews up and spits out girls like her by the dozen. Do you know what kind of lives these models have? They're out all night partying and taking drugs. Most of them are washed up by the time they're twenty-five."

"Hannah has a good head on her shoulders. And you'll be there with her," Dad said.

"For now! What about in two or three years?" Peyton asked, her voice rising.

Dad held up his hands, palms facing out. "I don't want to fight, Peyton. I just think you're doing the right thing by being supportive of her dreams."

But Peyton was too angry to hear him. "How would you feel if it was your daughter? What if, instead of becoming a doctor or mathematician, or whatever it is you see Miranda doing with her life, she threw it all away to chase a crazy dream?"

"I don't want to be a doctor or mathematician. I want to be a writer," I said quietly.

Neither Peyton nor my Dad heard me.

"I'd like to think I'd support her in whatever she chose to do," Dad said. "As long as it was safe and productive."

Peyton snorted. "That's easy for you to say. It's not like Miranda could ever be a model."

I'd been about to sneak out of the kitchen—it was my normal course of action when Dad and Peyton started fighting—but at these stinging words, I froze. Her meaning was crystal clear: With my big nose and frizzy hair, I wasn't pretty enough to model. Maybe I was cute, or even attractive on a good day. But I'd never compare to Hannah. I knew it was true, but, even so, it hurt to hear it put so bluntly. Even worse, I hated that it mattered to me—I was smart and nice and a good friend. What should it matter what my hair looked like, or how big my nose was?

"Peyton!" Dad's voice cracked across the room like a whip.

Peyton looked up, the anger in his voice startling her midrant. "What?"

"Don't talk about Miranda like that!" Dad said.

"What? What did I say?" Peyton looked genuinely confused.

Dad sighed irritably. "You owe my daughter an apology," he said. When Peyton continued to look mystified, he said, through tightly clenched teeth, "For saying she could never be a model."

Peyton looked at me for the first time, as though she were surprised to see me standing there. "Do you *want* to be a model, Miranda?" she asked.

"No," I said.

"Then what's wrong with saying that she wouldn't ever be a model?" Peyton asked my father.

Dad stared at her levelly. Then he turned to me. "I apologize on behalf of my wife, Miranda. You're a lovely girl. I hope you know that."

I shifted uncomfortably on my bare feet, while a flush spread over my face and neck. "Thanks, Dad," I muttered, wanting very much to be anywhere other than where I was at the moment. "I'm, um, going to go to my room."

I strode away as fast as I could, but even so, I could still hear them arguing.

"I still don't know what I was supposed to have said that was so offensive," Peyton said.

"And that right there is the whole problem," Dad retorted.

Hannah was just coming out of her room as I was passing by. Tears were stinging in my eyes, but I quickly wiped at them with the backs of my hands before Hannah could see.

"I thought you were calling your friends," I said to distract her.

"Tiff's calling me back in a minute," Hannah said, waving her baby blue cell phone. "Did I hear my mom shouting?"

"She and my dad are fighting," I said.

"Again?" Hannah asked.

I nodded. "Again," I confirmed. "It's been pretty much non-stop while you were in New York."

Hannah leaned against the wall. "This sucks," she said.

I nodded. "Yes, it does."

We stood there quietly for a moment, hearing the sound of muffled, raised voices in the background.

"How was that party you went to?" Hannah asked.

"It was okay," I said. "I didn't really know anyone."

"Weren't Tiff and Britt there?"

I nodded. "But they were hanging out with Avery, and she wasn't what you'd call friendly. Not to me, at least."

Hannah snorted. "She's just jealous that Dex is going out with you instead of her."

"Yeah, I sort of got that impression."

The shouting voices stopped abruptly as a door somewhere slammed shut. Both Hannah and I winced.

"Do you think we should do something to help them?" Hannah asked.

"Why?"

"I don't want them to get divorced. Richard is way nicer than any of the guys my mom dated before she married him. You don't want them to break up, do you?"

I wasn't so sure. Peyton had always treated me like the ugly stepchild. Then again, I wanted my dad to be happy. And the constant fighting and door slamming was wearing on my nerves.

"How could we help them?" I asked doubtfully.

"I don't know," Hannah admitted. "Maybe we could arrange a romantic dinner for them."

I shook my head. "I think they need a marriage counselor more than a romantic dinner."

"Really?" Hannah asked interestedly. "Would that work?"

"My parents went to marriage counseling when they started to fight like this. They still got divorced, obviously. But, yeah, they were getting along better for a while," I said.

"Tiff's and Brit's mom is a therapist. I wonder if she does marriage therapy," Hannah mused.

"I don't think you should get involved," I cautioned. "It's really none of our business."

"None of our business? We have to live with them fighting all the time. It's very stressful," Hannah said.

"That's true," I agreed.

"And everyone knows that stress is terrible for your skin. And if I'm going to model, I can't risk getting zits," Hannah said.

I had to stop myself from rolling my eyes. Hannah really was pathologically narcissistic.

Hannah's cell phone began ringing. She glanced at the caller ID. "Oh, good, it's Tiff. I'll ask her if her mom counsels married couples. If so, I'll make an appointment for my mom and Richard."

"I really don't think you should," I began, but Hannah already had the phone pressed to her ear.

"Hey, you," she said into the phone. "What sort of therapy

does your mom do? Only kids? Really? So she doesn't do, like, couples counseling?" There was a pause, and then Hannah laughed. "No, not for me and Emmett. My mom and stepdad." Another pause. Hannah suddenly brightened. "Yeah, definitely ask her for a referral."

Hannah gave me a thumbs-up.

"Don't you think—" I began again.

But before I could convince her to mind her own business, Hannah turned and walked into her room, still talking on her phone. "New York was amazing. Wait until you see my new portfolio. It's amazing! You're going to freak out."

Hannah closed the door behind her with a click.

Chapter Twelve

"Hello, Miranda," Mrs. Fisher said when she opened the door. Today, she was wearing a pink button-down shirt, black capri pants, and black flats with shiny white patent toes.

It was Monday morning, and I was hopeful that my second week taking care of Amelia would go smoother than the first. It seemed like she'd started to thaw out a bit by the end of our bowling excursion. Either that, or I was finally wearing her down with my charm offensive.

"Hi, Mrs. Fisher," I said, stepping into the house. Something seemed a bit off. Then I realized what it was: It was too quiet. For the first time, Amelia wasn't at her piano when I arrived.

"Where's Amelia?" I asked.

"I asked her to wait upstairs for a few minutes so I could have a chance to talk to you alone," Mrs. Fisher said. Her expression was pleasant, but I suddenly had the feeling that I was in trouble.

"Did I do something wrong?" I asked nervously.

"No, no, of course not. Why don't we sit down for a moment?" Mrs. Fisher said, gesturing toward the cluttered living room. I perched uncomfortably on the seat of a wing chair.

Mrs. Fisher sat on the sofa, and smiled at me. "You don't have to look so worried, Miranda. You're not in trouble. I just wanted to talk to you about how you and Amelia are spending your days. She told me you took her bowling on Friday."

"She wasn't really big on the idea at first, but once we played a few games, I think she had fun," I said.

"Amelia said that you were at the bowling alley for such a long time that she had to cut her afternoon practice short," Mrs. Fisher continued.

"Maybe a little," I said. "We were at the bowling alley for a few hours."

"And that's just it," Mrs. Fisher said, raising one finger. "Amelia really can't afford to take that much time off from practicing."

I was so startled, I just saw there blinking at Mrs. Fisher.

"I know it sounds strict, but the thing is, Amelia is a profoundly gifted child. It's my job—" Mrs. Fisher stopped, and smiled at me. "*Our* job to make sure that her talent is nurtured and not wasted."

"But Amelia's only ten," I said.

Mrs. Fisher nodded solemnly. "I know. And she didn't start seriously practicing until she was eight. She has a lot of lost time to make up for. Many children who are musical prodigies are well versed in their instrument by the time they're four."

I tried again. "I thought you wanted me to encourage her to take a break from practicing," I said, now thoroughly confused. "I thought you wanted her to have some fun."

"I do," Mrs. Fisher said. "Absolutely. It's just that the fun can't cut into her practice time."

I nodded, as though I understood, even though I had no idea what she was talking about. I thought that I'd been hired to entertain Amelia. I thought I was supposed to get her to ride her bike, and run through the sprinkler, and eat ice cream like any other kid would in the summer.

It started to dawn on me that maybe Amelia's obsession with

the piano wasn't entirely self-driven. Maybe her mother was also applying pressure to her.

"So you don't want me to take Amelia bowling again?"

"Well, I suppose you could," Mrs. Fisher said doubtfully. "If you could do it in a way that wouldn't take quite so much time."

"Okay," I said.

"This is a very important time in Amelia's career. She can't afford to let up right now. There will be plenty of time for things like bowling and fun when she's older and her career is established," Mrs. Fisher explained.

Up until just that moment I'd thought Amelia was a spoiled brat. Talented, yes, maybe even brilliant. But still a brat. Now I was starting to wonder if maybe I'd been unfair.

I looked up, and saw that Amelia was lingering at the doorway, listening to her mother. Her eyes were large and dark, and she looked very, very young.

"There you are, Amelia," Mrs. Fisher said. "I was just talking to Miranda about how you need more time to practice. We've worked it all out." Mrs. Fisher glanced at her watch. "I have to run. You two have a nice day," she said, standing. As she passed by Amelia, she laid a light hand on her daughter's cheek. "You'd better start your morning practice, honey. It's getting late."

•

"So, what did you do then?" Charlie asked.

We'd met at Grounded, a coffee shop located near Geek High. At the end of the school year, Charlie had declared the coffee shop off-limits, because Mitch—Charlie's ex-boyfriend—used to work there as a barista. Luckily, Mitch had gotten a job as a counselor at a summer camp and quit his job at the coffee shop, so we were now allowed back. I was glad. I was addicted to their frozen lattes.

"What do you mean?" I asked, bending forward to slurp my latte through a straw.

"Did you and Amelia do something non-piano-related today?"

I shrugged. "We played Boggle for twenty minutes. Does that count?"

"No, Boggle doesn't count!"

"Why are you yelling at me?" I asked, blinking at her in confusion.

"Because it's your responsibility to help that girl," Charlie said. "And now that we know she has a pushy stage mother, she obviously needs your help more than ever."

"What are you talking about?" I asked. I shook my plastic cup and slurped up the last of the frozen coffee slush.

"Miranda! Amelia's only ten years old, and she's basically being handcuffed to her piano! Forced to practice for hours and hours, while her whole childhood passes her by," Charlie said. She was talking really fast, and was gesturing a lot with her hands. I wondered if she was entering one of her manic periods. Or maybe she'd just had too much coffee.

"I think 'handcuffed' is a bit strong," I said mildly. "Her parents may be putting some pressure on her, but Amelia seems pretty dedicated. Maybe she wants to be a famous pianist just as much as they want her to be."

"No ten-year-old is that dedicated to anything," Charlie said. "And I should know. I was painting seriously at that age. But I took breaks from it, joined in other activities. I played soccer, and swam, and took dance classes."

"You danced?" I asked. I hadn't known Charlie when we were ten; we'd met in the seventh grade when I first transferred to Geek Middle. "For some reason, I can't see you as a ballerina. Did you wear a pink tutu and wear your hair up in a bun?"

Charlie gave me a withering look. "I didn't take ballet," she said. "I took tap and jazz."

"No kidding! Stand up and show me something," I said. "Can you do that shuffle-ball-change thing?"

"Can we please stay on topic?" Charlie asked, making a karate chop gesture with one hand to signal that she was cutting off the dance segment of our conversation. "Seriously, Miranda, you have to help Amelia."

"What am I supposed to do? Stage a coup against her parents? Kidnap her and bring her to live at the beach house? I'm sure the Demon would love that," I said. "She hates having Willow and me there as it is. I can't imagine what she would say if I smuggled a bratty ten-year-old in, too."

"I'm not suggesting you kidnap Amelia. *Obviously*," Charlie said. "But I think you have to do whatever you can to help her break out and start thinking for herself."

"Ah. You want me to undermine her parents' authority," I said.

"Exactly," Charlie said, pointing at me.

"No," I said.

"What?"

"No," I said again. "I'm not going to undermine Amelia's mother."

"Why not?"

"Because, she's her mom. I'm just the babysitter."

"I thought you were an au pair?" Charlie interrupted.

"Whatever. Either way, I'm not the one who gets to decide whether or not Amelia's going to be a concert pianist. That's up to her and her parents. And anyway, I think it's what Amelia wants, so what right do I have to interfere with her dreams?" I said.

"I'm not saying she shouldn't follow her dreams. But if she doesn't learn how to take a break from practicing every once in a while, she's going to burn out. So think of it this way—if you teach her how to relax and do normal kid stuff, you'll actually be helping her fulfill her dreams," Charlie said.

"If I keep her from practicing, I'll be out of a job," I pointed out.

"That just means you have to be extra sneaky about it," Charlie said.

"I don't like the sound of that," I said. I glanced at my watch. "And speaking of extra sneaky, where's Finn? I thought he was meeting us here at four."

"He said he was," Charlie said.

"He's late. It's four thirty," I said. "What's he been up to lately? He's been oddly absent. Normally, I'm tripping over him every time I turn around."

"He's probably with that Phoebe McLeod chick again," Charlie said. There was a definite edge to her voice.

"Are they an item now?" I asked interestedly. I hadn't heard from Finn all weekend, and had wondered how his date with Phoebe had gone.

Charlie shrugged. "No idea," she said moodily. She picked up her cup of coffee and drained it. "I'm going to get another. Want another one?"

"No, thanks," I said. I thought Charlie would be better off getting a decaf, but I knew she'd be irritated if I mentioned it. She probably wouldn't listen to me anyway.

I watched Charlie head to the counter to order her latte, and wondered if she was right about Amelia. Should I make more of an effort to encourage her to be a regular kid? Even if that meant going against Mrs. Fisher's wishes?

Charlie returned to the table, paper cup in hand. She popped off the top and took a sip.

"What you need to do is find something that Amelia will like just as much as playing the piano," Charlie said, returning to her pet subject of the day.

"That's just it. She doesn't like doing anything else," I said.

"She'll suffer through a board game if I make her, but she doesn't even pretend to enjoy it."

"How about computer games? You could give her one of Finn's games to play."

"I don't know. His games are pretty violent. I don't think Mrs. Fisher would approve," I said. "Besides, I think Amelia was developing a little bit of a crush on Finn. I don't want to encourage it."

Charlie snorted. "She has a crush on Finn? I thought you said this girl was bright. So video games are out. What else? Does she like animals?"

"I don't know. The Fishers don't have pets."

"Art? Dance? Music?" Charlie asked. "Other than the piano, I mean."

I shook my head. "Not that she's admitted to. I was thinking about taking her to the pool. She's never learned how to swim, so Dex said he'd give her some lessons." I scanned the blackboard menu over the counter. "I'm hungry. I wonder if the blueberry coffee cake here is good. Have you ever tried it?"

"That's a great idea! You should definitely get her swimming," Charlie exclaimed, ignoring my question about the coffee cake. "It's the perfect solution. Her mom can't possibly object to her learning. And what kid doesn't like to swim? When I was her age, going to the pool or the beach was the coolest thing ever."

"Maybe she has a water phobia. When I was a kid, I used to freak myself out pretending that the pool was full of barracudas," I said.

"Invisible barracudas?" Charlie asked, one eyebrow raised.

"Hey, don't mock my phobias," I said. "You're the one who breaks out in hives if you see a clown."

"Clowns are incredibly creepy!" Charlie said. "They paint smiles on their faces! Who does that?"

"Remember that time when you slept over at my house, and I convinced you that a clown lived under my bed?" I said, giggling.

"Yes, I remember. I didn't sleep for a week straight. Thanks for that," Charlie said. "And stop trying to change the subject."

"Okay, okay," I said, sighing. "I'll take Amelia to the pool to-morrow. Even though I think I'll probably live to regret it."

•

As Dex and I walked Willow on the beach that evening, I told him about my talk with Mrs. Fisher.

"She sounds pretty tightly wound," Dex said.

"She is, a bit," I said.

We held hands, our fingers lined loosely together. Willow stopped every few steps to investigate an interesting smell or nudge a clump of seaweed with her long nose, slowing our progress down the beach.

"Poor Amelia," Dex said.

"Her mom's not that bad. She's not mean to her."

"She is putting a lot of pressure on Amelia, though. What if Amelia doesn't want to be a star pianist? Is she going to be expelled from the family?"

A big wave crashed into shore, and the water lapped up over our bare feet. Willow, who hates to get her paws wet, leapt to the higher, dryer sand and froze, nose twitching. I had to tug her leash to get her moving again.

"Do your parents put pressure on you? To get good grades or to be good at lacrosse?" I asked.

Dex hesitated, and when I looked sideways at him, he had a strange expression on his face.

"My parents want me to do my best," he finally said. "But they don't put pressure on me to be the best. There's a difference."

"Is something wrong?"

"No, why?"

I shrugged. "Nothing."

"How about your parents? Do they put pressure on you to be a math superstar?" Dex asked.

"Never," I said, shaking my head. I found myself feeling unexpectedly grateful to my parents. Sure, they weren't perfect—my mom was flighty and self-centered, my dad distant—but they'd never put pressure on me to be anyone other than who I am. Even when I first started at Geek Middle, it wasn't because they were pushing me to become a world-famous mathematician. "Are you still up for giving Amelia swimming lessons?"

"Sure. When does she want to start?" Dex asked.

"Want might not be the right word. In fact, I have a feeling Amelia's going to be resistant to the idea. But I was hoping we could start tomorrow."

"Don't worry. Women of all ages love me," Dex said, with a cocky grin.

I stuck out my foot, intending to trip him as a punishment for his smugness, but Dex jumped deftly out of the way.

"Ha-ha," he said. "And I have ninjalike reflexes."

Just as the words left his mouth, another wave lapped up on shore. Willow skittered to the side, this time bumping into Dex's legs and knocking him off balance. Dex fell sideways, landing on the soft, hot sand. He lay there for a few moments, blinking with confusion.

I grinned down at him. "Ninjalike reflexes, huh?"

Chapter Thirteen

"Do you have a swimsuit?" I asked Amelia at lunch the next day.

Amelia looked at my suspiciously, but nodded and said, "Why?"

"I thought we might go to the pool today," I said.

"I don't want to go to the pool."

"Why not? It's going to get really hot today. A dunk in the water will feel great."

"I can't swim," Amelia said flatly.

I shrugged. "You don't really have to know how to swim just to paddle around in the shallow end. It's not deep. You can stand up in it without any problem," I said.

"What's the point?"

"Fun?" I suggested. When she looked at me blankly, I sighed. "I thought you'd like it better than playing another board game."

This time it was Amelia's turn to shrug. "Not really."

"Ah," I said. "I get it."

Amelia looked at me sharply. "Get what?"

"You're afraid," I said.

"Like that's really going to work," Amelia said, rolling her eyes.

"What do you mean?" I asked innocently.

"You think that by calling me chicken, you'll manipulate me into going swimming," Amelia said. "I'm not stupid, you know."

I shook my heard. "No, you are definitely not stupid. But being afraid of something doesn't mean you're weak or bad. It's just something you have to get past."

"I'm not afraid!" Amelia exclaimed.

"Then why haven't you ever learned how to swim?" I asked.

"I don't know. I guess I've never really wanted to," Amelia said defensively.

"You live in Florida. It's ninety-five degrees outside. Who wouldn't want to cool off in a pool unless they were afraid of the water?" I asked. "Anyway, it's not a big deal. We can just play Monopoly. Again."

Amelia groaned. "I *hate* Monopoly."

"That's why I suggested the pool. But it's up to you. If you'd rather hang out here, that's fine, too. Maybe we could try playing Jenga today," I suggested, picking up my turkey sandwich and taking a bite.

We ate in silence for a few minutes. Finally, Amelia said, "Okay. Let's go to the pool."

"Great," I said.

•

After lunch, Amelia found her bathing suit, and I changed into the one I had packed in my backpack, and together we biked over to the community pool.

Dex was on duty when we got there. I waved at him but didn't stop to talk. He wasn't supposed to socialize while he was in the chair and I didn't want to get him in trouble. Dex grinned and gave me a thumbs-up when Amelia was turned away.

I did a quick scan of the chaise longues. Although there were a fair number of bikini-clad sunbathers, Wendy Erickson wasn't among them, nor were Felicity and Morgan. I was glad. It was going to be hard enough to give Amelia a swim lesson—without her noticing that she was having a lesson—without doing it in front of a hostile audience.

We put our bags down and spread our towels over two chaise longues, and then I headed straight for the pool. It was a hot, muggy day out, and I'd worked up an uncomfortable sweat on the short bike ride to the pool. I couldn't wait to get into the water and cool off. I was on the pool steps, ankle-deep, before I noticed Amelia wasn't following me in. She was sitting on the chaise, still wearing her T-shirt and shorts, and looking absolutely terrified. I stepped out and walked back over to her.

"What's wrong?" I asked.

Amelia shrugged and stared resolutely down at her feet.

"Amelia?" I persisted.

"Remember how I said I wasn't afraid of swimming?" she asked in a small voice.

"Yes," I said.

"Well . . . I sort of lied," Amelia said.

"You are afraid of the water?"

"Not so much of the water," Amelia said. "It's more that I'm afraid of *drowning*."

"You're tall enough to stand up in the shallow end. I don't think there's any real chance that you could drown."

Amelia looked doubtful. "What if I slip and fall?"

"Then you just stand back up."

"What if I slip and fall, and hit my head on the side of the pool, and get knocked unconscious so I can't stand back up?" Amelia countered.

I pointed toward the lifeguard stand. "See that guy up there?"

Amelia squinted in Dex's direction, shading her eyes with one hand. "You mean the lifeguard?"

"Yes. I know him. I promise he won't let you drown. If you hit your head and get knocked unconscious, he'll dive in the water and save you," I said.

"What if he's looking in the other direction, and doesn't see me get knocked unconscious?" Amelia asked.

"Water safety *is* important, but I think you're focusing on this getting knocked unconscious thing a little too much," I said. "Especially since we're just going to putter around the shallow end of the pool."

I could tell Amelia still wasn't convinced.

"Why don't we just go over to the stairs and wade into the water slowly, one step at a time?" I suggested.

After a long hesitation, Amelia finally nodded. She shucked off her T-shirt and shorts, exposing a purple-striped tank suit, and then stood uncomfortably, her arms wrapped around her thin body. She was all painful angles—pointed elbows, narrow shoulders, sharp shoulder blades.

This time when I stepped in the pool, Amelia followed me in. I waded into the shallow end, where the water came up to my waist. But then I turned and saw that Amelia had frozen on the first step.

"Come on," I encouraged. "The water's really nice. It feels great."

Amelia face had gone very pale, and her eyes were even larger and darker than usual. I tried to remember back to when I had first learned to swim. I had a vague memory of green water wings, and being hugely proud at the independence they had given me to float around by myself. It was too bad they didn't make water wings for kids Amelia's age, I thought. Then I had a brilliant idea.

I swam over to the edge of the pool, under the lifeguard chair.

"How's it going?" Dex asked.

"So far, so good," I said. "Are there any noodles around here?"

"Yeah. Back there by the office," Dex said, pointing to a large plastic trunk. "There are noodles inside that box. Kickboards, too."

"Perfect," I said. I climbed out of the pool and, dripping water as I went, headed over to the trunk. A moment later, I returned with a long pink noodle. It really did look like a noodle—round, with a hole in the middle, and nearly as long as I was tall. It was made out of some sort of material that floated in the water. If you draped yourself over it, or threaded it through your arms, you floated, too.

I walked back to Amelia, who was still standing on the first step.

"I brought you a noodle," I said, handing the pink floatie to her.

Amelia took the noodle from me, but looked at it blankly.

"It'll help you float," I said. I took the noodle back from her unresisting hands and waded back into the water. I leaned forward on the noodle, kicking my legs behind me, demonstrating its use.

"You try," I suggested, stepping forward to hand her the noodle once more.

Amelia finally moved cautiously forward. Down one step, and then another, and another, until she was standing in the pool. Her body was stiff and her arms were raised up as though the chlorinated water might be toxic, but even so, she was in the pool. It was definite progress.

"Just put the noodle down and sort of lean forward on it," I suggested.

Amelia hesitated, but finally set the noodle down on the water and cautiously leaned against it. Unfortunately, she started to tip forward and immediately panicked, flailing to right herself and succeeding only in falling face forward into the water. I rushed to her side just as she righted herself, wet hair flattened against her face, her eyes glittering with unshed tears.

"I want to go home," Amelia whispered.

My heart sank. It was a disaster. Instead of teaching Amelia how fun swimming was, all I'd succeeded in doing was making her even more afraid of the water.

"Hi," a voice said.

I looked up and saw that Dex was wading through the water toward us. I glanced at the lifeguard chair and saw that his replacement—the athletic girl I'd seen last week—was already sitting there.

Amelia blinked at Dex uncertainly. Her lower lip was trembling, but I could see she was trying to fight back the tears. I felt an unexpected rush of pride at her bravery.

"This is my friend Dex," I told her. I smiled at Dex. "This is Amelia."

"Hi, Amelia," Dex said.

"Hi," Amelia muttered, looking away shyly.

"Miranda told me you're a new swimmer," Dex said.

Amelia nodded, still not looking up.

"Maybe I could give you some pointers," Dex suggested.

"No, that's okay," Amelia said, shrugging away the offer.

"Suit yourself," Dex said. "But if you stick with me, I can teach you how to do this."

Dex suddenly dove forward. A moment later, his large feet stuck up out of the water as he performed an underwater handstand. Amelia seemed to forget her shyness for a moment while she watched Dex. He finally resurfaced. "Ta-da!"

"Ta-da?" I snorted. "Anyone can do that."

"Oh yeah? I'd like to see you try," Dex said.

"Okay," I said. I took a deep breath and plunged into the water, landing hands first in a handstand. When I couldn't hold my breath any longer, I popped back up, dipping my head back to keep my hair out of my face. Dex applauded, and Amelia almost smiled.

"Do you want to try?" Dex asked her.

She shook her head. "I can't," she said.

"I'll bet you an ice-cream cone that I can teach you how to do a handstand in one day," Dex said.

"No way," Amelia said.

Dex nodded solemnly. "I'll pinkie swear on it," he said, holding up one hand, pinkie crooked.

"Nobody pinkie swears anymore," Amelia said. A faint smile appeared on her face.

Dex looked at me for confirmation.

I nodded. "She's right. No one pinkie swears."

"Okay, fine, we'll just shake hands, then." Dex stuck out his hand. After a long hesitation, Amelia shook it.

I spent the next half hour watching Dex give Amelia her first official swimming lesson. His first goal was to get her comfortable in the water. He had her practice putting her face down and blowing bubbles in the water and then bobbing up and down like a cork, sinking down to the bottom of the pool and then pushing off the bottom to buoy herself back up. Once she was comfortable being immersed in the water, he kept his word and taught her how to jump forward and place both hands on the bottom of the pool. It took Amelia a few tries—she kept panicking and resurfacing right away—but finally, she managed one, wobbly handstand before bobbing back up.

"I did it!" she exclaimed, beaming happily.

Dex raised his hand, and she gave him a high five.

"Excellent work. You owe me an ice-cream cone," he told her.

Amelia giggled. "I thought you owed me an ice cream," she said.

"No way. I bet that I could teach you, and I did. Do you want to try again tomorrow?"

Amelia looked at me. I nodded at her. "That would be great," I said. "If you have the time."

"How about tomorrow at eleven?" Dex said. He glanced up at the clock. "My break's just about over. I have to get back up on the chair."

Dex patted me on the arm, and I smiled at him.

"Thanks," I said.

"It was fun," Dex said. "I'll pick you up at seven. Okay?"

I nodded and then turned back to Amelia, who was looking much more comfortable floating on her noodle.

"Are you hungry?" I asked. "Your mom said there were grapes and cheese sticks in the fridge for a snack."

"Can we stay for just a few more minutes?" Amelia asked. "I want to practice floating on my back."

"Okay," I said, smiling at her. "A few more minutes."

Chapter Fourteen

As I biked home that afternoon, I was feeling very smug from the success of the swimming lesson. Dex had been amazing with Amelia, and—miracle of miracles—she'd actually had fun. She'd been so bright-eyed and animated after our outing that she hardly seemed like the same kid.

My dad was pulling into the driveway just as I reached the beach house.

He rolled down the window. "Hey, kiddo," he said. "How was work?"

"Great!" I said, still bubbling with enthusiasm over the breakthrough I'd had with Amelia.

"Do you want to go practice your driving?" he asked.

"Really?"

"Isn't your driving test coming up?"

This quickly grounded me, and my stomach gave an unpleasant shift. "Yes," I admitted. "But there's no way I'm going to pass. I'm terrible."

"You just need some practice," Dad said. "Come on, climb in. We'll take a few laps around the neighborhood before dinner."

"Okay," I said reluctantly.

My dad got out and walked around the car to the passenger side. I got in the driver side and adjusted the seat and mirrors.

"Whenever you're ready," Dad said.

"Okay." I inhaled deeply, put the car in reverse—thankfully, Dad's car had an automatic transmission, so I didn't have to worry about a clutch—and gently put my foot on the gas pedal. Too gently, as it turned out.

"You have to push down a bit harder on the gas pedal if you want the car to move," Dad suggested.

So, taking another deep breath, I pushed my foot firmly against the gas pedal. Several things happened at once: The car lurched backward, its wheels spinning in the gravel. My dad yelled something indistinct. And, finally, there was a loud, sickening thud from the back of the car.

I slammed my foot down on the brake pedal. The car stopped abruptly, throwing Dad and me back in our seats. There was a long moment of stunned silence.

"What happened?" I finally asked.

Dad turned to look first dazedly at me and then back over his shoulder. "I think you hit the mailbox."

"I did?"

"Put the car in park," Dad said.

We both got out and walked around to the rear of the car. The back passenger-side wheel was firmly planted in the small decorative bed of petunias that ringed the mailbox. Or, I should say, that *used* to ring the mailbox. The mailbox itself was no longer there. It was sitting in the middle of the street, black paint dented and the red flag hanging off. Only the post was left, now bent at an awkward angle.

At the same time, Dad and I turned to look at the back of his car. There was a large dent there that corresponded with the general size and height of the mailbox.

"Oops," I said.

"Oops?" Dad repeated.

"I'm so, so sorry. *So* sorry," I gabbled. "I didn't mean to run over the mailbox. Or dent your car."

Dad sighed. "I know you didn't mean to, honey. I'm just not sure why you decided to reverse the car at fifty miles per hour."

"You told me to step down on the gas pedal," I reminded him.

"What I meant was for you to put enough pressure on it to actually make the car move. I didn't mean you should floor it."

I crossed my arms over my chest and stared at the dent miserably. "I'm sorry," I said again.

My dad glanced at me and sighed. "It's okay," he said. "And it's not *that* noticeable. You can really only see it if you stare at it straight on."

We both leaned to the right to stare at it from an angle. The dent was still pretty obvious. Flakes of black paint from the mailbox had transferred to the back corner of the car.

"I'll take it to my mechanic tomorrow," Dad said, sounding resigned. "He should be able to hammer out the dent."

"I'll pay for it," I said quickly. "Out of the money I've been making babysitting Amelia. It was my fault."

"No, that's okay. You save your money."

I shook my head. "No, this is the point where you're supposed to punish me. Ground me, or make me clean up my room. If you let this slide, I may end up becoming a drug addict or going to jail."

"Really?" Dad asked.

I nodded. "Yeah. You're supposed to crack down on teenagers. It's the only way we learn not to be reckless."

My dad put his arm around me. "Something tells me that you'll turn out just fine, even if I don't ground you forever. But do me a favor, kiddo?"

"What's that?"

"Next time you're backing up, look in the rearview mirror first, okay?"

•

"Guess what," Hannah said, bursting into my room without knocking.

"You ran over the mailbox, too?" I asked. I was lying on my stomach, rereading my driver's manual. I hoped that if I read it often enough, the information might actually stick. It was the only hope I had of passing my driver's test.

Hannah's mouth dropped open. "You ran over the mailbox?" she asked. "Does Mom know?"

I shrugged. "I don't know. Have you heard any high-pitched screeching yet?"

"No," Hannah said. "But you never know with my mom. She only yells when she's just normally mad. When she's really, really, *really* angry, she goes silent. It's actually a lot scarier when she does that."

"Good to know," I said, closing the manual with a sigh.

"Anyway, I set the whole thing up," Hannah said proudly.

I blinked at her, having absolutely no idea what she was talking about. "What whole thing?"

"Marriage therapy for my mom and your dad," Hannah said.

"You *what*?"

"Just what I said," Hannah said impatiently. "I made an appointment for Richard and my mom to go see a marriage therapist. Tiff's and Brit's mom gave me the referral."

"Do they know about this?" I asked.

"Who? Tiff and Brit?"

"No," I said. It was my turn to struggle for patience. "My dad and your mom."

"No, not yet. I was going to tell them tonight at dinner. Although if they're still mad about the mailbox, maybe I should wait,"

Hannah said. She frowned at me. "You know, this wasn't the best time for you to knock it over."

"Sorry. Had I only known that you were going to set up a counseling session for them without their permission, I would have waited to have my minor traffic accident," I said.

"It's okay," Hannah said, missing the sarcasm altogether. "I'll see what kind of mood everyone's in. If I have to, I'll wait until the morning to tell them. I can't wait too long, though. Their appointment is Thursday afternoon."

"That soon?" I asked, wondering how my dad and Peyton were going to take to this interference.

"They need the help now," Hannah said. "It can't wait. Besides, I have my first modeling job next week. I need to be well rested and destressed before then."

"You got a modeling job?"

"Well, the job's not mine yet. It's just a casting call," Hannah amended. "But still, it's a start, right?"

She glanced at me, brushing her hair back from her face and holding it back in a ponytail.

"Absolutely! That's great news!" I said.

"Thanks," Hannah said. She smiled and let go of her hair. It fell back around her face with a silky swish. "Won't it be amazing if I got the job? Just imagine—getting paid to have my hair and makeup done, and wear nice clothes!"

"Hmm," I said, realizing just what a stark difference this was to my summer job of spending long days trying to coax a moody girl away from her piano. Still, I thought, with modeling, you don't get the sort of job satisfaction I'd had today. Or, at least, probably not. Then again, maybe all of the money and glamour made up for the lack of social relevance.

"Hey, what was Dex doing at the mall today with Wendy Erickson?" Hannah asked, jarring me out of my contemplation.

"What?" I stared at Hannah, as cold horror mixed with a sense of unreality hit me square in the stomach. *Dex* . . . was with *Wendy Erickson* . . . at the *mall?* Why? When? When we had left the pool, Dex had told me his shift was ending at three. Had he gone straight to the mall? He hadn't said anything about it to me. Had he arranged to meet her ahead of time? It would be bad enough if he'd just run into her and they decided to hang out together. But if they arranged it ahead of time . . .

"What were they doing there?" I croaked.

"I don't know," Hannah said. She had drifted over to admire her reflection in the mirror that hung over my dresser. "I didn't really talk to them."

"What does that mean? How do you not really talk to someone?" I asked. I realized that my teeth were clenched together, my teeth grinding down.

"I saw them in the food court, and I just sort of waved at them, and they waved back at me," Hannah said. "I think Dex said hi. Does that count as talking?"

"I don't know," I said miserably.

Hannah, finally hearing the anguish in my voice, turned to look at me. "I don't think they were together," she said. "I mean, they were sitting at the same table, but it didn't look at all romantic."

"How can you tell?"

Hannah shrugged. "I just can. Body language, stuff like that. You know what probably happened? Dex was probably there buying T-shirts at the Gap or something, and got hungry. And then Wendy was probably passing by when she saw him at the food court, and she ended up sitting down at his table for a minute. And then I just happened to pass by at that exact moment," Hannah said. She smiled encouragingly. "I'm sure that's all it is. Don't worry. Dex really likes you. I can tell. I'm sure he's not interested in Wendy anymore."

"Maybe he is. She's really pretty," I said.

"So? You're pretty, too," Hannah said.

I managed a smile. It was one of the nicer things Hannah had ever said to me.

"Or at least you would be if you defrizzed your hair," she continued. "You know, there are products out there that would help with that. And why don't you use the straightening iron on it like I showed you to?"

Before I could respond, there was a knock at the door.

"Come in," Hannah said.

The door opened, and my dad stuck his head in. "Dinner's ready," he said.

"Okay, we'll be right there," Hannah said.

"I won't. I'm having dinner with Dex," I said in a hollow voice.

"More for me, then," Dad said.

His head disappeared, and Hannah headed off to the bathroom to wash her hands. I was slower to move. I couldn't get the image of Dex and Wendy together out of my mind. They were so alike—both of them popular, funny, attractive. I knew Wendy would have fit in easily with Dex's friends at the cookout. She would have joined the group of chattering girls, and known all about the clothes and makeup they were discussing. She would have flirted with the guys, who would have brightened under the attention and envied Dex for getting to go out with her. She wouldn't have made Dex feel like he had to watch over her, as he had with me.

The mental image of Dex and Wendy together caused a sharp, shooting pain to stab in my chest. I couldn't help wondering: What if it was Wendy—and not me—that Dex was meant to be with?

Chapter Fifteen

Dex and I went out for pizza that night. We ordered a large supreme with extra cheese and pepperoni, but for once in my life, I had no appetite. I picked at my pizza, and half listened to Dex telling a story about his friend Luke, who once attempted to make an enormous bowl of Jell-O in his family's hot tub. Apparently, the Jell-O never set, and the experiment only succeeded in staining the tub purple. I nodded at intervals as Dex talked, the whole time imagining him and Wendy together at the mall, having a romantic liaison in the food court.

Finally, Dex asked, "Is something wrong? You've been really quiet all night."

I didn't know what to say. Obviously, something was wrong. He'd just spent the afternoon hanging out with his ex-girlfriend. What's more, he knew that I knew, since my stepsister had seen them together. And yet neither one of us had said anything about it. I knew why I hadn't—I was too scared to hear what he'd say. Was he just waiting for the right opportunity to break up with me? Was he about to tell me that I was a nice girl and he liked me well enough, but not in a way that could compete with the feelings he had for Wendy Erickson?

But why hadn't he brought it up? I wondered. If it had all been some huge coincidence—if Hannah was right, and Dex and Wendy just happened to run into each other while buying sodas at the food court, and just sat down together for a few minutes . . . well, then, why didn't he tell me about it? The fact that he was being so tight-lipped just proved that there was something to hide.

I realized Dex was waiting patiently for me to answer his question.

"I'm fine," I said.

"Why are you being so quiet?" Dex asked.

What was I supposed to say? *Are you breaking up with me? Are you in love with Wendy Erickson? Are you in love with me?* What if he said yes, yes, and no? I'd be stuck there, sitting in the middle of the pizzeria with a broken heart. But I also couldn't just ignore what had happened.

So, keeping my voice as casual as possible, I said, "Hannah told me she saw you today. At the mall."

"That's right. I forgot I saw her," Dex said, his voice even more casual than mine. So casual, in fact, I wanted to scream. "She had about twenty shopping bags with her."

"That sounds like Hannah," I said.

There was a long pause, where I waited for him to continue. He continued to eat his pizza. Finally, I realized he wasn't going to say anything about being there with Wendy. My stomach gave a sickly twist.

"Hannah said she saw you there with Wendy," I finally said, somehow forcing the words out of my too-tight throat.

"That's right," Dex said easily.

I took a sip of my Coke and waited for him to elaborate. But Dex just continued to eat his pizza.

"This is really good. I think they put extra cheese on it," he said.

For the first time since Hannah had told me about seeing the two of them together, anger broke through the murky, sickly dread. Dex seemed to think that it was no big deal that he was hanging out with his ex-girlfriend. Who was a *model*. And who was obviously still in love with him.

Well, he was wrong. It *was* a big deal. To me.

I set my Coke down on the table with a loud thump.

Dex looked up, startled. "What's wrong?"

Was he being purposely obtuse, or was this one of those weird guy deficiencies I'd heard other girls complain about, but had never experienced myself? I decided it was time to be direct.

"Why were you at the mall with your ex-girlfriend?" I asked.

"I asked her to meet me there," Dex said.

He'd *asked* her to meet him? *Ugh*. Ugh, ugh, ugh. The whole conversation was causing an unpleasant, sickly sensation to spread through my stomach.

"You did?" I asked. Then, taking a deep breath, I asked the question that was more to the point. *"Why?"*

Dex looked down at the slice of half-eaten pizza on his plate. After a long pause, during which Dex seemed to be deliberating something, he finally said, "Do you mind if I don't tell you?"

I blinked at him. What was I supposed to say to that? Of *course* I minded.

"It has nothing to do with you and me," Dex said. "Not directly anyway."

What did that mean? But before I could ask him what was going on, the waitress appeared at our table.

"Can I get you anything else? Dessert or coffee?"

Dex looked at me. I shook my head.

"Just the check," Dex said.

The waitress took a stack of checks out of her apron pocket

and flipped through them until she found ours. She set it facedown on the table. "Whenever you're ready," she said.

After the waitress left, taking our empty pizza pan with her, Dex looked at the bill.

"I'll pay half," I said, reaching for my wallet.

"No, I've got it," Dex said. He took out some money and set it on top of the bill.

The waitress reappeared. "Do you need change?"

"It's all set," Dex said.

"Y'all have a good night," the waitress said.

"Thanks," Dex said. And then, after she'd bustled off, he looked at me. "Are you ready to go? Or do you want to finish your soda?"

Before I could stop myself, I blurted out, "Do you still have feelings for her?"

"Who?"

"Wendy!"

"Wendy?" Dex blinked, and looked confused. Then he started to laugh.

"Why are you laughing?" I asked.

"I'm sorry. I just realized how it must look to you," Dex said. "You thought that I was *with* Wendy. Like on a date or something."

"So you weren't?"

"No! Not at all. No. I was just . . . well, I had to talk to her about something. But it wasn't at all romantic. It had nothing to do with her and me, or you and me. I needed some advice about something. Something she has firsthand knowledge of," he said, as though this clarified everything.

"What?" I demanded.

Dex hesitated. He picked the straw up out of his Coke and twisted it. "That's the part I don't want to tell you."

I stared at him for a long moment; then I stood abruptly, turned around, and marched out of the restaurant.

"Miranda, wait," Dex said, following me out.

"No. I don't want to talk to you anymore," I said. I knew I sounded childish, but I didn't care. I was fed up. First, he'd acted like it was no big deal that he'd been off with his ex-girlfriend, and then it turned out that they'd had some sort of private, personal conversation that I wasn't allowed to know about.

"I swear, I will tell you what Wendy and I talked about! Just not right now," Dex said. He caught up with me and put his hand on my shoulder.

"Why?"

"I have to make a decision about something first," Dex said.

"About what? Whether you want to break up with me?" I asked, my anger making me reckless.

"No! It has nothing to do with you, or breaking up, or anything like that. I promise," Dex said. He finally reached out and took my hand. "Miranda . . . I love you."

This time, it wasn't just my feet that stopped moving. My heart felt like it stalled in my chest . . . and then it suddenly exploded, racing at full speed. A warm, tingly sensation rushed through me, causing my hands to shake and my knees to go wobbly.

"You do?" I asked, looking up at him.

Dex nodded. Even in the dim light, I could see how serious his expression was, his eyes pale and intent on my face. He meant it. He was *in love* with me.

"Oh," I said softly. "I love you, too."

Chapter Sixteen

The next few days passed in a happy blur. Dex loved me! I loved him! How could life possibly get any better?

Okay, so there was still the lingering issue of whether I was going to London in the fall. But now that the L-word had been said, how could I possibly go? Which wasn't to say I'd definitely made up my mind, but all of the reasons to go to London—the culture, the excitement, the adventure—seemed insignificant when compared to love.

I still hadn't gotten to the bottom of why Dex and Wendy had been together at the mall the other day. All of my concerns that night had been swept away after Dex told me he was in love with me, and it hadn't felt right to bring it up again since then. But I had to believe that Dex was telling the truth about not being romantically interested in Wendy. He wouldn't have told me he was in love with me if he still had feelings for her.

But other than my lingering worries about Wendy, everything—for once—seemed to be going my way. I'd been taking Amelia to the pool every day, and under Dex's tutelage, she was turning into a little fish. She clearly liked Dex better than she liked me. She laughed at his jokes and obviously wanted to please him with her progress during her lessons. Still, I thought that maybe she was lowering her defenses a bit with me, too. I wasn't sure if Amelia's mom knew about the swimming lessons. I'd mentioned we'd been to the pool, which had surprised Mrs. Fisher, although she hadn't objected, especially once I'd assured her there were lifeguards on duty.

I was getting a lot of writing done while Amelia practiced. I'd been slowly expanding on *How to Get Noticed*, and was pleased with how well it was coming out.

At the beach house, there had been a sharp decrease in the amount of fighting. In fact, I hadn't heard a raised voice since the night Hannah came home. Surprisingly, Dad and Peyton hadn't been at all upset with Hannah for setting up an appointment with the marriage counselor. They'd just nodded thoughtfully, and said it was something they'd been thinking they should do, and thanked Hannah for her help. I couldn't believe it. If I'd been the one to make the appointment, Peyton would have thrown a hissy. It seemed to be working, though. After only one counseling session, Peyton and Dad were going out of their way to be polite to each other and to us. Peyton even offered to make me toast one morning before I went to work, which nearly caused me to fall over in shock. Coming from Peyton, this was tantamount to her making a tearful announcement that she wanted to adopt me.

Finally, I was starting to think that maybe—just maybe—I might possibly pass my driving test after all. Or, at least, I was no longer convinced I would fail. Despite the mailbox incident, my dad had taken me out every night to practice driving, and I was definitely getting better. I could now perform a three-point turn, change lanes without sideswiping another vehicle, and had even successfully merged into traffic on the highway once. Still, success was by no means guaranteed. The looming possibility of epic failure continued to gnaw at me.

"What if I fail?" I said during dinner Sunday night.

Dad had grilled some fish, which we were eating taco-style, folded into tortillas with cheese, diced avocados, and sour cream. Or, at least, Dad and I were eating. Peyton never ate anything. She mostly just pushed her food around on the plate. Hannah, too, was picking at her food.

"Aren't you hungry, Hannah?" Dad asked.

Hannah shook her head and pushed her plate away. "My casting call is in the morning. I don't want to look bulgy."

"I don't think that's a word," I said. "Besides, even if it was, you're not."

"But I will be if I eat a taco," Hannah said.

"Why don't you take the fish out and eat that?" Dad suggested.

Hannah considered this, and finally nodded, pulling her plate back and picking out the slices of white fish. This problem solved, Dad turned to me.

"You won't fail," he said. "You're doing great."

"I hit the garbage can when I was backing up today," I reminded him.

He'd set up two garbage cans a few car lengths apart so I could practice backing up in a straight line. Instead, I'd backed into one garbage can and then, panicking, pulled forward, overcorrected, and backed up into the other.

Peyton noticeably stiffened, and I thought her eye might have twitched, but rather than criticizing me, she just took a deep breath and continued to pretend to eat.

That was unusual, I thought. Normally, Peyton relished every chance she got to criticize me.

"You've gone from mailboxes to garbage cans. That's an improvement," Dad said cheerily. "Besides, we needed a new garbage can anyway. The old one had a crack in the lid."

I glanced at Peyton again. Still no reaction.

"I'm going to have to back up on a real road around actual cars during my driver's test," I said.

"We'll keep practicing," Dad promised. He glanced at Peyton. "Do you like your tacos, honey?"

"They're wonderful, dear," Peyton said smoothly, although I hadn't seen her take a single bite. "Thank you for making dinner."

"You're welcome. Thank you for setting the table," Dad said.

"Happy to help," Peyton replied.

Hannah and I glanced at each other. They were being bizarrely polite. It was the nicest they'd been toward each other in ages.

"Are you excited about your first modeling assignment tomorrow?" Dad asked Hannah.

"It's just the casting call. I haven't been hired yet," Hannah said. But her smile and the small wriggle gave away how excited she really was.

"What time do you have to be there?" Dad asked.

"Nine o'clock. And it's down in West Palm, so we'll have to leave early," Hannah said. "Right, Mom?"

"I think we'll be fine if we leave by eight," Peyton said.

Dad frowned. "Don't forget there'll be heavy traffic. You'll be right in the middle of the morning rush hour."

"I know how to drive, Richard," Peyton said, in the cold tone I was more used to hearing her speaking in.

"I *know* you know how to drive. But I don't think you've ever had to drive south during the morning rush, have you?" Dad asked. There was a definite edge to his voice.

Peyton's eyes flashed, and she opened her mouth, clearly getting ready to blast Dad with a stinging retort. But instead, she closed her mouth, drew in a deep breath through her flared nostrils, and said in a very calm voice, "When you say I've never driven in rush hour, I feel like you're implying that I've never had a real job. And that makes me feel as though I'm being criticized."

Hannah and I both stared at her. It was such an oddly un-Peyton-like thing to say.

Dad cleared his throat. "I didn't mean to diminish what you do. I very much appreciate all of the hard work you do running our home. I'm just concerned that you won't give yourself enough time to get there, and will end up rushing. I don't want you getting into an accident."

Hannah's and my heads swiveled from my father back to Peyton, as though we were spectators at a tennis match. I wanted to ask my dad what exactly he was talking about in regard to Peyton's hard work in running the house. She didn't really do anything, other than writing out checks for the various housekeepers and gardeners she employed. But I figured this wasn't the best time to bring it up.

"I appreciate your concern. Would it make you feel better if Hannah and I leave at seven thirty instead?" Peyton asked.

"Yes, it would," Dad replied.

"All right, then, we'll leave at seven thirty, Hannah," Peyton said. She took a sip of water and pretended to nibble on a black bean.

"Um, okay," Hannah said, shooting me another confused look.

•

"That was weird," Hannah said, walking into my room without knocking after dinner. I was sitting on the floor, rubbing Willow's stomach, while she lay on her back, all four legs waving in the air. Willow grunted with bliss.

"Very weird," I agreed. "I guess they learned to talk like that in therapy."

Hannah sat on my bed. "Do you think it's working?"

"Probably too soon to tell," I said. "But at least it's better than listening to them yell at each other."

"That's true." Hannah looked around my bedroom, which was very white and very modern. There was a low platform bed covered with a white duvet, a dresser, and a boxy white chair that was too uncomfortable to sit on. Before I'd moved in, it had been the guest room, and when Peyton was feeling particularly malicious, she still called it that. "Why don't you redecorate in here? I'll help. We could paint the walls. Blue maybe. Or do you like purple?"

I glanced around. "I don't know. When I first moved in, I didn't think I'd be here long enough to personalize it. And then I guess I got used to the whiteness."

Hannah wrinkled her nose. "It's just so cold and impersonal."

I was about to point out that the whole beach house was cold and white and impersonal—much like Peyton's personality—but bit back the remark. Despite a bumpy patch when I first moved in, Hannah and I had been getting along pretty well in recent months. I didn't want to ruin our good mojo by making mean comments about her mom, no matter how truthful they were.

"And you'll be here next year, too, right? Didn't you say your mom was staying in London?" Hannah asked.

I hesitated—I still hadn't told anyone but my dad about London—but I decided I could trust Hannah.

"Actually, my mom wants me to move to London to live with her," I said.

Hannah's mouth dropped open. "Are you serious?"

I nodded. "I probably won't go, though. I mean, I haven't decided. But I probably won't."

"Are you *insane*?"

The force of Hannah's words took me by surprise. She was looking at me as though I'd just announced that I'd just been asked out on a date by Robert Pattinson and had turned him down.

"You have a chance to get out of this hick town and go live in a glamorous, international city and you're not going to take it?" Hannah continued.

"You would go if you were me?" I asked.

"Are you kidding? Of course I would!" Hannah said. "That's, like, the opportunity of a lifetime."

"Even though it would mean leaving behind all of your friends and Emmett?" I continued.

"Well, sure, that would be hard. I mean, I do love Emmett," Hannah said, tossing her hair back. "But he's going away to college in a year, and let's face it—most high school couples break up as soon as one of them leaves for college. And if by some chance we are meant to be together, well, then, we'd be together even if I moved to Paris, right?"

"Paris?" I frowned at her. "What do you mean Paris?"

Hannah flushed, a pretty pink tinge covering her cheeks and the tip of her nose. "That's where I would move if I could live anywhere," she said. "I'd go to Paris and be a model. It's the fashion capital of the world."

"Okay, well, that makes sense. You'd be moving to follow your dream, right? But that doesn't really apply to me. I want to be a writer, and I can write here as well as in London," I said.

"But isn't part of being a writer having amazing life experiences, so you have something to write about?" Hannah said.

"I guess," I said slowly. "But I'd be giving up a lot."

I didn't have to mention Dex by name. Hannah immediately knew what I meant.

"If Dex and you are meant to be together, you'll be together," Hannah said. "Trust."

"And if we're not?" I asked.

Hannah shrugged. "Then you're not. And it won't matter if you're here or in London."

I nodded. I still wasn't sure what I should do, but Hannah was—shockingly enough—making a lot of sense.

"Don't tell anyone, okay?" I said. "I haven't told anyone other than my dad, and now you. I don't want Dex or anyone else to know until I've made up my mind one way or the other."

"Really? You told me, but not your friends?" Hannah asked, her eyebrows rising in two perfect blond arches.

"Yep."

"Why me?" she asked.

"I trust you," I said simply. And I couldn't help but feel a glow of goodwill when I saw how pleased she was to hear me say it.

Chapter Seventeen

When I arrived at the Fishers' house Monday morning, I could hear someone inside—I was pretty sure it was Amelia—shouting. I hesitated for a moment, not sure whether I should interrupt. Then, finally deciding I had to—it was my job to be there, after all—I pressed the doorbell. The shouting stopped. There was the sound of advancing footsteps in the hallway, and then the door swung open.

Mrs. Fisher stood there, smiling at me as usual. The smile was a bit tense, and Mrs. Fisher's cheeks were very red, but she said, "Good morning, Miranda," in a calm enough voice.

"Hi, Mrs. Fisher," I said, walking inside and dropping my knapsack by the front door.

Mrs. Fisher winced as a door on the second floor of the house slammed shut.

"Amelia's upstairs. She's a bit upset at the moment," she said.

"What's wrong?" I asked.

"We decided to engage a new piano teacher for Amelia—someone who has more experience with advanced students. Amelia is rather attached to her old teacher, and so, naturally, she's unhappy at the change." Mrs. Fisher sighed and ran a hand through

her short, wiry bob, causing the bangles on her arm to jingle together. "Maybe you could talk to her, Miranda. I know she looks up
to you."

She does? I wanted to say. Because even though Amelia had
ratcheted down her hostility toward me since I started taking her to
the pool, I thought we were a long way off from her looking up to
me. I was pretty sure I was someone she barely tolerated.

The phone rang, and Mrs. Fisher turned toward the kitchen,
tapping down the hallway in her heels, calling back over her shoulder to me, "Go ahead upstairs, Miranda. Amelia should be in her
room." A moment later, I heard her answer the phone. "Hello? Oh
yes, hello, Janice. I'm glad you called. I need to talk to you about
the fabric samples I got in for the window treatments for your living
room. . . ."

I trudged up the stairs. I hadn't been on the second floor of the
Fishers' house before. There was a long central hallway, carpeted
in beige, with framed family photos hanging on the walls. The pic-
tures were mostly of Amelia taken at what looked like piano recitals
and concerts, with Amelia up on a stage, wearing a full-skirted
dress and sitting at a large black piano. There was one shot of all
three Fishers, standing on a dock with boats behind them, smiling
at the camera. I hadn't met Mr. Fisher yet, but I could see Amelia in
his face—he had the same stubborn chin, the same large brown
eyes. Mr. Fisher had an arm slung around Mrs. Fisher's waist; she
had her hand on Amelia's shoulder. They looked like a happy family, I thought.

I continued down the hallway, passing the master bedroom
and a bathroom, until I reached the only closed door. By process of
elimination, this had to be Amelia's room. I knocked softly.

"Go away!" Amelia called through the door. Her voice sounded
ragged, as though she'd been crying.

"It's me. Miranda," I said.

I wasn't surprised when she said, in an even louder, more aggressive tone, "I said, *go away!*"

I considered my options. I could go back downstairs, but then I might have to talk to Mrs. Fisher some more when she got off the phone. That wasn't so bad in itself—Mrs. Fisher had always been nice to me—but she would realize that Amelia and I weren't nearly as close as she thought we were. She might even decide that I was a terrible au pair and fire me. I didn't know why this would bother me so much—taking care of Amelia hadn't exactly been fun. But I didn't want to be a failure at my first official job. So I knocked on the door again.

"Look, I'm not going away, so you might as well let me in," I said.

I didn't expect this to work, but after a brief pause, the door swung open. Amelia stood before me, her face pale and streaked with tears, her dark hair falling messily over her shoulders, her hands fisted at her sides. She was wearing a pink T-shirt with a glittery rainbow on it. This was unusual for her. Amelia didn't normally wear a lot of pink, or sparkles, or anything so overtly girly.

"Hi," I said. "Can I come in?"

Amelia shrugged, but stepped aside. I took this as an invitation and stepped into her room. Much like the pink T-shirt, Amelia's room didn't look like Amelia to me. The walls were pale blue, and the furniture—a bed, a dresser, a small desk—was white and edged with gold. The bedspread and curtains were both navy blue. On the wall, there was a series of framed black-and-white photographs of ballet shoes. I looked at these, surprised.

"Do you dance?" I asked.

"No," Amelia said. "My mom picked those out."

"Oh," I said. "That makes sense. She's an interior decorator, right?"

I thought it looked like the sort of bedroom you'd see in an advertisement—pretty but impersonal. I was suddenly reminded of my own room, back at the beach house. Maybe Amelia and I were more alike that I'd thought. We could both live in rooms and fail to make any impression on them.

In fact, the only bits of Amelia I saw in her room was a stack of sheet music piled up messily on the desk, a cuddly stuffed monkey propped against the pillow, and a book on the bedside table. I looked closer. It was *Anne of Green Gables*. I touched it, and remembered telling Amelia that the book had been one of my favorites.

"Are you enjoying the book?" I asked.

Amelia shrugged again, but then she nodded. "It's okay, I guess."

My spine stiffened. Who could possibly read *Anne of Green Gables*, and call it just *okay*? But then I reminded myself that Amelia was upset, and took a few deep breaths to keep my temper in check.

"Do you want to talk about it?" I asked.

Amelia looked at me strangely. "The book?"

"No, not the book. Why you're upset."

"Oh." Amelia looked away and began wrapping a long tendril of hair around one finger. "My mom didn't tell you?"

"She said you're changing piano teachers."

At this, Amelia looked up sharply, her eyes slanted with anger. "And I get no say in it! None at all. It doesn't matter that I want to stay with Miss Kendall, who's been my teacher forever. My mom just announces that I have to start taking lessons with this Ian Gregory guy, even though he lives in Miami, because he's famous."

"Miami?" I asked. "How often will you have to go down there?"

"Twice a week!" Amelia said. "Which means I'll be spending hours and hours in the car, which is time I won't have to practice."

"Have you tried talking to your mom about how you feel?" I asked.

"Duh," Amelia said, rolling her eyes at me. "That's why we're fighting. She won't listen to me."

"Sometimes when I get upset, it's hard to find the right words to express what I'm feeling. When that happens, I think it helps to write it down—the reasons why I'm upset, what I think the best solution to the problem is. You could try doing that," I suggested.

"What's the point? My mom's already made up her mind," Amelia said.

"Maybe. But maybe she's more open to hearing your side than you think. And even if she doesn't ultimately agree with you, at least you'll know that you made your best case," I said.

Amelia thought about this, still curling her hair around her finger. Her hair was straight as a pin, unlike my unruly, wavy mess. In fact, she had the sort of hair I'd always coveted—glossy and thick, the kind that always looks perfect in a ponytail.

"I suppose I could," Amelia said slowly, as though agreeing that my idea had merit was physically painful for her.

"And if you're still worried about talking to your mom, you could always just show her what you wrote," I suggested.

Amelia went to her desk, opened a drawer, and pulled out a spiral notebook and a pen. She sat down, cross-legged in the middle of the floor, the notebook balanced on her lap. Then she looked up at me expectantly.

"What should I say?" she asked.

I sat down next to her. "Why do you want to stay with your current teacher?"

Amelia considered this, tapping the end of the pen against her knee. "She always tells me the truth about what I need to work on, but she's never mean about it."

"So you trust her," I said.

"I trust her. Yeah, that's exactly it."

"Write it down."

Amelia obediently scrawled the words into the notebook.

"What else?" I asked.

"She's supportive," Amelia said. She thought for a minute. "And when she explains something, it makes sense to me. Should I write that down, too?"

"Definitely. She's supportive and you like her teaching style," I said. "Those both seem like really important points. What else?"

•

By the time we'd finished, Amelia had a detailed list of all of the reasons why she preferred to stay with her current piano teacher. I thought she made a compelling argument. We headed downstairs, but Mrs. Fisher had already left for work, leaving a note on the counter to let us know she'd be home a bit later than usual and that there was sliced turkey in the cold cut drawer for lunch. Amelia's shoulders drooped.

"I wanted to show her my list now," Amelia said.

"Look at this way—you'll have extra time to plan your strategy," I said.

"What strategy?"

"Exactly," I said.

"Huh?"

"This gives you more time to figure out how to best approach your mom," I explained. "You were just fighting, right?"

Amelia nodded.

"Well, now you'll both have time to cool off. If she's anything like my mom, by the time she gets home, she'll be feeling bad that you fought and will want to make up with you. So if you catch her in the right mood, she might be more receptive to hearing your side of things," I said.

"Wow. You're really good at this whole dealing with the parents thing," Amelia said, looking impressed.

I shrugged modestly. "I've had a lot practice with parental conflict," I said. "My parents are divorced and I have a stepmother."

"Do you fight a lot with your parents?"

I considered this. "My mom and I used to argue a lot when I was younger. But I live with my dad now, and he and I have never fought as much. Then again, we're also not as close as my mom and I are."

"I hardly ever see my dad," Amelia said.

"Why?" I asked.

"He travels a lot for business. And when he is home, he's always jet-lagged and wants to be left alone so he can rest."

"Could you talk to him about the situation with your piano teacher?" I asked.

Amelia shook her head. "There's no point. He'll just take my mom's side. I'm better off trying to convince her."

We were both quiet for a minute. "Do you want to go to the pool?" I finally asked. Then, remembering that she hadn't practiced at all that morning, I said, "Unless you'd rather practice. It's up to you."

Amelia thought for a minute. "Actually, I'd sort of like to go swimming. Will Dex be there?"

"He's off this morning. If there's enough wind, he was planning to go parasurfing."

"What's that?" Amelia asked,

"It's sort of like surfing—you're on a board, riding the waves—but you also wear a parachute. When a burst of wind comes, it lifts you right off the water," I said. "It's pretty cool."

"Do you do it?"

I laughed and shook my head. "No way. I'm a total klutz. I can barely stand on a regular surfboard."

"Can we go watch him?"

"Sure, why not? The beach where he usually surfs is right near the pool. We'll go see him, and then go for a swim. I'll make some sandwiches that we can take with us. How does that sound?"

"Great!" Amelia said, and she ran upstairs to change into her swimsuit.

Chapter Eighteen

Amelia and I biked over to the public beach. The boardwalk arched up over grass-covered dunes, and it wasn't until we reached the top that we could see the ocean, vast and dark and shimmering where the sun touched upon it. It was a windy day with big waves churning toward the shore, so there were a lot of surfers out, both the regular kind and a smaller number of parasurfers. I immediately picked out Dex's blue sail flying high above the others.

Amelia and I sat on towels and ate the turkey sandwiches I'd packed. We watched the surfers, who were mostly teenage guys, with the exception of one or two girls and a few men my dad's age. They took turns paddling out through the surf to wait for the best wave to ride in on. Dex and the rest of the parasurfers were a bit farther out, and they were clearly the most talented surfers out there. They jumped and flew through the air, nimbly touching down on the water before leaping back up again. Even if I hadn't known which sail was Dex's, I would have been able to pick out his coppery red hair, which gleamed in the bright sunlight.

And then I saw someone else I recognized. My heart skittered for a moment before sinking like a rock. *Wendy Erickson.*

Why was it that wherever Dex was, Wendy just happened to

show up in the very same place? I wondered. Was it a coincidence, or by design?

I watched her through narrowed eyes. Today, Wendy was wearing a long-sleeve surf shirt over tiny orange bikini bottoms, and her hair was tied back in a single thick braid. Surfboard in hand, she headed confidently into the water, where she jumped on and paddled through the surf until she was close enough to the parasurfers to call out to them. I couldn't hear what she said—or what any of them might have said in response—but even at this distance, I thought I could see Dex's teeth flash white in a smile.

Wendy sat up, straddling her surfboard, and looked back over her shoulder. A large wave loomed behind her. She deftly jumped to her feet and leaned forward, extending her arms out to either side for balance.

A not-very-nice part of me was silently rooting for her to be swept right off her board by the wave. I wanted to see her emerge from the ocean with bits of seaweed stuck in her hair and mascara running down her cheeks. But, disappointingly, Wendy rode the wave in looking like a pro. She reached the shore and leapt off her board, cheered on by the surfer guys, who clearly all had massive crushes on her. Wendy smiled broadly at them, and waved like a newly crowned beauty contestant.

I glowered, bending my knees in front of me and wrapping my arms around them.

"What's wrong?" Amelia asked.

"Nothing."

"You look like you just swallowed your tongue," Amelia observed.

"How flattering." I stood up and shook the sand off my towel. "Come on, let's go to the pool."

"Don't you want to wait until Dex finishes?" Amelia asked.

I shook my head. "No, that's okay. He probably won't come in for ages."

The truth was, I didn't want to see Dex and Wendy together again. Every time I saw the two of them in the same vicinity, I had the stomach-sickening realization of what a perfect couple they must have made. Also, I wondered if Dex knew Wendy would be at the beach today, and, if so, why he hadn't mentioned it to me when I spoke to him the night before. Was this yet another planned meeting, so he could talk to Wendy about whatever it was he felt comfortable telling her, but not me?

"Hi, Miranda."

I looked up from the towel I was folding, and saw Wendy looming over me, looking annoyingly pretty. She'd put on mirrored sunglasses, and I could see my reflection in them, looking distorted with an oddly big head.

"Hi," I said. Then, worrying that I sounded as unfriendly as I felt, I added, "I saw you surfing. You're really good."

"Thanks," Wendy said. "I didn't get much of a chance to surf while I was at school. It was nice to get out on the waves again. I keep telling Dex how much he'll miss it."

"Miss what?" I asked, confused.

"Surfing," Wendy said.

"You mean when he goes to school?" I asked. Like me, Dex was going into his junior year of high school, so he wasn't going to college for another two years. So why was she bringing it up now? Was it just a way to remind me that she and Dex had long, secret conversations about his future?

She needn't bother, I thought bitterly. It wasn't like I was about to forget.

Wendy nodded. "Especially if he's in the Northeast. You can't surf much when there's three feet of snow out."

My throat felt prickly, as though I'd just swallowed a pinecone.

So Dex was confiding to Wendy about where he was planning to apply to college. He and I had barely discussed it. I knew he was hoping to get a scholarship to a school with a strong lacrosse program, but it would be at least another year before recruiters started contacting him.

"He's got a lot of time to surf between now and then," I said.

"You think so now, but the summer has a way of going by quickly," Wendy said. "I'm only going to be here for another five weeks before I have to head back. Although I'm not going directly to school. I have a few photo shoots scheduled in Manhattan before the semester starts. Speaking of which, how did Hannah's casting call go today?"

"I don't know. I haven't talked to her." Then I frowned. "Wait—how did you know she had a casting call?"

"She told me last night. She called for some last-minute advice—what she should wear, what to expect. I used to work with her agency, before I switched to one in Manhattan," Wendy explained.

Typical. Just when I thought Hannah was someone I could trust, she had turned to the enemy for advice.

"Anyway, I'm going to head back out and catch a few more waves. Are you waiting for Dex?" Wendy asked.

"No, we're going over to the pool," I said. I looked down at Amelia, whom I'd forgotten until just that moment. She was standing to one side, looking up at Wendy with frank interest. "This is Amelia. Amelia, this is Wendy. She's a . . ." I hesitated. "A friend of Dex's."

"Hi, Amelia," Wendy said, smiling broadly at the younger girl.

"Hi," Amelia said.

"Do you want me to give Dex a message for you?" Wendy asked.

"No," I said, and then realized that—while perfectly true, the last thing I wanted was for Wendy Erickson to pass messages between Dex and me—I'd been a bit to abrupt in my refusal. "I mean, sure, just tell him we were here and I'll talk to him later," I said.

"Okay, will do," Wendy said. "Bye."

And with one last friendly smile and wave, she turned and headed back to her surfer friends.

"She's really pretty," Amelia said admiringly. "I think she's the prettiest girl I've ever seen. Well, in real life, I mean. I suppose there are movie actresses who are prettier. But not by much."

I was so not enjoying this conversation. I stuck my rolled-up towel and the remains of our lunch in my backpack.

"Come on, let's go," I said. I glanced back at the water once. Dex was still out there, riding his board and leaping through the air. Wendy was paddling out again on her surfboard, headed in his direction. And I was just standing on the beach, watching them, and feeling a million miles away.

"Are you coming?" Amelia asked.

"Yep," I said, turning and following her across the hot sand to the boardwalk.

Chapter Nineteen

"I'm home," I called out, slamming the front door behind me.

My voice echoed in the empty foyer. A minute later, Willow came padding out, wiggling happily when she saw me.

"Hi, girl," I said, patting her head. "Are you the only one home?"

"No, I'm here, too," Hannah said, appearing from the back hallway. "Mom and Richard had an appointment with their marriage therapist, so Mom said we should order from Mario's when we get hungry."

"I'm hungry now," I said.

"Big surprise. You're always hungry," Hannah said, turning and heading toward the kitchen.

"Didn't they just go to see their therapist?" I asked, following her.

"She wants them to meet with her a few times a week," Hannah said.

"Wow, they must be in even worse shape than we thought," I said.

"They left right after Mom and I got home from the casting call," Hannah said. She moved her hand over her shoulder, as though to flip back her hair—a habit she'd had as long as I'd known her—before remembering that her hair was now too short to flick. She instead tucked a tendril behind one ear. "Aren't you going to ask me how it went?"

"Oh, right. I forgot. How did it go?" I asked, climbing into one of the high bar stools that were lined up by the granite-topped island.

"I got the job!" Hannah announced. "It was amazing! It was a catalogue shoot, but for amazing, totally high-end dresses. It was at this gorgeous house, and the backyard was all done up like there was a big party going on, and I had to act like I was a mysterious woman who was gate-crashing the party. No one knew who I was, but everyone was intrigued by me. I was like a modern-day Cinderella."

"Wow, and you were able to act all of that out?" I was impressed. I'd thought modeling was just standing in front of the camera.

"I hope so! I mean, I was mostly just posing, but that's what the photographer—his name was Jojo, and he was super nice—told me I should be thinking about," Hanna said. She hopped up onto the stool next to me and sighed happily. "It was amazing, even better than I imagined. Although it was sort of hard to hold certain poses, but Jojo told me I did a really good job and that he'd like to work with me again."

"That's great," I said.

"I have to call Wendy and tell her," Hannah said happily.

I narrowed my eyes. "Speaking of which, I wanted to talk to you about that."

"About what?"

"I can't believe you called Wendy Erickson to ask her for advice!"

"Who else would I ask? She's the only working model I

know," Hannah said. "Or, knew. I met some really cool girls today. One of them told me a trick she had for losing five pounds in a hurry—"

"You know why! She's Dex's ex-girlfriend!" I said, cutting her off.

"So?"

"So she wants to get back together with him!"

"Why do you think that?"

"I can just tell. She oozes all over him every time they're together," I said.

Hannah sighed. "Miranda, Dex is with you. You have to trust him."

"I do trust him! *She's* the one I don't trust," I said.

"Wendy's actually really nice. Plus, she has a boyfriend at school. They're really serious," Hannah said.

This stunned me into momentary silence.

"Really? How do you know that?" I finally asked.

"Duh." Hannah rolled her eyes in a most annoying way. "She *told* me."

"What did she say exactly?"

"Hmmmm." Hannah reached behind her to grasp her hair into a stubby ponytail while she considered my question. "Her boyfriend's starting college in the fall. She said that he's going to Oberlin, but they're going to try to figure out how to do the whole long-distance relationship thing. She also said he's gorgeous and brilliant, and that they're madly in love."

"She said that? That she was in love with this other guy?"

Hannah nodded. "Mm-hmm. I'm telling you, you have nothing to worry about. She's not after Dex, and besides, Dex likes you. He's way more into you than he ever was with Wendy."

"You really think so?"

"Definitely. Tiff and Britt were just telling me how smitten he seemed at that cookout you all had at the beach. Don't you just love that word? *Smitten*."

"They said that? Really?" I asked. A warm, rosy glow spread through me.

"Yep," Hannah said.

"Oh. Well, okay, then. I guess you can call her," I said, with only a trace of reluctance.

Hannah laughed. "You're giving me permission?" she teased.

I smiled. "No, but I will give you my blessing. Let's order dinner."

But before I could find the take-out menu for Mario's, the doorbell rang.

"Can you get that?" Hannah asked. "It's probably Emmett. He said he might stop by after work."

She headed off to the bathroom—probably to touch up her lip gloss—and I went to answer the door. But it wasn't Emmett.

"Hi," Charlie croaked. Framed in the doorway, she looked absolutely wretched. Her face was pale and blotchy, and tears streamed down her cheeks. "Can I come in?"

•

I called back to Hannah, letting her know it wasn't Emmett, and then led Charlie to my bedroom. Willow followed us, looking worried and thrusting her long nose into Charlie's hand in an offer of canine comfort.

As soon as we were in my room with the door shut behind us, I turned to Charlie.

"What's wrong? What happened?" I asked anxiously. Although Charlie had a manic-depressive disorder, she rarely ever cried, even during her depressive periods. Normally, she just got really quiet and tired and spent a lot of time in bed. Seeing her like this, in floods of tears, was alarming.

Charlie sat heavily on the edge of my bed and covered her face with her hands. I sat down next to her, feeling almost numb with worry.

"Are you hurt? Do you need me to call your parents?" I asked.

Charlie looked up, wiping at her cheeks with the backs of her hands. "What? No. I'm fine. I mean, I'm not fine, obviously, but I'm not hurt."

"Then what's wrong?"

Charlie looked down, staring at her feet. "I feel stupid telling you."

"You can tell me anything," I protested.

"I don't know if I can tell you this."

"Okay," I said.

We sat there quietly, side by side. I wasn't sure how I could help if Charlie didn't want to tell me what was wrong. But I thought that if she really hadn't wanted to talk to me about it, she wouldn't have shown up on my doorstep in tears. The best thing to do was just wait her out.

Finally, Charlie took in a deep breath, slowing the ragged gulps of air she had been taking. "Here's the thing . . . I think I might . . ." She stopped and shrugged. "It feels weird to say out loud."

"Do you want to write it down?" I asked, thinking back on my advice to Amelia that morning.

Charlie gave me a withering stare, looking much more like her old self. "Don't patronize me," she said in an acid tone.

"There's the Charlie I know and love," I said. I nudged her. "Just tell me."

"I think . . . the thing is . . . I think I have feelings for Finn," Charlie said. She started off slowly at first, but then the words suddenly came out in such a rush, it took me a few beats to process what she'd said.

Charlie had feelings for *Finn*? It wasn't like I hadn't suspected it. But I'd never, not in a million years, *ever* thought Charlie would admit to it.

"Say something!" Charlie cried.

"I think . . . wow. I mean . . . that's just . . . *wow*," I said.

Charlie looked at me. "Wow?" she repeated. "All you can say is wow?"

"Give me a minute. I have to adjust to the news that one of my two best friends is in love with the other one," I said.

"Love? I didn't say *love*," Charlie said quickly. "I said, *have feelings. Have feelings* is not the same thing as *love*. It's an entirely different state of being." But despite her words, Charlie simultaneously blushed the color of a ripe tomato and shifted uneasily in her seat.

I couldn't help grinning. "You've got it bad, huh?" I said.

"Are you going to help me or what?" Charlie growled.

There was a knock on my door. "Come in," I called out.

Hannah opened the door. "Hey, are you ready to call in our dinner order?" she asked, poking her head in. She saw Charlie and smiled a little shyly. "Hi."

"Hi," Charlie said, still sniffling a bit.

"Hannah, this is my friend Charlie."

"I know, we've met before," Hannah said. She looked more closely at Charlie, taking in her tear-streaked face. "Oh my gosh, are you okay?"

Charlie nodded. "Guy problems," she said.

"What happened?" Hannah asked.

"There's just this guy . . . he's a good friend of mine. Of ours," Charlie said, flicking a glance at me.

Hannah, taking this explanation as an invitation to join the conversation, walked in and curled up on the opposite end of the bed, cuddling my pillow in her arms. "Go on," she said, nodding. "Tell me everything. I'm really good at solving relationship problems. Just ask Miranda."

I nodded. "She does have a knack for it," I said.

"There's nothing much to tell. I have feelings for this guy," Charlie said awkwardly. She looked sharply at me to quell any comments I might make. "I'm not *in love* with him, I just . . . well, I guess I realized I like him more than I previously thought I did."

"And he doesn't feel the same way about you?" Hannah sympathized.

"No. He doesn't," Charlie said sadly.

"I don't think that's necessarily true," I chipped in. "I think Finn might have feelings for you, too."

"You do?" Charlie asked.

I nodded. "When you were going out with Mitch, it drove Finn crazy. That's why he kept picking fights with you. I think he was jealous."

"Really?" Hannah said, drawing the word out. "This sounds promising."

But Charlie shook her head. "That was then. Now Finn's going out with someone else. He's infatuated with her."

"Who? Do I know her?"

"You might. She goes to Orange Cove High. Her name's Phoebe McLeod," Charlie said.

"Phoebe McLeod? Yeah, I know her," Hannah said. "She's pretty nice. A little ditzy, maybe."

"She does seem ditzy," I said loyally.

"She's not very smart," Hannah continued. "In fact, I think I heard she's in summer school, taking some classes she failed."

"It's hard to imagine Finn with someone who isn't smart," I said.

"No, it's not," Charlie said with a faint smile.

"No, it's not," I agreed, smiling, too.

Finn was brilliant, but he was a total goofball. And, like many of the guys we went to school with, he was self-conscious about being thought of as a geek. If a pretty girl showed interest in him *and* laughed at his jokes, he wouldn't care if she had the IQ of a cantaloupe.

"What you need is a plan," Hannah said.

"A plan? What do you mean?" Charlie asked, perking up a bit.

"First of all, you need to get his attention," Hannah said. She looked Charlie over critically. "You're cute, but the purple hair needs to go."

"Hannah!" I said.

"It's okay. I want her to be honest," Charlie said to me. Looking at Hannah, she said, "What would you suggest?"

"You should get it dyed a normal shade," Hannah advised her. "You'd look good as a blonde. But not too light—that would just wash you out. A dark blond with chunky highlights."

"This is ridiculous," I said. Turning to Charlie, I said, "You shouldn't try to be someone you're not."

I wanted to remind her of what had happened when she was dating Mitch. She'd dyed her hair red to please him and, in the process, had morphed into a different person altogether. Charlie seemed to be thinking along the same lines, because she reluctantly shook her head.

"Miranda's right. I can't change who I am," she said.

"Well, in that case, we're going to have to be a little devious," Hannah said, drumming her fingers against the pillow.

Charlie and I looked at each other.

"Devious is good," Charlie said.

"Devious may be the best way to get Finn's attention," I agreed.

"What would I have to do?" Charlie asked.

"You said Finn was jealous when you were dating someone else, right? Then you just need to make him jealous again," Hannah suggested. "Find a cute guy and flirt with him like crazy. Then when Finn sees you with the other guy, it'll snap him out of his infatuation with Phoebe."

"Do you think that will really work?" Charlie asked doubtfully.

Hannah nodded. "Guys are so predictable."

"I don't know," I said. "Wouldn't she be leading on the other guy? The one she was using to make Finn jealous, I mean. That doesn't seem very nice."

"Nice?" Hannah looked at me incredulously. "They're guys. You're not supposed to be *nice* to them."

"You're nice to Emmett," I countered.

"That's different. We're in love," Hannah said contentedly. "When you're officially with someone, then you can be nice to him."

"Hmm," I said, not quite buying this. After all, I'd been nice to Dex, and I'd still gotten his attention. Then I remembered all of the mix-ups Dex and I'd had before we got together—including his thinking I was dating another guy—and wondered if Hannah had a point.

"Come on," Hannah said, standing. "Stay for dinner, and I'll give you some pointers."

"Great, thanks," Charlie said, looking happier.

Chapter Twenty

A few days later, Amelia and I met Dex at the pool for her swimming lesson. Dex looked especially cute in his red lifeguard trunks. All of the hours he'd spent out in the sun that summer had tanned his chest a golden brown and bleached the hair on his arms a pale blond. I was wearing a turquoise tankini that Hannah had helped me pick out. Actually, she'd tried to talk me into a tiny string bikini version, but I'd taken one look in the dressing room mirror and turned the color of a ripe tomato. The tankini was as bare as I was willing to go.

"Dex, will you teach me how to surf?" Amelia asked.

Dex thought about it for a minute, but then shook his head. "I don't think you're a strong enough swimmer yet," he said.

"Yes, I am!" Amelia said. "I can swim a full length of the pool! Watch me!"

She dove forward, and began swimming down the length of the pool, arms churning and legs kicking. Dex looked at me. He knew that Amelia's new enthusiasm for the water was a big step for her, and I could tell he didn't want to discourage her.

"She's doing great. She's really come a long way," I said.

"Yeah, but swimming in the pool is a lot different from swimming in the ocean," Dex said. "I don't want her to get hurt."

"Maybe you could teach her some basics, like how you stand on a board and keep your balance. Not on the actual ocean, but here, standing on the deck of the pool," I suggested.

Dex nodded. "I could do that. And I could take her to the beach and get her started on a boogie board. You don't go out as far, and you ride in on your stomach. It's a good way to get used to the rhythm of the waves."

"I'm sure she'd love that," I said. I smiled at Dex and, with a sweep of one hand, splashed some water at him.

"Hey," he said, reaching out and grabbing hold of my wrist so I couldn't splash him again. "What did you do that for?"

"I was just thinking how nice you are to spend so much time teaching Amelia," I said.

"I'm nice, so I get splashed?" Dex said, grinning at me. He was wearing sunglasses, so I couldn't see his eyes, but I knew they were crinkled with humor.

"That's right," I said.

Dex squeezed my wrist, and then let it go as Amelia returned from her swim.

"Did you see me?" she panted.

"You were great," I said.

Dex nodded. "You need to reach a bit more," he said, demonstrating the crawl stroke in the air. "Like this. Reach and pull. You'll go a lot faster."

"Okay," Amelia said. She was still out of breath, and her face was pink with exertion. "So can I start surfing?"

"I'll tell you what. You keep working on your swimming, and I'll start teaching you the basics of surfing on solid ground," Dex said. "Then by the time you're a stronger surfer, you'll be ready to start riding the waves."

Amelia pouted. "But I want to surf now!" She stamped her foot, although since we were in the pool, it didn't have much of an effect.

"Amelia, Dex is trying to help you," I said.

"No, he's not! I know I'm ready to surf, and he's telling me I can't!"

"No, he's not," I said, irritation swelling. "He said he'll teach you the basics now. You should thank him."

"Thanks for nothing!" Amelia said, and she turned and stomped off toward the stairs.

Dex and I watched her climb out, huff over to the chaise where we'd left our bags, and wrap herself in a pink-and-green-striped beach towel, her back pointedly turned to us.

"Well," Dex said mildly. "I guess she told me."

"I can't believe she's being such a brat!" I said, shaking my head. "Actually, I can believe it—she's not exactly the most gracious kid I've ever met—but that doesn't make it any better. I'm so sorry."

"It's not your fault. And I get where she's coming from. When I was a kid, I always hated it when people told me I couldn't do something because I was too small or too young. It's frustrating."

"Yeah, but she shouldn't take it out on you. And after everything you've done for her. She and I are going to be having a conversation about this when we get home," I said grimly.

"Don't be too hard on her," Dex said. He grabbed my hand and laced his fingers through mine. "Are you busy later on? You want to do something?"

"I can't. My dad said he'd take me out driving. My test is in two days, and I need all the practice I can get."

"I'll take you driving," Dex offered. But then he hesitated. "As long as you promise not to kill my car."

I shook my head again. "Thanks, but no. You make me too nervous."

"*I* make *you* nervous?" Dex pointed to himself.

"Yes, you," I said. "Don't look so surprised. I don't want you to witness the epic fail that is me driving."

"You're not an epic fail. You just need more self-confidence," Dex suggested.

I snorted in disbelief. "Yeah, that's the problem. My lack of self-confidence. Not the fact that I run over mailboxes and garbage cans and sidewalks."

"You ran over a garbage can?"

"I don't want to talk about it," I said, and decided to change the subject. "How about tomorrow? It's penny pin night at the bowling alley, and Charlie's getting a group together to bowl. My friend Finn and the girl he's dating will be there, too."

"I was supposed to do something with Luke and Brian, but maybe we can meet up with you."

"Which ones are Luke and Brian?" I asked.

"They're both on the lacrosse team with me. I don't know if you've met Luke, but Brian was at that barbecue at the beach a few weeks ago," Dex said.

The guys at that party had all blurred together. They were all athletic, all wore plaid shorts and graphic T-shirts, and all called each another *dude*. Oh well. Their presence would make Charlie happy. I knew she was eager to try Hannah's strategy of making Finn jealous.

"Sure, bring them along. Hannah and Emmett are coming, too."

"Hannah bowling? Somehow I can't see that," Dex said.

I decided not to explain about Charlie's crush on Finn, and how Hannah had decided to make getting the two of them together her personal pet project for the summer. Charlie had asked me not to tell anyone, and besides, the whole situation weirded me out.

"Yeah, well, maybe she's looking for a new hobby," I said. I glanced at the big clock hanging behind the lifeguard stand. "I suppose I should get Amelia home."

I glanced over at my young charge. She was sitting on the recliner, hiding behind a pair of round sunglasses, her arms crossed in front of her. Even from a distance, I could tell she was glowering. I sighed.

"This should be a fun afternoon," I said.

"That's why they pay you the big bucks," Dex teased me. "Hey! Stop splashing me!"

•

"You're not hungry?" I asked.

Amelia and I were sitting at the kitchen table at her house. I'd made us grilled cheese sandwiches and heated up tomato soup for lunch.

"My sandwich is burnt," Amelia said, staring at her plate with disgust.

"It's not burnt," I said. "It's just a little brown."

"It's burned," Amelia said again, and pushed her plate away from her.

"Well, then, just eat your soup," I said.

"I don't like soup," Amelia complained.

"Then I guess you can just starve," I said, taking a bite of my grilled cheese sandwich.

The words sounded familiar to me, and I realized that I'd probably heard my mother say something similar, when I was acting like a brat at mealtime. Did this mean I was turning into my mother? What a horrible thought.

I expected Amelia to push her chair back and stalk off to her piano. But instead, she just sat there, her shoulders slumped and her mouth a tense line. My irritation dissipated a bit. She was so talented and so driven, sometimes it was hard to remember that she was just a little girl.

"Is everything okay?" I asked, forcing myself to use a kinder, gentler tone.

Amelia shrugged.

"Did you ever talk to your mom about not wanting to change piano teachers?"

"She didn't want to hear it," Amelia said. "She said I've outgrown Miss Kendall, and Ian Gregory will help me to maximize my potential. End of discussion."

"Did you show her the list we made?"

Amelia shook her head. "There was no point. She'd already made up her mind."

"And what do you think?"

"I don't even want to play anymore," Amelia said.

We both went silent under the weight of this admission.

"I didn't mean that," Amelia finally said. "I don't know why I said it."

"It's okay if you feel that way," I said.

Amelia snorted her disbelief. "No, it's not. My mom would freak. Besides, I don't really want to stop. I love playing. I just . . . well, sometimes I wonder what it would be like not to feel so . . ." She stopped, grappling for the right word.

"Pressured?" I suggested.

Amelia nodded. "But then I feel guilty for thinking that. It's like, because I have this gift, all of the decisions about my whole life have already been made. What I'm going to do, what I'm going to be."

"But they haven't, really," I said. "You still get to make choices for yourself."

"It doesn't feel that way," Amelia said softly. Tears glittered in her eyes.

"I really think you should talk to your mom about how you're feeling," I said.

"I tried that. Remember? She wouldn't listen to me."

"You talked to her about changing piano teachers. This is a

little different. I think she'll have to listen to you talk about your feelings on this," I said. "It's your life, Amelia. You get to decide what you're going to do with it. If you don't want to be a concert pianist, you don't have to be."

"I can't tell my mom that. She'd be so disappointed," Amelia said. She wiped at her eyes, looked up at me under a damp fringe of lashes.

"I know, it's hard," I said. "But I think you still have to talk to her."

Amelia nodded. And, strangely enough, this decision to confront her future—or, at least, to confront the possibility of a different future than the one she'd had for as long as she could remember—seemed to steady her. Her shoulders relaxed, and she reached for her grilled cheese sandwich.

"I thought it was burned," I teased her as she took a big bite.

Her cheeks were bulging, chipmunk-style, but even so, she managed a weak grin. "I guess it's not as bad as I thought," she admitted.

Chapter Twenty-one

"Who's coming tonight?" Charlie asked as she tied the laces on her red bowling shoes.

"Dex said he's bringing some friends," I said. We had arrived early to claim two side-by-side lanes. The bowling alley tended to get crowded on penny pin nights.

"Are they cute?" Charlie asked.

I rolled my eyes. It was such an un-Charlie-like thing to say. "I have no idea," I said.

"You haven't met them?" she persisted.

"I think I have, but I don't really remember them. Dex said they're both on his lacrosse team, though, so they're probably not your type."

"Why wouldn't they be my type?"

"Aren't you the one who said that all jocks have IQs roughly equal to their jersey numbers?" I asked.

Charlie considered this. "I may have said that," she admitted. "But I don't want to date them for their minds. I just want to use them to make Finn jealous."

"Make me jealous of what?" Finn asked, appearing behind Charlie.

Charlie jumped, and let out a small scream. She stared at me, wide-eyed, silently begging me to fix it.

"Yeesh, what's up with you?" Finn asked. "And what would I be jealous of?"

"Charlie made it to level five on Arachnozombies," I lied quickly.

I wasn't that into gaming, but close proximity to Finn over the years kept me more up to date on the gaming world than I ever wanted to be. Arachnozombies was Finn's current obsession. He'd bragged endlessly when he made it to level four. I had no idea if there even was a level five, but it was all I had.

"You did not," Finn said accusingly. He stared at Charlie as though she'd personally wounded him.

Charlie managed to compose herself quickly. She shrugged modestly. "It wasn't all that hard," she said.

"I didn't even know you played!"

"You never asked," Charlie said.

"Prove it," Finn said. "Show me how you get to level five right now."

Charlie looked around pointedly. "Um, hello? We're in a bowling alley."

"So?" Finn asked.

"There aren't any computers here."

"I have a laptop in my car," Finn said, turning. "I'll go get it."

Charlie and I exchanged an alarmed glance. I was pretty sure that she had never even played Arachnozombies before. Chances were she wouldn't get past level one. Luckily, we were saved by the timely appearance of Phoebe McLeod, wearing a short denim skirt that showed off her long tan legs.

"Hi," Phoebe said, giggling a little as she greeted Finn.

"Hi, yourself," Finn said, sidling over to her for a kiss, all thoughts of Arachnozombies forgotten.

Charlie looked like she wanted to vomit at this scene. I tried to distract her.

"Do you want to be the scorekeeper?" I asked as I signed our names into the computer that kept track of the bowling scores.

"No, thanks," Charlie muttered.

"But you love being scorekeeper," I said.

Finn and Phoebe started whispering into each other's ears, causing Phoebe's giggling to become even louder and more giddy.

"No, I need to concentrate on my goals for the evening," Charlie said. She straightened suddenly and waved. "Oh, good, Hannah and Emmett are here. Hannah! Over here!"

I turned and saw Hannah and Emmett strolling toward us, hand in hand.

"Hi, Bloom," Emmett said to me. Emmet Dutch was as gorgeous as ever—tall, broad-shouldered, and tan. He had blond hair that curled back from his face and eyes the color of the ocean at sunset. There was a time, pre-Dex, when hearing Emmett Dutch call me Bloom and seeing him holding hands with my stepsister would have caused my insides to shrivel up with jealousy. Happily, he no longer had that affect on me.

"Hi, Emmett," I said. "Are you having a good summer?"

"Pretty good," Emmett said cheerfully.

"Is he here yet?" Hannah asked Charlie.

Charlie widened her eyes and looked meaningfully in Finn's direction. He was so absorbed in Phoebe, he didn't notice the exchange.

"Him?" Hannah asked, surprised.

With his shaggy hair and goofy smile, I knew Finn was not what Hannah would consider much of a catch. Still, she'd given her word, so she shrugged off her surprise and got to work.

"Where's Dex?" she asked me. "I thought he was bringing Luke and Brian."

Hannah, of course, knew both guys. She went to school with them at Orange Cove High, and was friendly with most of the jocks.

"He said he'd be here," I said.

"Good," Hannah said. She turned to Charlie and began pelting her with instructions in a low, fierce whisper. "Luke's a lot more outgoing than Brian, so he's probably the better bet. Still, you never know who you'll have better chemistry with, so flirt like crazy with both of them. Touch your hair a lot, make eye contact, find reasons to touch his arm. Guys love that. Oh, and I brought you this." Hannah handed Charlie a tube of lip gloss. "Put it on."

Charlie looked doubtfully at the tube. "I don't usually wear lip gloss. My hair gets stuck in it," she said.

"You're as bad as Miranda," Hannah said, rolling her eyes.

"Hey!" I said.

Hannah ignored me. "Trust me. Put it on. You can't flirt without glossy lips," Hannah said with such authority that Charlie meekly obeyed.

I saw Dex enter the bowling alley, flanked by two guys who looked vaguely familiar. As I'd suspected, they were both of the typical high school jock variety. One was thicker through the chest and had very dark hair. The other had longish blond hair, and was even taller and lankier than Dex.

"Hey," he said when they'd reached us. He smiled down at me.

"Hi," I said.

"This is Luke and that's Brian," Finn said. "And this is Miranda."

We all said hello. Luke was the dark-haired one, and he stood with his hands in his pockets, his eyes roaming over the crowd. They rested briefly on Hannah, again on Phoebe, and then lingered when they got to Charlie. I turned and saw that Charlie was smiling at him, while tilting her head to one side and tucking her purple hair behind her ears, as per Hannah's instructions.

"Hey," he said to her.

"Hey yourself," Charlie said flirtatiously.

Hannah looked pleased, but I couldn't help feeling uncomfortable. I didn't think anything good could come of Charlie acting like anyone other than herself. Charlie seemed to read my thoughts, and winked at me.

Don't worry, the wink said. *I've got a plan.*

I rolled my eyes. *That's exactly what I'm worried about.*

Charlie grinned at me and then turned her attention back to Luke. "Let's have a bowl-off," she suggested. "We'll pick teams, and then the team with the highest score has to buy wings and cheese fries for the other. The shoe rental is over there."

Everyone who hadn't already gotten their bowling shoes obediently went off to rent some, accompanied by Finn, who didn't seem willing to leave Phoebe's side for even a moment. Only Hannah remained at the lane with Charlie and me.

"No way," she said, shaking her head, so that her platinum hair swished around her face. "I am absolutely not wearing rental shoes. That's totally gross."

"You have to or they won't let you bowl," Charlie explained.

"Fine, then I won't bowl," Hannah said.

"This was your big plan," I reminded her. "You can't not participate."

"I'll just watch, and give advice where needed," Hannah suggested.

"No way," I said. I pointed to the shoe rental. "Go rent a pair of bowling shoes. We're all in this together now."

Hannah pouted, but gave in.

"She really doesn't have to bowl if she doesn't want to," Charlie said as we watched her join Emmett in line.

"Yes, she does," I said. "I'm not missing a chance to see Hannah in ugly footwear for the first time ever."

"I thought you two were getting along better these days," Charlie said.

"We are. But even so, it's too good an opportunity to pass up," I said. I glanced at my friend, who looked pale and nervous, but also determined. "You don't have to go through with this if you don't want to."

"I absolutely want to," Charlie said firmly. "Finn's not going to know what hit him."

⚫

At first, Charlie's prediction seemed to fall flat. We divided up into two teams. Dex, Brian, Hannah, Emmett, and I bowled on lane two, while Finn, Phoebe, Luke, and Charlie bowled on lane three. Hannah tried to talk Brian into joining the other group—"We're two couples over here. You don't want to be a fifth wheel," she said—but he wouldn't budge.

"It looks like there are two couples over there, too," he said, nodding at Luke and Charlie, who were talking animatedly. Charlie was incorporating all of Hannah's flirting tricks, touching her hair and making lots of eye contact. Luke definitely seemed interested in her, I thought, but for all the good it seemed to be doing—Finn was so wrapped up in Phoebe, he didn't seem aware of their existence.

"I'll be a fifth wheel either way," Brian continued, sitting down at our lane.

Hannah didn't seem overly pleased by this, but the sight of Charlie's successful flirting with Luke seemed to mollify her.

"Who wants to go first?" I asked as I began signing everyone up on the electronic scoreboard.

It turned out to be pretty fun for a while. Dex was a terrible bowler, which was a surprise, considering how athletic he was in general.

"Stop laughing at me!" Dex demanded as he guttered the fifth ball of the night.

"Sorry," I said, still giggling. "It's just that you bowl about as well I drive."

Hannah got the hang of it, under Emmett's tutelage, and Brian was pretty good, too. But I seemed to be having the lucky streak of the night, hitting strike after strike, and easily taking first place.

"Yes," I said, raising a fist of victory as I downed all of the pins in a spare.

"It's just pure luck. There's no skill involved at all in this game," Dex grumbled as he stood to take his turn.

"So says the guy with a score of twenty-seven," I teased.

I sat on one of the benches behind our lane and took the opportunity to glance over at the other group. Phoebe was bowling. Behind her, Finn sat alone on one bench, while Luke and Charlie, deep in conversation, sat close together on the other. Luke had slung a casual arm over the back of the bench, as though he were working his way up to shifting it onto Charlie's shoulders. Finn seemed to have finally snapped out of his Phoebe-induced trance. Instead of watching his girlfriend bowl, he had his eyes pinned on Charlie and Luke.

Maybe Hannah's plan is working, I thought with a jolt of shock.

"He's really bad at this," Brian said, sitting down beside me.

I turned and saw Dex shank the bowling ball straight into the gutter. I laughed.

"Yeah. He's pretty awful," I agreed.

Brian smiled at me. Like Dex, he didn't have the typical jock, meathead look about him. His brown eyes were thoughtful, and he seemed almost uncomfortable in his body, as though it had grown too quickly for him to get used to it. His legs were folded in front of him, and his long arms rested on his knees.

"Are you on the lacrosse team, too?" I asked.

Brian nodded. "I'm not that good," he admitted. "I'm a second stringer. Or, actually, more like a third stringer. I really just play to stay in shape for the fall soccer season."

"They seem like they're a lot alike, soccer and lacrosse," I said.

"Yeah, except that in soccer, no one tries to whack you in the knees with a long stick," Brian said. "Which is a good thing, I think."

"I can see that," I said.

"The team is really going to miss Dex next year," Brian said.

It's weird that how when you know you're about to hear something you really don't want to hear, everything seems to slow down a bit. Noises get a bit dimmer, people seem to move slower. It's almost as if there's a slight hiccup in time. This was one of those moments. Even though I didn't know what Brian was talking about—miss Dex? Why? Where else would he be?—I instantly knew it was going to be something dreadful. And I also knew that there was no way I would be able to swallow back my next question, as much as I might want to.

"Where is he going to be next year?" I asked quietly.

Brian looked surprised. "You don't know?"

I shook my head. "No."

Brian looked at Dex's back, his expression shifting to one of uneasiness. "Oh, man. Maybe I shouldn't have said anything. I didn't realize . . . I mean, I thought you knew."

"Knew what?" I asked again. My skin felt like it was both hotter and more sensitive than usual. My cheeks burned, and the tension of my hair pulled back in a ponytail suddenly made my scalp ache.

"Miranda, what's wrong?" Hannah asked sharply, looking from Brian to me. "Brian, did you say something rude to her?"

Brian held up his hands, and stood. "No way. I just . . . look. I'm going to go get a soda."

He bounded off, throwing one worried glance back at us over his shoulder. I sat frozen in place. Where was Dex going? Was his family moving? Was that what he had talked to Wendy Erickson about, but hadn't wanted to tell me?

Hannah stood, and plopped down in Brian's vacated seat. "What's going on?" she asked.

"I don't know. Brian said . . ." I stopped, my throat closing, refusing to let out the words.

"Brian said what?" Dex asked, suddenly in front of us, looking down at me, his face creased with worry. I started at his sudden appearance—I hadn't even noticed that he'd finished his turn.

I stared back up at him. "Brian said you're not going to be here next year," I said quietly. "Is that true?"

"What? I'm sure Brian was just kidding," Hannah sad quickly. "Right, Dex? I mean, where would you go?"

But Dex had gone pale. He swallowed, and then took in a deep breath.

"I was going to tell you," he said.

I nodded, even though it felt as if all of the air had been sucked out of the room. "Tell me what?"

"I got a scholarship to the Brown Academy. It's a prep school up north. They want me to play lacrosse for them," Dex said.

I nodded again and tried to think of something to say. Nothing came to mind. He was leaving town. And he was leaving me. I stood suddenly, surprising Dex so much that he took a step back. Hannah was staring up at us with her mouth agape.

"I have to go," I said. My voice sounded weird to my own ears—thin and high-pitched.

Dex laid a hand on my arm. "Miranda," he began.

I shook his hand off. "Please don't. Not right now."

"We should talk about this," Dex said softly.

I knew that if I stood there much longer, I was going to cry. I could already feel a burning sensation in my chest, pushing upward through my lungs and filling my throat. I turned and started to walk away.

"Where are you going, Miranda?" Hannah called after me. "It's your turn!"

I didn't look back. And Dex didn't follow me.

Chapter Twenty-two

Although it was almost unbearably hot and muggy out, I decided to walk home. I knew I could call my dad for a ride, but I didn't want to have to explain the tears sliding down my cheeks.

Dex had lied to me. He'd let me think that things next year would go on just the same as they had that summer. He'd let me think that we'd be together.

If it had been the other way around, if I were the one leaving, I'd have told him, I thought. And then I suddenly realized that this wasn't entirely true. I hadn't, after all, told Dex about the possibility that I might be moving to London for the upcoming school year.

But it wasn't the same. Not at all. For one thing, I hadn't decided yet whether I was actually going to move to London. Once I had made that decision, I would have told Dex immediately. The only reason I had kept the possibility from him was that I couldn't figure out what I wanted to do. He, on the other hand, had already made his decision . . . and he hadn't told me. He'd told Brian, and probably told his other friends, also. But he hadn't told me.

Why had Dex told me he was in love with me if he knew he was leaving? I wondered as a spasm of pain shuddered through me. Maybe if he hadn't told me that—hadn't used the word *love*—I could have protected my heart.

A car drove past me, its headlights glaringly bright, its wheels spinning through puddles left over from a late afternoon storm. I ducked my head to avoid the lights, and trudged on.

This must have been what Dex and Wendy had been talking about when they met at the mall food court, I realized. I remembered what Wendy had said when I saw her surfing at the beach. *"It was nice to get out on the waves again ... I keep telling Dex how much he'll miss it ... Especially if he's in the Northeast ... You can't surf much when there's three feet of snow out."* So she'd known, too. She'd known before me.

I didn't hear the second car approaching until it slowed down next to me. I glanced up at it and recognized Emmett's Jeep even before I saw Hannah in the passenger seat. She leaned out the window to talk to me.

"Get in, Miranda. We'll drive you home," Hannah said.

"That's okay. I'd rather walk," I said.

"It's raining," Hannah pointed out.

"It is?" I looked up. It had started raining, heavily, without my noticing.

"You're freaking me out. Get in," Hannah ordered.

I obeyed her, climbing in the back of the Jeep. The top was on, but the windows and back were open, and the resulting breeze felt good on such a humid, airless night.

Hannah twisted around in her seat.

"That was a dramatic exit," she said. "You pretty much brought the bowling party to an end."

"Sorry," I said.

"Don't be. I think everyone was bowled out," Emmett said, glancing at me in the rearview mirror.

It was the first time I'd ever ridden in a car with Emmett. A year ago, this would have made my life. It was amazing how much things had changed in such a relatively short amount of time.

"Dex was pretty upset that you left," Hannah said.

"He was?"

Even though the mere mention of Dex's name caused a fresh wave of throbbing pain in the general region of my heart, I still wanted to hear every detail. Luckily, Hannah instinctively understood this without my having to ask.

"Yeah. He looked really sad. And then Brian came back, and Dex was furious at him for telling you. They got into a big fight," Hannah reported.

"It's not Brian's fault that Dex has basically been lying to me," I said.

"Yeah, well, Dex didn't see it that way. For a minute there, I thought Dex was going to punch him. But then Dex just turned around and walked off, without saying good-bye to any of us. And then Brian took off, and then Emmett and I left," Hannah said.

"What about Charlie?"

"She was still there. She and Luke seemed to be hitting it off," Hannah said, sounding pleased with herself. "And the other guy, the one she likes—what's his name?"

"Finn."

"Right, Finn. He was definitely jealous. My plan totally worked. I told Charlie to report in tomorrow, so we'll find out what happened," Hannah said.

When we got back to the beach house, Emmett started to turn off the car, but Hannah put her hand on his arm. "Why don't you just drop me off? I think Miranda needs some girl time."

"That's okay," I said quickly. "I'm fine. Really."

"No, it's cool. I have an early shift in the morning," Emmett said. He gave Hannah a quick kiss.

She made a face. "All you do is work," she complained as she unlatched her seat belt.

"We can't all have cush jobs standing in front of a camera looking pretty," Emmett teased her.

"Gag," I said, climbing out of the Jeep. Hannah giggled and climbed out after me.

"Bye," she said, waving as Emmett drove off. Then she turned to me. "Come on. Let's go see if there's any ice cream."

"Ice cream?" I asked.

"Yes, ice cream. That's what girls are supposed to eat when they've had a romantic crisis," Hannah informed me as she opened the front door. "It's, like, a rule or something."

"I'm not hungry," I said. My stomach felt so cramped and sour, I doubted I'd ever be hungry again. "But you can have some if you want."

Hannah looked shocked. "I don't eat ice cream. Do you have any idea how many fat grams are in it?"

"You have got to stop obsessing about your weight," I began, but then stopped. I heard voices coming from the kitchen. Angry voices. More specifically: Dad and Peyton. "Oh no. Are they fighting again?"

"Let's go see," Hannah said, heading off in the direction of the kitchen. I reluctantly followed her.

". . . can't believe you told that to Dr. Patel!"

"He told us to be honest with our feelings!"

Dad and Peyton were sitting on opposite sides of the kitchen table. As soon as Hannah and I entered the room, they stopped fighting abruptly.

Peyton cleared her throat. "Hi, honey," she said to Hannah, ignoring me as usual. "Did you have a fun night?"

"Sort of. We went bowling. I had to wear the ugliest shoes," Hannah said.

"Is that sanitary?" Peyton asked.

"Doubtful," Hannah said.

"Hello, girls," Dad said, pointedly stressing the plural.

Peyton started. "Oh! Hello, Miranda," she said stiffly. "I didn't see you there."

This was an obvious lie. I was standing right next to Hannah. Peyton would have to be blind to have missed me.

"Hi," I said.

"Did you go bowling, too?" Dad asked.

I nodded.

"So you two are fighting again?" Hannah asked, hopping up onto one of the tall stools.

"No. Richard and I were having a discussion," Peyton said stiffly.

"It sounded like you were fighting," Hannah continued. She twirled a fine strand of pale blond hair around one finger. "I thought you weren't doing that anymore."

"Everyone gets into arguments from time to time," Dad said mildly.

Hannah and I exchanged a look.

"Yeah, but it hasn't really been, has it? Time to time, I mean," I said.

"More like all the time," Hannah said. "It's getting annoying to live with."

I nodded. "She's right. It is."

Dad and Peyton exchanged a look, and, surprisingly, Dad smiled at Peyton. Peyton didn't return the smile, but that might be because her face was paralyzed by Botox (which she adamantly insisted she didn't use, but totally did).

"We're sorry we've been annoying you," Dad said.

"And we've been trying to work out some of our issues with our therapist," Peyton added.

"Is it helping?" Hannah asked.

"I think so," Dad said carefully.

"I do, too," Peyton said. She reached a hand across the table. Dad took it, holding it gently in his hand.

Hannah smiled at me, looking pleased.

I didn't smile back. My head had started to pound. Too many thoughts were bouncing around it, too many emotions were slamming up against one another. Suddenly all I wanted to do was to crawl into bed, pull the covers over my head, and shut out the rest of the world.

"I'm going to bed," I said abruptly.

Everyone looked at me, surprised. "Are you okay, honey?" Dad asked.

"I'm fine. Just . . . tired. Really, really tired," I said. I turned and left without another word.

Chapter Twenty-three

Charlie called me on my cell phone as soon as she got home. I was already in bed with my lights out, but I hadn't been able to fall asleep. Instead, I just lay there staring up into the darkness, while thoughts of Dex—his leaving, his hiding it from me, the way we'd parted that evening—clattered around in my head.

"Hi!" she said when I answered. "Where did you go?"

I didn't feel like getting into everything that had happened, so I just said, "I had a headache, so I went home."

"You could have said good-bye," Charlie said accusingly.

"Sorry."

"You would not believe how well our big plan went," Charlie said happily. "Luke was all over me! And Finn was *so* jealous!"

"Why? What did Finn do?" I asked.

"He started to completely ignore Phoebe. And he kept trying to get my attention."

"How?"

"You know, typical Finn stuff. He kept saying how goofy I look when I bowl, and making fun of how I throw the ball. You know, generally insulting me. It was great."

"Sounds like it," I said dryly. "Um, Charlie?"

"Yeah?"

"You used to want to rip Finn's face off when he insulted you. How did that suddenly become a turn-on for you?"

"This was a different kind of insulting. This time he was obviously trying to divert my attention away from Luke. And poor Phoebe," Charlie said.

"Poor Phoebe? I thought we hated her." Charlie had told me this many, many times, refusing to be swayed by the apparently irrelevant fact that I couldn't hate Phoebe, as I didn't even know her.

"We used to hate her. Now we feel badly for her," Charlie corrected me. "She just sat there, her arms crossed, looking like she was on the verge of bursting into tears."

"Oh, that's terrible!" I exclaimed. "Charlie!"

"What? It's not my fault that Finn was neglecting her," Charlie said defensively.

"Of course it was your fault! It was exactly what you were hoping would happen!"

"Do you want to hear the rest of the story or not?" Charlie demanded.

"Fine, go ahead."

"I'm not going to tell you if you don't want to hear."

I was *so* not in the mood for this. "Okay, then don't tell me."

"Okay, okay. So anyway, we finished the game, and Phoebe got all pouty and said she wanted to go home. And Finn said, okay, but then he didn't leave. He just stood there and looked at me. Phoebe asked him what he was doing, and Finn asked me if I was coming, too," Charlie said.

"I thought you drove to the bowling alley," I said.

"I did. That's what I told Finn, that I had my car there. And he got all huffy. He was crossing his arms and shooting Luke suspicious looks. Finally, Finn asked if he could talk to me in private. I said fine, so he pulled me aside and told me that he didn't trust Luke and he didn't want to leave me alone with him. I told him I was perfectly capable of taking care of myself. And Phoebe finally got fed up and walked off. And Finn didn't even notice that she'd gone!" Charlie was triumphant. "I knew it would work! Your stepsister is a genius."

"So what happened after that?"

"We all left. Finn, Luke, and I walked out to the parking lot together, but neither of the guys would leave—Luke was obviously hoping Finn would get the hint and go away, but Finn just stood there, glaring at us, refusing to leave us alone. So finally Luke had to ask for my phone number right in front of Finn," Charlie said.

"Did you give it to him?" I asked, curious as to how far Charlie was willing to take this.

"Of course! Why wouldn't I?"

"But Luke's going to think that you like him."

"So?"

I closed my eyes and pressed a thumb and forefinger over them. A muscle next to my right eye had begun to twitch.

"Miranda? Are you there?" Charlie asked.

"I'm here."

"So, what do you think?" Charlie was beginning to sound impatient.

I took in a deep breath. "I think that you should stop playing games before someone gets hurt."

"Who's going to get hurt?" Charlie scoffed.

"Luke. Phoebe. They're both actual people with actual feelings," I pointed out.

"Well, obviously, I don't want anyone to get hurt. But how else am I supposed to make Finn realize how he feels about me?" Charlie asked.

"Have you considered telling him how *you* feel?" I asked.

This was met by an absolute silence that ticked on for so long, I wondered if Charlie had hung up on me.

"I can't do that," she finally said.

"Why not?"

"Isn't it obvious? The only way that would turn out well is if Finn responded by telling me he felt the same way about me. Otherwise, it would be an absolute nightmare. He might think I'm joking, and just laugh at me. Or he might say he doesn't have feelings for me, and then he'd feel sorry for me. Or he could just say nothing, and everything would always be weird between us forever," Charlie ranted.

"I still think it's better than playing games with everyone," I said. "You said that Phoebe almost cried tonight."

"You're supposed to be on my side!" Charlie said.

"I am on your side—" I began, but Charlie interrupted me.

"No, you're not! You more concerned with Phoebe's feelings than you are with mine! Besides, I can't believe you're being such a hypocrite."

"Hypocrite?" I repeated, stung. "How am I being a hypocrite?"

"Because you're giving me advice to do something that you would never have the guts to do!" Charlie continued, her voice thin with anger. "Do you remember when you had a crush on Emmett Dutch for, what, two full years? You never told *him* how *you* felt."

"That was different. Emmett and I weren't friends. He didn't even know who I was," I protested.

But Charlie wasn't listening. "And then when you first liked Dex, you never came out and told him how you felt about him. And when he didn't e-mail you while you were in London, you just automatically assumed that it was over. All because you were too afraid to just talk to him about it."

I wasn't really enjoying this trip down memory lane. It had been a stressful enough night already, without adding this to the pile.

"What's your point?"

"You're not in a position to be giving relationship advice. Unlike Hannah, who clearly knows what she's doing."

"Fine!" I said. "Then why don't you just call Hannah?"

"Maybe I will!" Charlie retorted.

There was another long pause, and I again wondered if Charlie had hung up. Then I considered hanging up. But then I decided that I wasn't up to getting into a big fight with Charlie right now. I had enough conflict in my life at the moment.

"Are you still there?" I finally asked.

"I'm still here. Do you really think I should tell him how I feel?" Charlie asked, in a very different sort of voice from the one she'd been shouting at me with a moment before.

"I don't know. You're probably right. I shouldn't be giving out relationship advice."

"I shouldn't have said that," Charlie said, sounding contrite.

"No, I mean it. I don't know what I'm talking about. I don't know about anything anymore," I said wearily. My eye was still twitching, and a headache had started to throb at my temples. "But I probably should go and try to get some sleep. I have to get up early for work tomorrow."

"Okay. Feel better. I'll talk to you tomorrow," Charlie said. Then she hesitated. "Sorry I yelled."

"No worries," I said. "Bye."

Chapter Twenty-four

When Mrs. Fisher answered the door the next morning, she didn't look happy. Her eyes were hard and narrowed, her mouth was a taut line, and her cheekbones were flushed high and bright. I took an involuntary step back from her, tripped over the edge of the step, and ended up stubbing my toe on the walkway.

"Ouch," I said, standing on one foot to favor my throbbing toe.

Mrs. Fisher did not seem to have noticed my lack of grace.

"Miranda," she said, "please come in. My husband and I would like to have a word with you."

"Mr. Fisher?" I asked tentatively. I'd never met Mr. Fisher. And, judging by how angry Mrs. Fisher seemed, I wasn't at all sure I wanted to meet him now. But I couldn't think of a way to gracefully bow out, so I limped into the house.

It was silent again, but, even so, I glanced through the French doors into the living room, half expecting to see Amelia at her piano as she almost always was when I arrived. The living room was empty.

"Where's Amelia?" I asked.

Mrs. Fisher didn't respond. Instead, she strode off to the

kitchen, heels clicking loudly against the tile floor, clearly expecting me to follow. My heart started to beat a bit faster. I had a bad feeling about this.

Reluctantly, I followed her. Amelia's father was sitting at the table, looking somber and vaguely uneasy, as though he didn't want to be there any more than I did. In person, he looked even more like Amelia than he did in the family photo I'd seen. They both had the same large, serious eyes, the same angular face, the same too-pale skin.

I managed a smile at Mr. Fisher, despite the nervous wriggling in my stomach. He didn't smile back at me. Instead, he just nodded, looking grave.

"Michael, this is Amelia," Mrs. Fisher said shortly. "Amelia, please sit down."

I sat in one of the ladder-backed kitchen chairs and folded my hands on my lap. Mrs. Fisher took a seat on the opposite side of the table from me, next to her husband. She sat very erect, her shoulders squared.

"Do you know what we want to talk to you about?" Mrs. Fisher asked.

I've always hated it when you know you're in trouble, and the person in charge—a parent or teacher—starts off with this question. What happened to my Fifth Amendment right not to incriminate myself? Sure, this might not be an official courtroom, but at the moment, it sure felt like one. Only Mrs. Fisher was the prosecutor and judge all rolled into one. What did that make Mr. Fisher? I stole a glance at him, and saw that he was gravely regarding me. He was the jury, I decided.

The thing was, I did have a pretty good idea why I was there—Amelia had talked to her mom about cutting back on the amount of time she spent practicing the piano, and somewhere in the midst of that discussion, my name had come up.

I drew in a deep breath. "Amelia talked to you about not wanting to practice quite as much."

Mrs. Fisher looked surprised. "So you don't deny that you know about it," she said.

I shook my head. "No."

"What business do you have telling an impressionable young girl that she should give up the great passion in her life, the one thing she's been dreaming of and working towards for years?" Mrs. Fisher asked. Her voice was as sharp and cold as an icicle.

"I didn't tell her that," I said indignantly.

"You just said you did!"

"No, I didn't. I never told Amelia that she shouldn't play the piano!" I said.

Mrs. Fisher's lips curled down, somewhere between a frown and a sneer. I could tell she didn't believe me, so I turned to Mr. Fisher.

"Amelia was upset. Partly because she doesn't want to change piano teachers, but also because she feels like she's under a lot of pressure and that all of the decisions about the sort of life she's going to lead have already been made for her. And I told her that she should talk to you about all of that," I said.

"Would it surprise you to hear that Amelia told us that you told her she doesn't have to be a pianist?" Mrs. Fisher asked.

I tried to remember if that was exactly what I'd said. "I guess I did say that, but I didn't mean—" Before I could finish, Mrs. Fisher cut in again.

"Your story keeps changing, Miranda. One minute, you say that you just told her to talk to us, and the next you're admitting that you told her to give up the piano. Which one is it?" Mrs. Fisher asked. She folded her arms over her chest and looked levelly at me.

I felt like I was standing on a hill of sand, and with every step up I took, I slid down even farther.

"It's neither. Or, I mean, it's both. Sort of," I said, starting to feel flustered. "The main thing I told her was that she should talk to you about her feelings."

"And that's exactly what she did do. At dinner last night, Amelia announced that she was tired of practicing, and that she wasn't going to play anymore. And she told us that you'd told her it was okay," Mrs. Fisher said.

"No! I just told that it was her life and she needed to be involved in any decisions that were made about her future," I said. "She's just under so much pressure—"

Mr. Fisher looked up sharply then, his eyes troubled. But Mrs. Fisher just pressed her lips into an even tighter line and said, "The only pressure Amelia is under is that which she puts on herself. And she's hardly an ordinary ten-year-old. She's a musical genius. It would be a tragedy for her to throw her gift away."

"I don't think she really wants to do that," I said, twisting my hands together my lap. "But she's getting burned out. She needs to have a life outside of the piano. To get away from it sometimes."

"You don't get to make those decisions for Amelia," Mrs. Fisher said coldly.

"I didn't want to . . . I really didn't mean to . . ." I gabbled. I wanted to say something that would fix this, that would assure the Fishers that all I had been trying to do was be a good friend to Amelia. But I couldn't seem to find the right words to explain this. It was especially hard sitting there in their gloomy gray kitchen, with Mrs. Fisher spitting-mad and Mr. Fisher so quiet and watchful.

Mrs. Fisher seemed to notice her husband's silence for the first time. She turned on him. "Don't you have anything you would like to say to Miranda?"

Mr. Fisher cleared his throat. "Perhaps it would be best if we found alternate child care for Amelia for the remainder of the summer."

I had been expecting this ever since Mrs. Fisher first led me back to the kitchen. Even so, hearing it said aloud—I was being *fired*—made my insides shrivel up. I'd been fired from my very first job. Epic fail.

I nodded and stood up, noticing that my legs somehow felt both shaky and wooden. I waited for the Fishers to say something further, but Mrs. Fisher seemed to have run out of steam—she stared down at the table, her arms still crossed, as though she couldn't bear to look up at me—and Mr. Fisher had returned to his mute, contemplative posture. When it became clear that they weren't going to say anything else, I turned and headed down the hallway, happy to see that despite the woodenness and shakiness, my legs were still capable of carrying me away.

When I got to the front door, I heard a noise from upstairs. I looked up, and there, sitting on the top stair, was Amelia. She looked very small and very sad, sitting hunched over, with her arms wrapped around her legs. I raised a hand in a halfhearted wave. Amelia waved back.

And then I turned away, opened the front door, and left.

Chapter Twenty-five

It wasn't that I was avoiding Dex. It was just that the first time he called, I was biking back from the Fishers' house, still reeling from having been fired. I looked at the caller ID, saw Dex's name, and decided that while of course I was going to talk to him—eventually—I wanted to be prepared and, if at all possible, somewhat poised when that conversation did happen. I stuck my phone back in my pocket and kept on biking, the ocean breeze drying the tears on my cheeks.

The second time Dex called, later that afternoon, I was sitting at the kitchen table in the beach house. I was trying to study for my driving test the next day, but was really just staring into space, contemplating everything in my life that had gone wrong over the past twenty-four hours and the very real possibility that it was going to get even worse tomorrow if I failed the exam. Which I was pretty sure was going to happen. This time when my phone rang, I was tempted to pick it up—my heart gave a small leap of excitement when I saw who was calling—but I hesitated, still unsure of what I should say to him.

Dex stopped calling after that, and instead began texting me.

I'm sorry, the first text read. *Can we talk?*

The second, which arrived five minutes later, read, *Please stop ignoring me . . .*

Then, a little while later, *If I don't talk to you, good luck tomorrow.*

"Don't you think you're being a little childish?" Hannah asked, reading over my shoulder. I jumped. I hadn't even heard her come into the kitchen.

"Are you training to be a ninja or something?" I asked, pressing one hand over my heart, willing it to slow back down to a normal rate.

"You have to talk to him eventually," Hannah said, ignoring my ninja crack.

"I know," I muttered. "I will."

"When?"

"When I can think of something to say. Besides, I have my driving test tomorrow. I need to stay focused on that. I'll talk to him after it's over."

"You're not seriously worried about your driving test, are you? I don't know anyone who's failed," Hannah said.

"Is that supposed to make me feel better?" I asked.

"Yes. Doesn't it?" Hannah asked.

"Not even a little bit," I said.

Hannah went to the refrigerator, opened the door, and stared in. Then, somewhat sadly, she closed the door.

"What's wrong?" I asked.

"I'm hungry," Hannah said.

"So eat something."

"Can't. I have a modeling job tomorrow," Hannah said.

"Another casting call?" I asked.

"No, I've already been hired! Didn't I tell you? Jojo, the photographer I worked with for the catalogue shoot, got me the job. It's for an advertising campaign for UFO Computers," Hannah said.

"Isn't that a national store?" I asked.

My stepsister nodded happily. "It's a really big deal that I was chosen. That's why I don't want to eat anything and end up with a tummy bulge."

"That's great about the job, but you can't go the whole day without eating," I said. It was a horrifying prospect. I get weak if I go more than three waking hours without eating.

"I'll have a salad or something for dinner," Hannah said vaguely. She got herself a glass of water and then sat down at the table across from me. Without asking permission, she picked up my phone and began scrolling through the messages Dex had sent me.

"Hey!" I said. "Those are private!"

Hannah ignored me. "If you're not going to talk to him, you have to at least text him back," she said bossily. "Hmm. What should you say? I know!" She began to type into my phone.

"Stop!" I said indignantly. I tried to grab the phone out of Hannah's hands, but she turned one shoulder away, deftly moving out of my reach. "What are you saying?"

"Here, see for yourself." Hannah handed me the phone.

Tx for the good luck! Let's meet up after my test. Beach at 2?

"You didn't send it, did you?" I asked.

"Not yet. Why, is there something you want to add?"

"Yes. I want to delete everything after good luck, including the exclamation point," I said. "And instead put in that I'll call him after my test is over. If I pass. If I fail, I'm going to spend the rest of my life hiding in shame."

Hannah grabbed the phone back, before I could type it myself. "I'll do it," she said. But instead of deleting what I'd asked her to, she instead hit a few buttons, and the phone let out a familiar chirp.

I gaped at her. "Did you just send your message?"

"Yep," Hannah said, tucking her hair behind her ears and looking generally pleased with herself.

"Without changing it like I asked you to?"

Hannah nodded. "It was better my way," she said.

I grabbed my phone out of her hand, wondering if there was some way to undo what she had just done, but the phone chirruped again, notifying me of Dex's response: *I'll meet you by the lifeguard shack. CU then! Love you. XXOO.*

Hannah leaned forward, so she could read, too. "Look. He sent you hugs and kisses. That's sweet," she said.

"I can't believe you!" I exclaimed, pulling the phone out of her reach and stuffing it in my pocket to prevent any further rogue texting on Hannah's part. Even so, I couldn't help feeling just the slightest bit better. And it wasn't just the L-word. I was going to see Dex tomorrow. And no matter what happened, no matter what we ended up saying to each other, it had to be better than the horrible uncertainty I'd been feeling ever since learning that he was leaving town. Nothing was worse than not knowing what was going to happen.

"Now we have to figure out what you're going to say to Dex when you see him tomorrow," Hannah said. "What's your goal?"

"What do you mean?"

"Are you going to ask him to give up his scholarship and stay in Orange Cove?" Hannah asked,

"No! Of course not!" I said. "I mean, I hate that he's leaving, but . . . no." I shook my head, resolute. "I would never ask him to give up such a good opportunity. I wouldn't want him to."

"Then why are you so mad?"

"I'm not mad. I'm just hurt that he didn't tell me himself, that I had to hear it from one of his friends," I explained. "And, yeah, I guess I'm also worried about what this will mean for us in the future. It's like we just got together, and it's been so great, and now he's going away." I shrugged, feeling tears start to prick at my eyes. "What happens now?"

"Do you think you'll break up?" Hannah asked.

"I don't know. I don't want to, but maybe . . . maybe it would be for the best," I said, feeling hollow.

"That's exactly what you should tell him!"

"I should tell him I want to break up with him?"

"No. Tell him that you don't want to break up, but you'll understand if he does," Hannah said. She leaned forward, her eyes bright. "Haven't you ever heard that saying about having a bird fly away from you?"

I blinked at her. "Huh?"

"You know. That thing about how if you have a pet bird, you should let it out of its cage and see if it flies away?"

"That's not exactly how the saying goes," I said.

"What is it, then?"

"Something along the lines of if you have a caged bird, you should let it fly free. If it flies away and never returns, you know it wasn't yours to begin with," I said.

"Exactly. But if it returns to you, then you know it's true love!" Hannah said, sighing happily. She took a sip of her water.

"Or that the bird got hungry, and didn't know how to find its own food out in the wild," I said. "And you do know it's a metaphor, right? You're not supposed to actually go around freeing birds."

"Maybe I should be a relationship counselor. What do you think?"

"I thought you wanted to be a model."

"I could be both! I'll model for a few years, and then when I get too old, I'll be a therapist. Just like Christy Turlington. Only she didn't go into therapy. She went into yoga. But it's practically the same!" Hannah said. "And look at all of the good work I've been doing around here. Speaking of which, have you heard from Charlie?"

"Yeah, she called last night. Luke asked her for her number, and Finn was really jealous," I said, even though I hated to encourage my stepsister in her meddling, especially after the texting incident.

"You see?" Hannah was delighted. "I have a gift for bringing people together! What do you have to do to become a relationship counselor?"

"I'm not sure. It's probably something you have to go to college for. Maybe even get a postgraduate degree," I said.

"Hmm." Hannah looked thoughtful, tapping her fingers on the table. "It's something to think about. That sounds like a lot of work, though. I don't know if I want to be in school for that long. I don't like studying."

"Speaking of which," I said. I waved my driving test manual at Hannah. "I have to read through this at least one more time before tomorrow. And then when Dad comes home, he's going to take me out for one last practice session. Until I get this driving exam over with, I don't want to think of anything but three-point turns and merging."

"Okay," Hannah said, standing. She picked up her glass of water and took one last, longing look at the refrigerator. "Do you think if I eat an apple it will make me look bloated tomorrow?"

"No," I said.

"I don't know if I should risk it," Hannah said.

"That's one thing in favor of a career in counseling—you wouldn't have to starve yourself," I said.

"That's true. On the other hand, you also don't get to wear designer clothes and have everyone tell you how beautiful you are all the time," Hannah said. She gave me a broad smile, grabbed an apple out of the fruit bowl on the counter, and swept from the room.

Chapter Twenty-six

TO: mirandajbloom@gmail.com
FROM: Della@DellaDeLaCourte.com
RE: Driving is Overrated

Darling,
Good luck on your driving test today!

But if you should happen to fail, remember that you
don't need a driver's license to get around London. You just
take taxis everywhere! It's much more chic than driving
yourself.

XXXOOO,
Sadie

P.S. You are coming, aren't you, darling? The suspense is kill-
ing me!

The examiner for my driving test, Mr. Greene, was a short man
with a large stomach, hunched shoulders, and a head that was completely bald except for some greasy gray-brown fringe that looped

from one ear around the back of his head to the other ear. Mr. Greene sat in the passenger seat of my dad's car, clipboard in hand.

"When you're ready, put the car in gear and head east on Ocean Drive," he said.

I looked over at my dad, who was waiting for me on a sidewalk bench, as I'd refused to let him sit in the backseat of the car during my test. He gave me an encouraging thumbs-up. I smiled back, drew in a deep breath in an attempt to quiet the butterflies zooming around my stomach, and shifted the car into drive. I was very glad I'd given up trying to learn how to drive Dex's stick shift car—this was going to be hard enough with the easier automatic.

I tapped my foot on the gas pedal a bit too hard, and the car jerked forward. Blushing, I compensated by pulling away from the sidewalk so slowly that a group of moms pushing jogging strollers blew past me.

Mr. Greene made a tick on his clipboard.

"What did you just check? I haven't failed already, have I?" I asked, my voice high and squeaky.

"Don't worry about what I'm writing," Mr. Greene said, in the sort of desperately-bored-bordering-on-clinically-depressed tone that made me think he was regretting his career choice. "Just focus on your driving."

"Okay. But do you mind if I ask what's on your checklist?" I asked hopefully.

"Yes," he said.

"Yes, you mind, or yes, I can ask?"

"Yes, I mind. Take a right at the stop sign."

I managed to switch on my right-hand turn signal and then come to a complete stop without causing either of us to get whiplash. I looked both ways to make sure there weren't any cars coming, and then successfully made the turn. My self-confidence grew. I hadn't hit anything yet! Or driven onto the sidewalk!

"Proceed to the traffic light and make a legal left-hand turn," Mr. Greene said.

"Okay," I said, wondering what exactly he meant by *legal*. Did that just mean I should wait for a green arrow? Or was something else involved? Panic welled up inside me, and I struggled to stay calm. I signaled a left-hand turn, moved over to the left-hand-turn lane, and waited for the light to turn. Next to me, Mr. Greene made another check mark. I desperately wished I knew what all of his check marks meant. Was there an automatic fail box? And if I did fail, would he tell me right away or would I still have to complete the test? And what would happen if I hit something? Or—even more horrific—some*one*?

"Have you ever had anyone get into an accident in the middle of their driving test?" I asked nervously.

"Yes," Mr. Greene said.

"Have you ever had anyone hit someone? A pedestrian or a bicyclist?"

"Yes," Mr. Greene said again.

I was instantly dying to know what had happened, but Mr. Greene didn't seem like the chatty type. In any case, the green arrow lit up, so I gently stepped on the gas and edged forward into the intersection. Happily, I managed not to hit any pedestrians, other vehicles, or signposts while doing so.

Mr. Greene continued to give me commands in a depressed monotone. I completed a three-point turn, backed up fifty feet, merged into a lane of traffic, and pulled into a parking spot outside a dry cleaner. This last task caused me the most problems—I pulled in just a tad too far, and the front tires bumped up against the edge of the sidewalk—but it was hardly noticeable. Or, at least, I hoped so. Mr. Greene simply made another check mark on his list. Luckily, I didn't have to parallel-park—the one driving task I'd never yet managed to do properly.

Mr. Greene finally told me to pull back up outside the Department of Motor Vehicles, where the test had begun. There were a few agonizing moments where he scribbled something on his clipboard with a ballpoint pen—What was he writing? *What?*—but then he capped his pen and then made rather a production out of blowing his nose on an old-fashioned cotton handkerchief. I had the feeling that he was enjoying himself—for the first time—by keeping me in suspense.

Well? Did I pass? Did I? I wanted to scream at him. But instead, I remained outwardly calm, my hands clenched on the steering wheel in the ten-and-two position, and waited while he tore off the top sheet of his pad. My dad was hovering anxiously outside on the sidewalk, peering into the car.

"You passed," Mr. Greene finally said, handing me the form.

"I *passed*?" I gasped.

Mr. Greene nodded dourly. I was so excited, I almost lunged forward to hug him, but managed to get a hold of myself in time. He smelled like cough drops, and besides, I didn't think he was the hugging sort.

"Thank you! Thank you so much!" I said.

Mr. Greene nodded again, and huffed and groaned as he climbed out of the car. My dad leaned forward into the car and looked at me. "Well? What happened?"

"I passed!"

"Yes!" Dad yelled, raising his hands in two triumphant fists. "You did it!"

"You don't have to sound so surprised," I said, but I was grinning, too.

Dad climbed back in the car and kissed me on the cheek. "Congratulations, sweetheart!"

"Thanks," I said. I could still hardly believe it. I'd really passed!

"So? Now what?" Dad asked.

"Now I have to park, and then go inside and have them process the paperwork and take my picture. And then I get my license!"

"My baby is getting her driver's license. It seems like just yesterday you were crawling around on those fat little hands and feet," Dad sighed.

"Dad!"

"This is cause for a celebration. What do you say we go in, get your license, and then later the four of us will all go out to dinner somewhere?" Dad asked.

I hesitated. Dinner out with Peyton was not my idea of a celebration. Dad seemed to read my mind.

"Or, if you'd rather, we can just go out on our own. Just the two of us," he suggested.

But that didn't seem right, either. And I had to admit that ever since Dad and Peyton had started seeing the marriage therapist, Peyton hadn't been nearly as critical and unpleasant as she normally was. Weeks had gone by without her suggesting I needed a nose job or remarking on how large my feet are.

"No, we'll all go together," I said, forcing myself to sound cheerful at the prospect.

"Are you sure?" Dad looked hopeful. "It's your celebration. We can do whatever you want."

"I'm sure," I said.

"Thanks, honey," Dad said, patting my hand. "And for the record, I'm really proud of you. And I'm officially terrified at the idea that you're now going to be out driving on the roads. I'll probably never have a peaceful night's sleep again."

"Thanks, Dad."

Chapter Twenty-seven

My dad offered to lend me his car so I could drive over to the beach to meet Dex. But the public beach was a little less than a mile away down the coast from our house, and I thought the walk would help clear my head. I tried not to mind how relieved my dad looked.

As I walked along the beach, my bare feet leaving a faint trail in the wet sand, lingering euphoria at having passed my driving test was quickly replaced by yet another bout of stomach-twisting anxiety. What was I going to say to Dex? What would he say to me? Were we about to break up?

I hadn't reached any conclusions by the time I spotted the lifeguard shack set up high on stilts at the back edge of the public beach. Brightly colored umbrellas were dotted along the beach. Sunbathers lounged in chairs, their faces turned up to the sky, while young children scooped sand into buckets with shovels as the water lapped up over their feet. There wasn't much wind today, and the waves rolling in were low and calm, so the beach was largely free of surfers. Only a few kids with boogie boards fastened to their ankles with Velcro cuffs were attempting to ride the gentle waves.

I scanned the beach, looking for a coppery redhead, and finally spotted Dex, sitting on a log at the bottom of the dunes, just to the left of the lifeguard shack. His long legs were bent in front of him, and he was resting his elbows on knees, his hands clasped together. I drew in a deep breath, steeling myself for whatever was about to happen, and, my heart thumping heavily, trudged up the beach toward Dex.

"Hi," I said when I reached him.

Dex looked up at me, squinting in the sun. "Hi," he said.

He looked unusually serious. His pale blue eyes were free of their usual glinting humor and he wasn't smiling. I sat down next to him on the log. My mouth suddenly felt very dry. This was it, I thought. Dex was about to break up with me. If everything was okay, he'd have been happier to see me. He would have stood and kissed me. Instead, he just sat there, not even taking my hand in his. It felt like we were already miles apart, even though he was sitting only inches away.

"Where's Willow?" Dex asked.

"I left her at the beach house. It's too hot to bring her, but she's furious that I left without her. I even heard her bark once or twice," I said. Willow rarely barked, not even when she saw her archenemy, Madonna the Cat.

"Poor Willow," Dex said.

I nodded and dug my toes into the hot sand. I wanted to ask him if he was breaking up with me. Part of me thought that if I never brought it up and he never brought it up, well, then, it would never happen. Even if he wanted it to. But a larger part of me didn't want to be the desperate girlfriend hanging on to a guy who didn't want to be with her. I had my pride. I hugged my arms around myself and tried to work up the courage to ask him.

But before I could, Dex spoke. "So I guess you're breaking up with me," he said, his voice flat.

"*What?*" I was so astonished that for a moment I forgot to breathe. When I remembered—I felt a searing pain in my chest—I let my breath out in a great whoosh.

"You're breaking up with me," Dex repeated. "Aren't you?"

"No," I said slowly. "I'm not. I thought *you* were breaking up with *me*."

"Why would you think that?"

"Why?" I repeated. *"Why?"*

"Yes," Dex said. "Why? And don't just repeat the word *why*. I mean, why would you think I wanted to break up with you?"

"You mean you *don't* want to break up with me?" I asked.

"No. I mean, yes."

"Yes?"

"I mean, yes, I really don't want to break up with you. And you don't want to break up with me?" Dex asked.

"No. I don't want to break up," I said. "Well, not unless *you* want to."

"I don't want to," Dex said again.

"Okay," I said.

"Okay," he said. He smiled. "I'm glad that's cleared up."

I grinned back at him, until I suddenly remembered what had led up to this conversation. Dex was leaving and he'd hidden it from me. The smile faded from my face.

"So you're really leaving?" I asked.

"Hi, Miranda."

Dex and I both looked up sharply. Amelia was standing there. She was wearing her purple-striped bathing suit and her dark hair was pulled back in a ponytail. A faded light blue knapsack was slung over one of her shoulders.

"Amelia," I said. "What are you doing here?"

"I called your house, and your dad told me you were here," Amelia said.

I glanced around, looking for her mom and not seeing her. "Wait. You came by yourself?"

Amelia nodded.

"How did you get here?"

"I biked over," Amelia said simply.

"Does your mom know you're here?" I asked.

"Of course not. She'd have never let me come. She thinks you're a bad influence on me," Amelia said.

"I'm not a bad influence!" I said indignantly.

"I think I'm missing something," Dex said, looking confused. "Why would Amelia's mother think you're a bad influence on her?"

"I forgot. You don't know—I was fired," I said.

"Seriously? Why?" Dex asked.

"Mrs. Fisher thought that I was interfering with Amelia's piano practice," I explained.

"Were you?" Dex asked.

"No! I just thought that Amelia should get a say in her life, that's all," I said. I looked at Amelia. "You shouldn't have come. Your mom wouldn't like it."

"It's okay. She doesn't know I'm here."

"That's not okay," I exclaimed. "Where does she think you are?"

"At home, practicing. She's there, too. But she was talking on the phone to one of her clients, and I knew she'd be on forever, so I plugged my iPod into the stereo, turned on some Vladimir Horowitz, and left."

"What's Vladimir Horowitz?" Dex asked.

"He was a really famous pianist," Amelia explained. "Anyway, my mom never bothers me while I'm practicing, so as long as she hears the music, she'll have no idea that I'm not home."

"That's brilliant," Dex said. He sounded impressed. I kicked him gently in the heel and shot him a quelling look.

"Amelia, your mom is going to freak when she finds out you're gone," I said. "Come on, I'm taking you home right now. Wait. I don't have a car." I looked hopefully at Dex. "Did you drive over?"

"No. I walked over from the pool. My sister needed to borrow my car today, so she dropped me off at work today," Dex said.

"You're going to have to bike home on your own," I told Amelia. I didn't like the idea, but it was either that or I'd have to call Amelia's mom to come pick her up. And even though it had been wrong of Amelia to sneak out, I didn't want to get her in trouble.

"No! I'm not going!" Amelia said, stamping her foot on the ground.

"Why not?" I asked.

"Because Dex promised he'd teach me how to surf," Amelia said.

"No, I didn't," Dex said quickly. "I told you I'd teach you the basics, on dry land, but that you had to wait to surf until you're a stronger swimmer."

"But I *can* swim," Amelia protested. "I'm ready now."

"Not well enough to surf. It can be really dangerous out there, even on a day like today." Dex gestured toward the seemingly calm ocean. "There's a strong undertow out there. The lifeguards posted a warning about it on the board."

"I can do it!" Amelia insisted.

Dex shook his head. "It's not safe," he said.

"You just don't want to bother teaching me!"

"Amelia, that's not fair," I said. "Dex taught you to how to swim."

Amelia took a step back. Her face was red and contorted with rage.

"He doesn't care about me, and neither do you! So stop pretending like you do!" Amelia shouted.

I grew aware of the looks we were getting from people sitting nearby. Some had even put down their books and magazines, and were craning around to get a better look at the commotion.

"I'm not pretending. I do care about you, and so does Dex," I protested. "But you shouldn't even be here, Amelia. I'm not your babysitter anymore."

Amelia looked as though I'd slapped her. She bit her lower lip, as though to hold in tears, and then turned and stormed away.

"Wait! I'll take you home," I called after her. We'd have to walk back to the beach house to get my dad's car, but that was better than having her go off by herself when she was this upset.

But Amelia didn't stop or turn around, or even acknowledge that I'd spoken.

I looked at Dex, feeling equal amounts of anxiety and exasperation. "Should I go after her?"

"How far away does she live?" Dex asked.

"Not far. Maybe a mile and a half?" I guessed. "She and I have biked it before."

"I'm sure she'll be fine, then. Besides, if you're the one to take her home, her mom might think you put her up to sneaking out," Dex said.

"That's true," I said. I sat back on the log next to Dex, wondering if I could have handled that better. Should I have reminded Amelia that it was no longer my job to take care of her? She'd looked so hurt.

Dex took my hand and gave it a squeeze.

"Don't worry. She'll be fine. When I was Amelia's age, I biked all over town by myself," Dex said.

"Yeah, I guess I did, too," I said, feeling a bit better.

We sat quietly for a few minutes, watching the sun sparkle on the ocean. A small girl with pigtails and a pink swim shirt was walking into the water, holding on tightly to her mother's hand.

"Why wouldn't you talk to me when I called you yesterday?" Dex asked.

"I wasn't sure what to say. Why didn't you tell me before that you were leaving?"

"I didn't know how," Dex said. "It's something I've wanted to do for a long time, long before I ever met you. This school, the Brown Academy, has a top lacrosse program, one of the best in the country. Getting on the team there would almost guarantee me a spot on a top college team. But I didn't think I'd ever be able to go, because there's no way my parents could ever afford it. Then my scholarship came through right after you and I got together, and I wasn't sure what to do."

"That's what you wanted to talk to Wendy about."

"She's been away at prep school for the past year. I wanted to know if she liked it."

"Not the same school you'll be going to?" I asked hopefully.

"No." Dex smiled faintly. "Her school is in New York. The Brown Academy is in Maine."

I nodded, glad for that at least. Wendy Erickson might have a serious boyfriend, but even so, I didn't relish the idea of her getting any closer to Dex. "So what did Wendy tell you?"

"She told me that there are things she likes and things she doesn't like about going away from school. She said that she really missed her friends and family at home, and that the academics were a lot harder. But she said she eventually adjusted and made friends up there, and that overall she was glad she'd gone," Dex said.

I tried to swallow down the walnut-sized lump in my throat. That's what would happen with Dex, too, I thought sadly. He'd go away, and at first he'd miss his life here, but gradually he would get used to it. And eventually, his life there would be his regular life, and this would just be a place he'd visit on holidays.

Don't go, I wanted to stay. *If you really loved me, you would stay*.

Except that I couldn't say that. I couldn't ask him to give up this amazing opportunity. And I wouldn't, because *I* loved *him*.

I inhaled deeply. "I think she's right," I said.

"You do?" Dex asked.

"I'm sure there's an adjustment period at first, but once you settle in and get to know the people at your new school, I'm sure you'll be really happy there."

Dex looked down, and nudged a piece of dried seaweed with his toe. "I don't know," he said broodingly. "I'm not even sure I want to go anymore."

"Why not?"

Dex looked at me, squinting against the bright sun. "I don't want to move away from you," he said softly.

Joy and pain swelled inside me, until I thought my skin would burst from trying to contain all of my feelings. Dex was thinking about giving up on his dream just to stay near me. The lump in my throat expanded. If I told him not to go . . . if I asked him to stay for me . . .

But I couldn't do that. I shook my head. "No. You're right, it *is* too good of an opportunity pass up. It's like you said, this could mean a full scholarship to college for you. It's a big deal."

"What happens with us?" Dex asked.

"We'll talk on the phone and on Skype. We'll make it work," I said.

And even though I'd worried about the exact same thing—how well could a long-distance relationship really work?—at that moment, it *felt* like the truth. We would figure out a way. Somehow.

"And we'll see each other during my vacations," Dex said.

I drew in a deep breath, and exhaled slowly.

"Actually, there's something I haven't told you," I said.

"What?"

"My mom wants me to move to London to live with her," I admitted. "I haven't decided if I'm going to go yet."

Ever since I found out Dex was leaving, I'd wondered if it changed how I felt about moving to London. Had I been lying to myself all along, thinking that there were more reasons than just Dex to stay in Orange Cove?

Oddly enough, the decision didn't seem any clearer. Sure, taking Dex out of the equation might tilt things in London's favor, but there were still reasons—good reasons—to stay. For one thing, my friends were here. Charlie and Finn could make me crazy at times—and I wondered if that would even get worse, now that Charlie had finally owned up to her feelings for Finn—but they were like family to me. It was impossible to imagine not seeing them almost every day.

And then there was my position at *The Ampersand*. The more I wrote—and I tried to write every day—the more it felt like it was the right path for me. And *The Ampersand* had won all kinds of awards and national recognition. Sure, a school magazine might not be the only chance I'd ever have to publish—hopefully it wouldn't. But having a position there, getting published in it, might help get me into one of the top writing programs in the country when I went to college. Going to London might be an interesting addendum to my college applications, but surely it wouldn't be quite as impressive.

"Wow," Dex said.

"Yeah, I know."

I turned to look at him. As we stared at each other, I thought I could actually feel my heart breaking. Tears welled up, stinging my eyes. Dex looked close to tears, too.

"Miranda—" he began.

But before Dex could finish whatever it was he was about to

say, shouts broke out, coming from the direction of the water's edge. We both looked up.

"There's a little girl out there! I think she's in trouble!" a man called out.

"Someone get the lifeguard!" a woman screamed.

Dex and I were both on our feet running before we heard another word.

Amelia, I thought. *Amelia.* Somehow, I just knew it was her, even before I saw the long dark hair floating up in the water and the glimpses of a purple-striped swimsuit amidst the white-foam-capped waves.

I heard the sharp blow of the lifeguard's whistle and knew the guards on duty were on their way, but Dex got to the water first. Without hesitating, he dove in, fully clothed, and began swimming out toward the small figure bobbing twenty feet out from shore. People crowded around me, pointing and shouting, as though this would somehow help Dex. I knew there was no way he could hear any of us over the roar of the ocean.

The two lifeguards on duty, each clutching a long red floatie, reached the water and dove in, swimming after Dex. But he'd already gotten to Amelia, and had turned her over, faceup, hooking one arm around her to keep her afloat.

"Over here!" Dex shouted to the lifeguards, waving his free arm in the air.

Even though it was a boiling-hot day, my entire body had turned to ice. Numbly, my hands clasped in front of me, I sent up a silent prayer, *please oh please oh please oh please*, as the lifeguards took Amelia from Dex, leaned her back against their red flotation devices, and together, swam her ashore.

There were gasps and muttering from the crowd as the lifeguards carried Amelia out of the surf and laid her down on the sand. She looked so small and helpless. A loose circle of observers formed around Amelia and her rescuers. I heard someone sob, and realized, distantly, that it was me.

"Stand back," one of the lifeguards shouted to the crowd, and everyone took an obligatory two steps back, without breaking the circle formation.

I couldn't move. I stood there, frozen in place, until Dex, his hair dripping wet and rivulets of water running down his arms, took my hand and pulled me to the side.

Amelia was breathing and had her eyes open. That was something, I thought. She seemed confused, though, as the lifeguards asked her questions, and she kept convulsing with body-racking coughs. Someone brought over a towel, which was draped over Amelia, shielding her pale skin from the sun.

"Is this girl's parent or guardian here?" one of the lifeguards asked.

I didn't respond—I wanted to, but I couldn't. I was vaguely aware that my legs, arms, pretty much every part of me was trembling. Dex put an arm around me—wet, but reassuringly solid— and pressed a hand on my shoulder.

"I'm her babysitter," I said.

This caused the crowd to start murmuring again, as everyone turned to look at me. Some of the gazes were curious, others were downright hostile, especially as they took in Dex's arm around me. I knew what they were thinking: *What kind of a horrible, irresponsible person hangs out with her boyfriend instead of watching the child in her care?* And they were right. It didn't matter that I hadn't brought Amelia to the beach. She had come there to find me. I should have seen her safely home. This was all my fault.

An ambulance was driven right onto the beach, and the medics jumped out and went straight over to Amelia. They checked her vitals and then moved her onto a stretcher and transferred her to the ambulance.

"I should go with her," I said to Dex through chattering teeth.

"Go ahead. I'll call my sister for a ride. I'll meet you at the hospital as soon as I can," he promised.

I climbed into the ambulance after the medics. Between Amelia's stretcher and the various equipment, there wasn't a lot of room to navigate, but one nodded toward a chair, complete with seat belt, off to one side.

"Take a seat," the medic said.

I sat, facing Amelia. She looked very small and very pale. Her wet hair was a tangle around her face. There was a dark bruise just under her right eye.

"Hi," I said softly.

"Hi," Amelia croaked.

"What happened?" I asked. "Why were you in the water?"

"I wanted to prove that I was a good enough swimmer to surf," Amelia said. "But then I got out there, and it felt . . . it felt like I was being pulled down . . . and I couldn't . . . I couldn't . . ."

Amelia broke off then, her eyes welling with tears. Her teeth were chattering, and I could see that despite the heavy gray blanket the medic tucked around her, she was trembling. I wasn't sure if it was from cold or from shock. I leaned forward and took her small hand in mine.

"It's okay. Everything's okay now," I said.

"I want my mom," Amelia said. Her face crumpled, and she began to cry.

Chapter Twenty-eight

The waiting room at the hospital emergency room had rows and rows of uncomfortable plastic seats, tables stacked with magazines three years out of date, and faded posters on the wall advertising blood pressure medication. Dex and I sat side by side, our hands clasped, both of us silent. I wasn't entirely sure why we were waiting there—I doubted anyone would tell us anything, or that the Fishers would even want to speak to me—but the idea of leaving was unbearable.

Someone—I wasn't sure who—had called the Fishers. I'd given the medics Amelia's contact information while we were on our way to the hospital, and Amelia's mother had arrived moments after the ambulance. She ran into the waiting room, her face white with shock, demanding to see her daughter. She was escorted back to the patient area through a heavy pair of automated double doors. Mr. Fisher had arrived separately, a half hour later, looking just as shaken, although he was far more soft-spoken when he talked to the nurse staffing the counter. The nurse gestured in my direction—I suppose answering his question about who'd accompanied his daughter to the hospital—and Mr. Fisher turned to look at me. I raised a hand in silent greeting, and he nodded solemnly at me, before disappearing behind the same double set of doors.

"This wasn't your fault," Dex finally said.

I didn't answer. My head bowed down, and my shoulders slumped forward.

"It wasn't," Dex insisted.

"I should have been watching her," I said. My voice was so thin, I didn't recognize it as my own.

"It wasn't your responsibility."

"But I was there. And I knew she was at the beach alone," I said.

"You didn't know she was going to go swimming by herself," Dex pointed out. "How could you have? She was supposed to be on her way home."

"I know how contrary she is. I should have known she'd head straight for the ocean," I said miserably.

"You're not a mind reader," Dex pointed out. "Besides, I was there, too. That makes me just as responsible as you are."

I knew he was trying to make me feel better, but it wasn't working. Right now I just wanted to know that Amelia would be okay.

"Isn't that your dad?" Dex asked.

I looked up to see my dad walking toward us through the waiting room. I'd called home when we first got to the hospital to let him know where I was and what was going on. Dad had offered to come right over to get me, but I told him I wanted to wait and see how Amelia was.

"Dad?" I said, standing up so he'd see me.

"Hi, Miranda," Dad said, heading toward us. When he reached me, he gave me a big hug, squeezing me extra hard.

"What are you doing here?" I asked.

"I thought you might need some moral support," Dad said. He smiled at Dex. "Hi, there."

"Hi, Mr. Bloom," Dex said, standing, too, and shaking my dad's hand.

"Have you heard anything about Amelia's condition?" Dad asked as we all sat back down on the hard plastic chairs.

I shook my head. "No. The nurses won't tell us anything, because we're not family, and the Fishers haven't come back out."

"Why don't you come home?" Dad asked gently. "There's no point in just sitting here."

I shook my head. "That wouldn't feel right," I said. "But you don't have to stay. Dex can bring me home." Dex nodded in agreement. After his sister picked Dex up at the beach, he'd dropped her back off at their house and then driven to the hospital. Dad shrugged.

"I might as well wait with you for a while," he said.

It should have been weird sitting there in the shabby waiting room between my dad and my boyfriend, waiting for news that we might not even hear. But for some reason, it wasn't. It was oddly comforting.

•

We'd been waiting for just over two hours when the heavy double doors opened and the Fishers came out. They both looked pale and tired. Mr. Fisher took Mrs. Fisher's arm and led her over to where Dad, Dex, and I were sitting. I stood up as soon as I saw them approach. Dad and Dex quickly got to their feet, too.

"How is she?" I asked when the Fishers reached us.

"Amelia's fine," Mr. Fisher said. "She's resting right now, but I think they're going to release her and let us bring her home today."

Relief flooded through me. She was fine. Amelia was okay. I drew in a deep breath and let it out in a whoosh.

"That's great," I said. "Thanks for letting me know."

"Actually, we're the ones who should be thanking you, Miranda," Mrs. Fisher said. "I had no idea Amelia snuck out of the house. I heard the piano music, and I . . . I just assumed . . . I didn't even check on her."

Her voice broke, and her eyes filled with tears. Mr. Fisher put an arm around his wife's shoulders to steady her.

"If you hadn't been there, I don't know what would have happened," Mrs. Fisher continued.

I couldn't bear hearing this undeserved praise. I shook my head. "I didn't do anything. I was just sitting there. I wasn't watching her. I hadn't even realized she'd gone in the water until she got into trouble. And even then, Dex is the one who saved her," I said, gesturing to Dex. "He's a lifeguard."

"You're the one who went in after her?" Mrs. Fisher asked Dex.

Dex nodded, and Mrs. Fisher lunged at him, pulling him into a bear hug.

"Thank you. Thank you so much," she said.

Dex looked a bit embarrassed when she finally let him go. A faint rosy blush spread over his nose and cheeks, and he rumpled a hand through his hair.

"You're welcome," he said.

"I'm Richard Bloom, Miranda's father," Dad said, reaching to shake Mr. Fisher's hand. "I'm very glad to hear that Amelia's well."

"It's nice to meet you," Mr. Fisher said. "We're very thankful that your daughter and her friend were there for Amelia today."

"But you don't understand," I blurted out. "It was all my fault."

"No, it wasn't," Mrs. Fisher said gently. She reached out and took my hand, which should have been weird, but was actually sort of nice. "Amelia told us what happened. She used very bad judgment. And you had no idea what she was going to do, or what would happen as a result. We're just glad that you were there with this young man." Mr. Fisher smiled warmly at Dex. "And that you were there to ride to the hospital with her. She told us what a comfort that was for her."

"She did?" I said.

"She did," Mrs. Fisher confirmed. She smiled at me, although tears still glittered in her eyes. Mrs. Fisher squeezed my hand and released it. "What happened today was my fault, Miranda, not yours. If I'd been watching her more carefully, she would never have been able to sneak out of the house."

"Amelia is pretty crafty," I said fairly.

"I know she is," Mrs. Fisher said with a faint laugh. "She's too smart for her own good."

"I know what that's like," my dad remarked.

Mrs. Fisher wasn't done, though. She took in a deep breath, let it out, and said, "I owe you an apology, Miranda. I should never have fired you. I've just been so caught up in the idea of Amelia having this great talent . . . I somehow let it take over everything else."

"It's okay," I said quietly.

"No, it's not okay," Mrs. Fisher said. "I'm not letting myself off the hook that easily."

Mr. Fisher put an arm around his wife's shoulders again. "We need to spend some time together as a family, I think."

"Speaking of which, we should be going," Dad said. He smiled at me. "The Fishers probably want to go back in to be with Amelia."

"Right," I said. I hesitated. "I don't suppose I could see Amelia, could I?"

"She's sleeping right now," Mrs. Fisher said apologetically. "That's why we were able to step away for a moment."

"I understand. But could you tell her hi from me?" I asked.

"Of course," Mr. Fisher said.

My dad waited for me in his car while I said good-bye to Dex.

"Do you mind getting a ride home with your dad?" Dex asked. "I have to get back to the pool. Jessie covered my shift, so I have to go take hers. If I leave now, I might just be able to make it."

"Absolutely," I said. I smiled up at him. "Thanks for waiting with me. I didn't realize you were missing work."

"No problem. Jessie didn't mind," Dex said, taking my hand. He hesitated. "So, we're good, right?"

"We're good," I said. I let out a small laugh and looked at the ground. "And I was so sure you were going to break up with me today."

"I thought you were going to break up with me," Dex said.

"I'm glad we were both wrong," I said.

"Me, too," Dex said. He rested one hand lightly on the back of my neck, and the other on my waist, and drew me toward him, resting his forehead against mine, so that our eyes were only inches apart. I could make out every feathery fine point on his eyelashes. Suddenly Dex drew back, looking wary. "Wait—where's your dad?"

"He's in his car back over there," I said, gesturing behind me. "Can he see us?"

I shook my head. "Nope."

"Good. Because I don't want him to see me do this," Dex said, leaning forward to kiss me.

Chapter Twenty-nine

Charlie came over that evening. I was feeling so wrung out that I was already in bed when she arrived, even though it was only seven o'clock. I leaned back against a pile of pillows with the snowy white duvet draped over my lap. Charlie camped out at the foot of the bed. She'd brought a bag of chocolate-covered pretzels as a treat, and we took turns reaching into the blue foil bag for the candy.

After I finished telling Charlie about Amelia nearly drowning, I filled her in on everything that had been going on with me and Dex—his leaving for school, my fears that he was breaking up with me, that for one wild moment I'd considered asking him to stay, but instead encouraged him to go. Then, even though I felt like I'd been talking for hours at that point, I went on to tell her that Sadie had asked me to move to London. I wanted to get it all out at once, and not hold back any secrets.

"Wow," Charlie said, her eyes wide. She shook her head. "How did I not know any of this was going on?"

"You've had a lot on your mind lately," I said. "And I didn't say anything."

"Yeah, what's up with that?" Charlie frowned at me. "Why

didn't you tell me you were considering moving out of the country? That's not exactly a small thing."

"I'm sorry. I should have. I guess I wanted to figure out what I was going to do first," I said.

"And what are you going to do?"

I shrugged. "I have no idea," I said. "Right now I'm so tired, I just want to curl up and sleep for a hundred years."

Charlie shook her head and popped a pretzel in her mouth. She looked thoughtful as she chewed and swallowed it.

"Isn't it easier to make up your mind now that Dex isn't going to be here?" she asked. "He would have been one of the reasons you stayed, after all."

"That's the weird thing. Even though I've tried really hard not to let him affect my decision—I want to go or not go because it's what's best for me—I know he has been a factor. A big one. But once I found out he was going away, it didn't seem to change how I felt about London. I'm just as unsure about it as ever," I said. "Don't you think that's strange?"

"Nah," Charlie said, reaching for another pretzel. "You've been talking about writing for *The Ampersand* for years, ever since we were at Geek Middle. Now that you've finally got your spot, I'm sure it would be hard to give it up. And then, of course, there's me." She patted her chest modestly. "Your best friend in the whole world. You'd be heartbroken to have to leave me."

I grinned at her. "That's true."

"And I seriously don't think I could survive another two years at Geek High without you," Charlie said. She shuddered. "What a hideous thought."

"You'd still have Finn," I reminded her.

"Right," Charlie snorted. Her eyes flashed.

"Uh-oh. What happened?" I asked.

"Are you sure you want to hear this?" Charlie asked. "I'd understand if you weren't up to listening to me moan about my pathetic love life right now."

Tired of dwelling on my own crisis, I jumped at the chance for a distraction. "No, tell me. What happened?"

Charlie held up one hand, touching her thumb and index together to form a zero. "A big, fat nothing is what happened," she said. "The brilliant plan that couldn't fail? Well, it failed."

"Finn wasn't overcome with jealousy?" I asked sympathetically.

"Oh, he was. Just not for me," Charlie said gloomily. "It turns out that Phoebe knows all about Hannah's trick. After she left the bowling alley the other night, she apparently called her ex-boyfriend for a ride home and then went out for a coffee with him the next day. At Grounded. When she knew Finn was going to be there."

"That's so obvious," I said, my estimation of Phoebe going down a few notches.

"I know, right? But apparently it worked. Finn flipped out, and he and Phoebe had a big talk, and now they're back together. Thus proving that Finn is as big an idiot as I've always said he is," Charlie said contemptuously.

"I thought you were in love with him," I said.

"I am. But that's in spite of his idiocy," Charlie said, not noticing that she'd just finally admitted that she was in love with Finn. "And meanwhile, Luke won't stop calling me. I finally gave in, and agreed to go to the movies with him tomorrow night."

"Is that good or bad?" I asked.

"It's terrible! I don't like Luke in that way. Which means, of course, he'll probably fall madly in love with me, because that's what guys always do—they go for the wrong girl," Charlie said. "It's practically a given."

"Not always," I said, thinking of Dex and the kiss we'd shared earlier that day. The memory caused a whoosh of happiness tinged with sadness to spread through me. It wasn't the last time I'd see

Dex—we still had weeks together before he left for school. But it felt like the beginning of a good-bye. I wondered if that was what it would be like from now on—if every moment we spent together, every kiss we shared would be bittersweet. I sighed and hugged my pillow to my chest.

Charlie just rolled her eyes. "It's probably a good thing Dex is going away to school. At least you won't be so nauseatingly happy anymore."

"Hey!" I said. I whacked her with my pillow.

Charlie just ducked and giggled. "It's true! When I'm feeling bitter, I need to have bitter people around me."

"I'm not bitter. I'm sad," I said.

"I'll take what I can get," Charlie said. "Hey! Stop hitting me!"

I put the pillow down and leaned back again. "You never know. Finn might surprise you."

"I don't think so," Charlie said, shaking her head sadly. "If he really had feelings for me, he wouldn't have run back to Phoebe."

"But Finn still doesn't know how you feel about him. He thinks you see him as just another friend. If you told him how you felt—"

"Absolutely not," Charlie said, cutting me off. She flopped on her back. "I would just be setting myself up for complete and utter humiliation."

There was a knock on the door, and then Hannah opened the door a few inches wide. "Hey," she said. "How did your driving test go?"

"I passed," I said.

"You did!" Charlie sat bolt upright. "You didn't tell me that!"

"I sort of forgot in all of the excitement," I said. "Why are you out in the hallway, Hannah? Come on in. Charlie brought chocolate-covered pretzels. Although I know you probably won't eat them, will you?" I rolled my eyes at Charlie. "Hannah thinks she's fat."

"That's crazy talk," Charlie said.

The door opened an inch wider, but Hannah still didn't come in. I could barely see her, hovering out there.

"Something sort of happened at the photo shoot today," she said.

"How did it go?" I asked. Then, seeing Charlie's confusion, I explained, "Hannah was hired to model for an ad campaign for UFO Computers. It's actually a really big deal that she was picked," I added, feeling an unexpected rush of pride for my stepsister.

"Very cool," Charlie said, clearly impressed.

"No, it was *not* cool," Hannah said. She finally opened the door all the way and stepped through.

The first thing I noticed was her hair. It was silver. And not its usual pale, silvery blond. It was now a metallic silver, complete with sparkles. And there was something odd about her face, too, although I couldn't quite figure out what it was. She was clearly distressed. Her eyes glittered with tears, and her mouth was a tight, pinched line.

"Cool hair," Charlie said appreciatively.

"It's not cool. It's horrible!" Hannah said. Her voice broke on the word *horrible*.

"I like it. How long will the sparkles stay in it?" Charlie asked.

"Probably forever." Hannah wrapped her arms around herself. "They said it could take twenty to twenty-five hair washes for it to all come out."

"That's not forever. If you wash your hair every day, it will be back to normal in a little under a month," I said encouragingly.

"A month! I'm not going to walk around with freak hair for a month!"

"You won't have to," Charlie said. Charlie had been dyeing her hair since the age of eleven and, as a result, was quite knowledgeable on hair color. "There's a shampoo that will take all of the color out in a wash or two. You can buy it at the beauty-supply store. You have to be careful, though—it's strong, and it can strip a lot of the moisture out of your hair. Make sure you condition well afterwards."

"Really?" Hannah looked slightly mollified. She crossed my room and collapsed on the hard white chair in the corner. She still looked to be on the verge of tears. Her face was pale—although that could just have been the heavy makeup she was still wearing—and her brow was furrowed. . . .

"Hannah!" I exclaimed, suddenly realizing what it was that was so different about her. "What happened to your eyebrows?"

Hannah looked up, her face crumpled with misery. "They waxed them off," she said. And then she burst into tears.

It took Charlie and me a few minutes to calm Hannah down. Charlie tried to force-feed Hannah pretzels while I fetched her a glass of ice water from the kitchen. When she'd finally recovered her composure, she told us what happened.

"I was supposed to be dressed up as an alien for the photo shoot. They had me wear this really weird silver dress that had all sorts of hoops around the arms and waist. And they did this to my hair." Hannah pointed to her head. "And then the makeup lady said she was going to wax my eyebrows. I thought she was just going to shape them up a bit, the way they do at the salon. But suddenly she just ripped them all off."

Charlie and I both cringed. *Ouch.*

"They said it would make me look more alien-like. But now I just look like a big freak!" Hannah continued.

"No, you don't," I said soothingly.

But I had to admit, it did look pretty weird. Hannah's forehead was completely bald, every last trace of eyebrow gone.

"Can they do that?" Charlie asked curiously. "Can they wax off your entire eyebrows without getting permission first?"

"I don't know if they are supposed to, but they did. My mom

freaked out when she saw. She started threatening to sue everyone. The photographer, the makeup artist, the computer store. So then they freaked out and fired me on the spot. It was awful. You cannot even imagine what a terrible day I had," Hannah said.

Charlie and I exchanged a look. Charlie raised her eyebrows. I smiled, shrugged, and handed Hannah a box of tissues. She took one and blew her nose daintily. "I am never modeling again."

"You're not? But I thought you loved it. Up until today, at least," I said.

"No one's going to hire me until my eyebrows grow back," Hannah said. "Besides, I'm tired of always being hungry."

Charlie handed her the bag of pretzels. Hannah took it gratefully and grabbed a handful.

"Mmm, these are so good," she mumbled through a mouthful of pretzels. She looked curiously up at Charlie. "What happened with you and Finn? Did he call you?"

Charlie and I exchanged a look.

"That's a bit of a sore subject at the moment," I said.

Hannah frowned—as best she could without eyebrows—and looked from Charlie to me.

"What happened?" she asked.

Charlie told her about Phoebe showing up at the coffee shop where she knew Finn would be with her ex-boyfriend in tow, and about Finn's jealous reaction, and that Luke had asked her to go to the movies with him. At this last news, Hannah brightened.

"But that's great! Do you know where Finn's going to be to-morrow night? Find out, and then you can arrange to accidentally-on-purpose bump into him while you're on your date," Hannah said.

"Do they teach a course on making guys jealous at Orange Cove High? That's exactly what Phoebe did," I pointed out.

"And it worked," Hannah said.

"But she looked ridiculous in the process. At some point, Finn's going to wake up and realize it," Charlie said stubbornly.

Hannah gave Charlie a pitying look. "No, he won't," she said. "He's a guy. He won't care that she was trying to make him jealous. If anything, he'll be flattered that she went to that much effort to get his attention."

"Really?" Charlie asked. She glanced at me. "Is that true?"

"You know what I think. I think you should just tell Finn how you feel," I said.

"Don't listen to her! That's terrible advice," Hannah said.

Charlie collapsed back on my bed and groaned.

"I don't know what to do. Maybe Finn and I have been friends for too long. They say that once you get into the friend loop, it's impossible to get out of it. Maybe I should just forget about him. Date Luke or someone else instead," she said in a hollow voice.

Hannah and I glanced at each other. Every time I looked at my stepsister, I got a shock of surprise to see her sparkly silver hair and eyebrow-less face. It was a little like looking at an alien.

"You can't just give up," Hannah said. "Right, Miranda?"

But I wasn't sure what to say. Maybe Charlie was right. Maybe she and Finn had been friends for too long to now make the jump into romance. And maybe I was wrong to advise Charlie to tell Finn how she felt—it could turn out terribly wrong, and maybe even ruin their friendship.

"I just don't know," I said, shrugging. "I don't know what the right thing to do is."

Charlie sighed. "This stinks," she said.

"Yeah, it does," I agreed.

"Look at the bright side," Hannah said.

"What's that?" Charlie asked.

"At least you two still have your eyebrows," Hannah said ominously as she popped another pretzel in her mouth.

Chapter Thirty

On a Saturday morning two weeks after Amelia's near-drowning scare at the beach, Amelia and I biked to downtown Orange Cove together. Downtown Orange Cove consisted of one main street—which was oh so originally called Main Street—that was lined with restaurants and shops. At the far end, there was an adjacent board-walk that jutted out into the Intracoastal Waterway. There was a music festival going on with a series of concerts at the stage down by the water, so Main Street was blocked off to traffic and dozens of people were milling around.

"I thought you said you got your driver's license," Amelia said as we dismounted from our bikes and locked them to the down-town bike stand.

"I did," I said.

"Then why are we biking instead of driving in a nice, air-conditioned car?"

"I have my license. What I don't have is a car," I said. "Or a job, for that matter."

Mrs. Fisher had decided to take the rest of the summer off work to spend time with Amelia. In fact, the Fisher family had just gotten back from a vacation to the Florida Keys. It was great for Amelia, but I was really missing the regular paycheck. I'd even put in an application at the bowling alley. Charlie was rooting for me to get the job. If I did, she informed me, I'd have to take over the shoe rental counter, while she would be promoted to the snack bar.

"Can we get an ice cream?" Amelia asked hopefully.

"If you're treating," I teased her. We started to walk up Main Street to Hudson's, which sold ice cream, fudge, and T-shirts to the tourists. "How was your trip?"

"Awesome. I got to go swimming with dolphins," Amelia said, skipping a bit.

She looked exactly the same at first glance, and yet there was something different about her. Maybe it was the sun-kissed glow on her formally pallid face, or maybe it was the relaxed line of her shoulders.

"No way!" I said. "Were you scared?"

"No, it was fun! And you have to tell Dex—I took a beginners' surfing class," Amelia said proudly. "I'm going to keep taking lessons here."

This surprised me, especially after her scare at the beach.

"My mom said that if I was so determined to learn how to surf that I'd sneak off to the beach and nearly drown, she said I should take lessons and learn how to do it safely," Amelia said. She grinned. "But she also said that I shouldn't think that in the future I'll be able to get my way just by doing something dumb and dangerous. Dex was right, by the way. They started off teaching us how to stand on the board while we were still on the beach. You don't get to move to actual waves until you pass a swimming test."

"Just do me a favor and watch out for the undertow," I said, shuddering at the memory of her being fished out of the water by Dex and the beach lifeguards.

"I will," Amelia promised.

When we got to Hudson's, Amelia ordered a mint chocolate

chip cone, while I opted for the peanut butter swirl. After I paid, we headed back out into the heat and strolled up the street toward the boardwalk.

"How are things going with your mom?" I asked, licking a dribble of ice cream off the side of my cone.

"Actually, really good. When I got home from the hospital, my parents and I had a big talk. They said they'd been putting too much pressure on me to be a concert pianist, and told me that I should have a say in what I do with my life. Which is exactly what you told me," Amelia said.

I remembered. I also remembered that Mrs. Fisher had been furious with me for saying these things to Amelia. But since the Fishers had been so nice not to blame me for Amelia nearly drowning, I decided that it was only fair that I didn't hold a grudge against them.

"What did you say?" I asked.

Amelia paused to take a bite out of her ice-cream cone. When she finished, she had a spot of ice cream on the tip of her nose.

"You have some right here," I said, pointing to my nose and handing her a napkin.

"Thanks," she said, wiping up the ice cream. "I told them I still want to play the piano. Just maybe not quite as much."

I nodded. I wasn't surprised. I knew how much she loved her music, and how talented she was.

"And what did they say?" I asked.

"They were actually really cool about it. I thought my mom would be disappointed, but she said the important thing is that I'm happy and healthy, and everything else will fall into place," Amelia said. She grinned at me. "And she agreed to the surfing lessons. I might even take up the drums. I've always wanted to play percussion."

"Really? The drums? I have a hard time picturing you as a rocker chick," I teased.

"Are you kidding? I was born to rock," Amelia boasted.

The strains of a funky jazz beat reached us before we got to the end of Main Street. We turned right and headed down a short side street and then down a flight of stone stairs to the boardwalk. The band came into view, set up on the riverside stage. Lots of people had come out for the concert. Some were sitting on the steps, some were lounging on folding chairs, and others stood to one side, clapping appreciatively as the jazz band finished its song. Amelia and I found space on the stairs to sit down. The band played for a while longer, and Amelia and I lounged in the sunshine, soaking in the music and finishing our ice cream.

When the band took a break, Amelia said, "They were really good. I haven't played much jazz. Maybe I should try it."

"Maybe you should," I agreed. It was good she was trying new things, I thought, although the vision of Amelia putting on a concert, complete with a classical piano concerto, followed by a drum solo, and then finishing up with a funky jazz piece made me smile. "Whatever happened with your piano teacher problem? Are you staying with your old teacher, or are you still going to take lessons from that teacher in Miami?"

"Didn't I tell you? After I got out of the hospital, I finally showed my mom that list we made with all of the reasons why I wanted to stay with Miss Kendall. My mom listened, and we came up with a compromise. I'm going to keep taking lessons with Miss Kendall, and then twice a month, I'll go down and take a lesson with Mr. Gregory, the teacher in Miami," Amelia said.

"That sounds like a good solution," I said. "Are you happy with it?"

"Yeah. We stopped by Mr. Gregory's school on our way down to the Keys, and he was actually a pretty good teacher. He was a bit scary at first—he had these weird, bushy eyebrows, with long hairs sticking out like antennas," Amelia said, giggling. She wiggled her fingers over her eyes to demonstrate. "But he was really nice. And a good teacher."

"And he probably can't help the eyebrows," I said.

"Probably not," Amelia agreed. "Although he could get some tweezers."

The next band was setting up. From the ripped denim and leather they were wearing, I guessed that they were probably a rock band. Something about them looked vaguely familiar. I frowned, trying to place where I'd seen them before.

"Miranda?" Amelia asked shyly.

"Yeah?"

Amelia was staring determinedly down at her feet, scuffing the toe of her canvas sneaker against the cement stair.

"I was just wondering," Amelia finally said. "You know next year?"

"Yes, I know next year," I said.

"I mean when we're back at school," Amelia clarified. She would be returning to Geek Middle, although she didn't know, of course, that I might not be back at Geek High next year.

"What about it?" I asked.

"Will you talk to me?" Amelia asked.

Surprised, I laughed. "What do you mean, will I talk to you?"

"You know. When you see me at school. Will you say hi to me, even though I'm just at Geek Middle?"

"Of course I'll say hi to you! Why wouldn't I?" I asked.

"There's a girl in my class—Madeline Davies—whose older sister, Milly, goes to the high school. Madeline says Milly never, ever speaks to her while they're at school," Amelia said.

"Maybe that's because they're sisters," I suggested. "Sisters tend to get weird around one another."

"Really? Oh. Well . . . good. I'm glad you'll say hi to me," Amelia said, sounding shy again. "I wasn't sure if you would, so I thought I'd ask."

"You don't have to ask," I told her. I still felt a little guilty for not confessing that I might not get a chance to say hi to her, since I might not be there, but then Amelia said something that made me forget my ongoing confusion over my future plans.

"It's just that . . ." Amelia began, then stopped. Her face flushed red.

"What?" I asked, poking her with my elbow.

"I thought maybe I could pretend that you're my sister," Amelia said in a rush. "I know, that sounds really stupid, but I just thought . . . well, since I don't have a sister, and you don't have a sister . . ." Amelia fell silent, clearly mortified.

I was so touched, it took me a moment to collect myself and speak. "I'd like that," I said.

"Really?" Amelia looked at me for confirmation.

"Absolutely," I said.

"But I forgot—you actually have a sister," Amelia said. "Or a stepsister anyway."

"I do. But I don't think Hannah would mind if I had an adopted little sister, too," I said.

"Adopted little sister," Amelia repeated. "I like that. It sounds better than being pretend sisters. What do adopted sisters do?"

"They hang out together sometimes. Just like this," I said, with a gesture around me. "And they can talk whenever they want. Adopted sisters don't ignore each other at school."

"Cool," Amelia said happily.

The people around us began to clap as the members of the rock band took their places.

"One, two, one two three," the lead singer called out, and the band began to play. The singer gyrated in front of the microphone, twisting his hips from side to side. I frowned. The band sounded oddly familiar. . . .

"Oh my gosh!" I said as it finally clicked. "That's Snake House!"

"What?" Amelia asked.

"The band! They're called Snake House. You see the guitarist with the piercings and the tattoo? His name is Snake," I explained. "Although I think that's just a nickname. He dates a girl in my class. They played at the Geek High Snowflake Gala last year."

Amelia wrinkled her nose. "They're not very good."

"No, they're not," I agreed. "But we might as well listen. We're in no hurry to get back home, right?"

Chapter Thirty-one

"Miranda, may I speak with you?"

I looked up from the book I was reading while lounging on my bed. Peyton stood at the doorway, looking uneasy. Her hands were clutched together and her bony shoulders were even more tense than usual.

"Um, okay," I said, putting down my book and sitting up.

Peyton walked into the room and glanced around. "You haven't changed much in here," she said. "Hannah thinks we should have your room painted."

"Yeah, she said something about that to me, too," I said cautiously. It was the first time Peyton had ever called it my room.

"Would you like to do that?" Peyton asked. Her tone was curt, almost testy.

"Would I like to do what?" I asked.

"Paint. The. Room," Peyton said, spitting out each word as though it tasted foul in her mouth. Her thin nostrils flared, and I could practically feel the waves of cold dislike rolling off her.

"Okay. Sure," I said cautiously.

Since the Peyton I knew would never voluntarily do anything nice for me, much less have a whole room painted to suit my tastes,

I had a feeling there was something more going on here than she was letting on.

Peyton stared at me for a long, cold moment. I stared right back at her, waiting for her to get to the point.

Finally, Peyton said, somewhat abruptly, "May I sit?" She nodded toward the uncomfortable modern white chair in the corner of the room.

Taken aback, I said, "Sure."

Peyton crossed the room and lowered herself onto the chair. She frowned. "This chair isn't very comfortable," she remarked.

"No," I agreed. "It's not."

"Why didn't you ever say anything about it?"

"I didn't think it really mattered."

"Well, you have to have a comfortable chair in your room," Peyton said impatiently. She sounded almost angry again. "With the amount of reading you do. And you should really have a desk in here, too, where you can study. Where do you do your homework?"

"Right here, usually," I said, patting the bed. I felt like I'd passed into some sort of alternate reality. When had Peyton ever cared about my comfort? Or where I studied? Mostly, she seemed happy—well, not *happy*, but less mean and twitchy—if I just stayed out of her way.

"We'll order you a desk," Peyton said with finality.

"Okay," I said slowly. "Can I ask a question?"

Peyton's nostrils flared. "All right," she said.

"Why?"

"Why what?"

"Why are you suddenly so interested in painting my room and ordering furniture? I've been living here for almost a year, and you've never shown any interest in whether I have a comfortable place to read or study before," I said.

Red spots flamed high on Peyton's cheeks, and her mouth

pursed even tighter. She and I had always lived by a code of sorts: While we didn't like each other, we also didn't talk about it. True, she put in her little digs now and again, and I did a lot of eye rolling and sighing. But we'd never addressed our enmity outright.

Peyton pursed her lips, and for a moment, I thought she was going to refuse to answer. But then she finally sighed and said, "Richard told me that you're considering moving to London. To live with your mother."

I nodded. "That's right. I was."

Peyton seemed to be struggling for the right words. I waited patiently, my hands folded on my lap.

"It's no secret that you and I have never been close," Peyton began.

I raised my eyebrows. "Okay," I said.

"But I love your father very much. And it's important to him that you—as his daughter—are welcome in our home," Peyton said. She swallowed. "I think that maybe, perhaps I haven't made you feel as welcome here as I could have."

That was the understatement of the year, I thought.

"I want to change that. I'd like you to stay here with us. If you want to," Peyton said. She looked like she'd just swallowed a porcupine.

I was getting the gist of what she was saying. She still didn't particularly like me, and would probably be happier if I moved to London with Sadie. But she was worried that her relationship with my dad would suffer—or perhaps even permanently rupture—if she didn't start making an effort with me.

"Thank you," I said. "I'd like that."

Peyton looked a little surprised by how quickly I was accepting her offer.

"So you're not going to London?" she asked.

"No," I said.

I could have sworn I saw a flash of disappointment cross her face.

"Well. Good, then," Peyton said, rising to her feet. She glanced around. "Why don't you think about what color you might want to paint your room?"

"I will," I said.

Peyton departed. Shaking my head, I picked my book back up. I'd only just started reading again when my door banged open and Hannah rushed in. She'd gotten most of the silver out of her hair, although in a certain light, you could still see the odd sparkle or two. Her face was still eyebrow-free, which I was still getting used to.

"Is it true? You're staying?" Hannah asked.

I nodded. "Yep," I said.

Hannah beamed at me. "I still think you're crazy. I'd totally go if I was you. But I'm so glad you're staying here."

"You are?"

Hannah nodded. "Yeah. I've gotten used to having you around."

I thought back to how quiet the house had been when Hannah was in Manhattan visiting her dad. "I know what you mean," I said.

"So when did you decide you were going to stay?" Hannah asked, flopping down on the end of my bed.

"You know, I'm not really sure," I said. "It was after I found out Dex was going away to school. I kept wondering what would happen with us if I left, and then I'd worry because I didn't want to be the kind of girl who wouldn't go do something she wanted to do because of her boyfriend. But then once I found out he wasn't going to be here, it was easier to make a decision." I shrugged. "If I was in London, I could still come back here in the summer and for holidays, which is when Dex would be home, too. And so once I took him out of the equation, I was finally able to think about what I really wanted to do."

"How did Orange Cove beat out London?" Hannah asked.

"I guess I don't feel like I've done everything I need to do here before I leave. Does that make sense?" I asked.

"No," Hannah said. "Not even a little bit. I think you're crazy to give up London. I bet the shopping there is to die for." She sighed longingly, thinking of a whole city full of stores, but then looked up sharply. "Not that I want you to change your mind or anything."

"It's okay. I won't. I've already told my mom," I said.

"How did she take it?"

"Sadie was disappointed, but she understood. She's only going to stay there for another year, and then she'll move back, so she'll be here for my senior year," I said. "Or, at least, that's what she says now. You never really know with Sadie."

Hannah wrapped her arms around her bent legs, pulling them into her chest. "I'm officially done with modeling. I called my agency this morning and told them," she said, abruptly changing the subject.

"The eyebrow thing?" I asked sympathetically.

"Well, there's that. But I'm serious—I really do think I'd be an amazing relationship counselor. I want to focus on that instead. Look at the success I had with my mom and your dad. I saved their marriage."

"Wait, what success?" I asked, trying to figure out what Hannah had done exactly.

"I'm the one who convinced them to go to marriage therapy, aren't I?" Hannah said. "And then there's you and Dex. I totally got the two of you talking again. And then there's Charlie and Finn."

"But Charlie and Finn aren't together. Your plan backfired," I pointed out.

"No, it didn't. It just hasn't played all the way out yet. Trust me, they're totally going to end up together all because of me," Hannah said, with breathtaking confidence.

"Right now Finn is head over heels in love with Phoebe," I said. "And Charlie's dating Luke. Who she doesn't even really like."

"Actually, I think Luke's growing on her," Hannah said.

"Really? Well, even so, she and Finn are obviously not together."

"They aren't now. But they will be," Hannah said. "And why are you pooh-poohing my dream?"

"I didn't realize that getting Finn and Charlie together was your dream," I said.

"Well, not just them. I meant more in the broader scheme of things." Hannah suddenly gasped, covering her mouth dramatically with one hand.

"What?" I asked, startled.

"I totally know what I want to do! I'm going to be a matchmaker. Like that woman on TV who fixes up women with millionaires," Hannah announced. "Wouldn't that be perfect for me? You get to match people up and counsel them along the way. I could use all of my skills that way."

"Actually, you know, I really could see you doing that," I said truthfully. Knowing Hannah, she'd probably get her own reality television series, too. It would be called *Hannah's Hotties*, or something like that.

"I'm going to totally start working on it now. There's no reason why I can't be a matchmaker at Orange Cove High, right?"

"Right," I said, somewhat more doubtfully.

"Do you know of anyone who needs to be fixed up?"

"No," I said.

"Hmm. It's too bad you're not single," Hannah mused.

"Thanks a lot!" I said.

"I just meant you'd be a good first project. Not that you'll need it. I'm sure you and Dex will stay together," Hannah said.

I smiled, feeling the odd mixture of happiness and melancholy that had become common whenever I thought of Dex these days. What did the future hold for us? Was there any chance a long-distance relationship would work? I kept telling myself that there was no reason to dwell on it now, while Dex was still here with the remaining weeks of the summer stretching before us. But it's hard to make yourself not think about something.

"We'll see," I said.

Chapter Thirty-two

I was in the kitchen, foraging in the fridge for a snack—I'd already uncovered a box of Parmesan crackers in the cupboard, and now discovered some hummus—when I heard the front door open and my dad call out, "Miranda! Where are you?"

"I'm in the kitchen," I called back. I closed the refrigerator door shut with one hip and put my snack on the counter.

"Can you come out here, please?" Dad said. He sounded excited.

"Coming," I said, although I dipped one cracker in the hummus and stuffed it into my mouth before heading out to the foyer. My dad was standing there, his hands in his pockets, rocking back and forth on his feet. "What's going on?"

"I have a surprise for you!"

This piqued my interest. "Really? What sort of surprise?"

"Close your eyes and I'll show you," Dad said.

"Okay?" I said. I closed my eyes and held out my hand.

I was expecting my dad to put whatever the surprise was in my hands. But instead, he took my hand in his and led me forward.

"Where are we going?" I asked.

"You'll see. Keep your eyes closed."

I heard the front door open again, and then felt the blast of hot air hit me as my dad led me outside.

"Keep coming, keep coming. Watch out, there's a step right there. Good. Now just a few more steps, and . . . open your eyes!"

I opened my eyes, and blinked in the dazzling summer sunshine. There, parked in the driveway in front of the beach house, was the ugliest car I had ever seen. It wasn't just yellow. It was the most obnoxious shade of neon, glow-in-the-dark yellow I had ever seen. Even worse, someone had, rather inexpertly, painted black racing stripes down the sides and hood. I wondered who it belonged to.

"Ta-da," Dad announced.

"Ta-da?" I asked.

"I bought you a car!"

"Wait. This car?" I asked, pointing at the yellow monstrosity.

"Do you love it?" he asked. "I thought the color was pretty. And you'll never lose it in the parking lot."

This was undoubtedly true. "Wow, thanks," I said, struggling to sound enthusiastic while simultaneously picturing Felicity Morgan's glee when she saw me drive into the Geek High parking lot in this car.

"I know it's not as nice as Hannah's car, but . . . well . . . ," Dad said, his voice trailing off.

Peyton had bought Hannah a silver Lexus SUV for her birthday. And even though, okay, yes, of course I'd prefer her car to this one—who wouldn't?—I wasn't about to let my dad know that. I knew there was no way he could afford such an over-the-top, extravagant gift. And I didn't want to hurt his feelings, especially when he was so excited by his gift. And any car—even an ugly yellow one—was better than having to bike it everywhere.

"I love it," I said firmly.

My dad's face cleared. "You do? Good," he said, clearly relieved. "I thought that since you were going to be staying here, instead of going to London, you needed your own car to get around."

"Thanks, Dad," I said, hugging him. My dad smelled like he had since I was a little girl—a combination of peppermint and lemon-scented aftershave. My heart gave a sentimental squeeze.

"Do you want to take it for a spin?" he asked, dangling the car keys from one hand. I took them from him. The key chain had a ratty-looking stuffed dolphin attached to it, the metal key ring impaling the dolphin through its gray head.

"Sure," I said, opening up the door.

The car was upholstered in dirty gray fabric, and there were long grease stains on the floor mat. A pine tree room deodorizer—piña colada scent—hung from the rearview mirror.

"The radio doesn't work," Dad said through the window. "But I don't think that's a bad thing. I don't like the idea of you driving around with music blasting so loud, you can't hear anything."

"Dad!" I said. "You have no faith in me."

"Of course I do. If I didn't have faith in you, I wouldn't have given you a car. Start her up."

I turned the keys in the ignition. There was a thumping sound, and then the engine roared to life.

"The engine sounds great, doesn't it?" Dad said happily.

I thought it sounded a bit like an old lawn mower. "Sure," I said, shouting to be heard over the roar. "It's kind of loud, though, isn't it?"

"That just means it has a powerful engine," Dad said. I was fairly sure he had no idea what he was talking about, but what was the worst that could happen? Other than the car exploding, or breaking down by the side of the highway late at night.

I waved good-bye and with a jerky start, drove the hideous yellow car—*my* hideous yellow car, I reminded myself, and an ugly car was better than no car at all—out of the driveway. Underneath the perfume of faux piña colada, there was another, stronger smell. What was that? I wondered. It was like an unpleasant combination of body odor, fast-food grease, and cigarette smoke. I rolled down the windows. Maybe it just needed airing out.

I drove to Grounded, parked, and headed inside. Charlie had said she'd be there, working on some sketches, and to meet her if I could. I saw her immediately, sitting at a corner table with Finn. I hesitated for a moment, wondering if I was interrupting them. But Charlie smiled when she saw me and waved me over.

"Hi," I said, sitting down next to Charlie.

"I'm glad you're here," Finn said.

"Why, thank you, Finn," I said. "That's an unusually nice thing for you to say."

"I need girl help, and Charlie's pretty much useless," Finn said.

"Hey!" Charlie said, looking affronted. "I can't believe you'd say that, especially after I just spent the last thirty minutes listening to you moan about your love life."

"It's not your fault," Finn told Charlie. "I'm sure you did your best, but let's face it—you're a virtual guy."

"And what exactly is that supposed to mean?" Charlie asked dangerously through clenched teeth.

"Well, I mean, you're not a guy—obviously—but you have the emotions of one," Finn said. "You know. You eat up men and spit them out."

"I do not!" Charlie said.

"Yes, you do. With the notable exception of your ill-fated—and I might add, ill-advised—relationship with that loser Mitch," Finn said.

"What guys have I eaten and spit out?" Charlie demanded.

"That Luke guy for one. You were totally leading him on at the bowling alley that night," Finn said.

Charlie smiled, suddenly pleased with the direction the conversation was going. "No, I wasn't," she said. "We're going on our third date tomorrow night."

Finn's mouth dropped open. "Please tell me you're not serious."

"Of course I'm serious. Why wouldn't I be?" Charlie asked.

"Because that guy is an idiot," Finn said. "He was so dumb, I think at one point he was actually drooling. He probably forgot to swallow."

"We've been through this before. Just because someone doesn't go to Geek High, it doesn't mean that he's stupid," Charlie said.

"Yes, it does," Finn said.

"Finn?" I said. "*You're* dating someone who goes to Orange Cove High."

"That's right, you are," Charlie said, taking a sip of her coffee.

"Yeah, but I'm not going out with Phoebe for her brains," Finn said.

"Nice," Charlie said.

"Finn!" I said. "You're such a pig!"

"No, I'm not. Someone can have a good heart and soul without being an intellect," Finn said loftily.

"And that's why you're going out with Phoebe? For her heart and soul?" I asked, amused.

"No, he's totally lying," Charlie said, before Finn could speak. "He just spent the last half hour complaining that Phoebe doesn't do anything but giggle when they're together."

"And that's a problem for you?" I asked Finn.

"I just wish she had some base of knowledge. I mean, she doesn't have to share my interests, necessarily, like computers or gaming. But how about a working knowledge of, oh, I don't know, *Battlestar Galactica*?"

"*Battlestar Galactica*?" Charlie repeated scornfully.

"It doesn't have to be *Battlestar Galactica*," Finn said fairly. "It could be *The Lord of the Rings*. Or Manga."

"So you don't really want to date a girl," Charlie said. "You want to date a girl who's basically you—a geeky guy—only with boobs."

"Exactly," Finn said, pointing at her.

"Are you going to break up with Phoebe?" I asked.

"No way! She's way too hot to break up with," Finn said.

I saw Charlie flinch, but Finn didn't notice.

"I just need to figure out a way to work my Jedi mind tricks on her, so I can mold her into the perfect girlfriend."

"I need a coffee," I said.

When I got back from fetching my frozen latte, Charlie and Finn were still arguing.

Big surprise, I thought.

"Well, I personally couldn't date someone who hadn't read the *Harry Potter* series," Charlie said. Her arms were folded over her chest, and she had a stubborn expression on her face. "But that's just me."

"Has Lukey-boy read them?" Finn asked slyly.

"First of all, don't call him that. His name is Luke," Charlie said haughtily. "And second, although we haven't talked about it, I'm sure he has."

"Call and ask him," Finn said.

"What?" Charlie looked taken aback.

"Call and ask him." Finn pushed his cell phone across the table to her. "Here, you can use my phone."

"No, thanks," Charlie said.

"Why not? Scared what you might find out?" Finn asked.

"No. But I also don't want to insult him by quizzing him about his reading habits," Charlie said.

"Bok bok," Finn clucked.

"Oh my God. You've officially regressed to the age of seven," Charlie said, shaking her head in disbelief.

I decided it was time to break in on the lovefest, before it came to blows.

"I have some news," I said. "My dad bought me a car!"

It worked. The magnitude of my announcement caused Finn and Charlie to stop sniping at each other and turn to stare at me.

"Are you serious?" Charlie said. "That's so cool!"

"A new car?" Finn asked.

"Not exactly," I admitted. "It's a new-to-me car."

"Can we see it?" Charlie asked.

"Sure. I parked out front. But I think I should warn you—it's yellow," I said.

"So?" Finn asked.

"It's very yellow," I said. "Very, *very* yellow."

•

Two minutes later, the three of us were standing outside Grounded, staring at my new car.

"The color's not that bad," Charlie said, in a lame attempt to be supportive.

Finn didn't even bother trying.

"This car makes my life," he said, standing with his hands stretched out in front of him, fingers spread. "If I died this moment, I would go out a happy man."

"It's bad, right?" I said worriedly. "I know it's a car, and any car is better than no car. But even so, it's still bad, right?"

"Are you kidding? It's *awesome*," Finn said gleefully. He ran a finger down the hood. "The racing stripes are just the best. I think I have to own this car. How much do you want for it, M?"

Could I sell it? I wondered. Finn could certainly afford it. He was a self-made millionaire, after all. And it would solve my ugly car dilemma. I could use the proceeds to buy a normal-looking car. But then I quickly decided that, no, I really couldn't do that. It would hurt my dad's feelings.

"I can't sell it," I said with a sigh.

"You have to! I'll give you ten thousand for it! No, twenty!" Finn announced.

"Really?" I asked.

"Well, no," Finn conceded. "But I will give you five hundred. And this Pez dispenser." He held up a Pez dispenser with a Tweety Bird on top. "It's vintage."

"No sale," I said, waving away the Tweety. And a vintage candy dispenser? Gross. "Do you guys want to go for a ride?"

"Shotgun," Finn said automatically.

Charlie gave him a withering look while he bounded around the car and hopped into the passenger side. "Does he have to be such an idiot all the time?" she remarked.

I just raised my eyebrows at her.

"I know, I know," Charlie said with a sigh. "What can I do? I can't help it."

"Next year should be pretty interesting," I said. "Come on, hop in."

Epilogue
Four Weeks Later

"I can't believe you're actually leaving tomorrow," I said.

"I know. The summer went by way too fast," Dex said.

We were sitting on a picnic table at a park that overlooked the Intracoastal Waterway. There was a playground nearby, although it was deserted now that it was past eight and the sun was setting. Over the water, the sky was a hazy smudged purple, ribboned with shots of orange.

"Are you all packed and ready to go?" I asked.

"I'm packed," Dex said. "I'm just not so sure about the ready-to-go part."

"I'm sure you'll love it there," I said.

"And if I don't, I can always come home," Dex said.

"I don't think you should go into it thinking that way. It might be hard at first. But once you adjust, I'm sure you'll be really happy."

"I hope so," Dex said. He flexed his hand and then drew it into a fist.

I reached out and took his fisted hand in mine. His hand instantly relaxed as we knitted our fingers together. "Don't worry," I said softly. "Everything will be fine."

"And we'll talk every day," Dex said.

"We'll e-mail, too."

"You'll tell me all about what's going on here."

"I will," I promised. "And Hannah will keep me up to date on all of the Orange Cove High news, so I'll be able to pass that on to you, too."

"Good," Dex said. "It'll be nice to hear what's going on. Even if it has a uniquely Hannahesque perspective."

The sun was sinking lower in the sky. The light began to fade into the soft darkness of twilight. The cicadas chirped around us, hidden in their treetop haunts. I wanted to hold on to this moment—to make the sun still on the horizon, to keep the next day from dawning—even though I knew it was impossible.

"I don't want to say good-bye," I said. A lump lodged in my throat.

"I don't, either," Dex said. His hand was firm against mine. "So let's not say good-bye."

I could feel a sob tearing in my chest. "What do you mean?"

"We'll just say, *see you later*, like we always do. And it will be true. We will see each other later," Dex said.

I took in a deep breath, pushing the sob back down before it could break free.

"I have something I need to tell you," I said.

"Okay. Wait, no, let me guess: You're really a superhero with incredible powers who was sent to Earth from a faraway planet to be raised by adoptive parents and eventually save the world from being attacked by an evil race of aliens set on taking over the planet?" Dex asked.

I laughed. "No."

Dex snapped his fingers. "Darn."

I braced myself for the words I knew I had to say out loud, no matter how painful they'd be to both him and me.

"I just wanted to say ... I know we already talked about this ... but I think maybe we were wrong. Maybe we should break up after all," I said.

Dex stilled beside me, although he didn't release my hand. His fingers were warm and strong, interlaced with mine. He smelled so good, like soap and lingering chlorine from the pool. I wanted to lean closer and inhale the scent of him, memorizing it for when he was gone.

"It's not that I want to," I said quickly. "Because I don't. But I also don't want you to feel that you're tied down here, when you're starting a new life up there. It's not fair to you."

Dex breathed in deeply, and then sighed on the exhale. "What if I want to be tied down here?"

"I know that's how you feel now, but you might feel differently in time," I said.

"I won't," Dex said in a voice that was soft yet fierce.

"You might."

"No."

I felt a squeeze of pleasure, but then reminded myself that it was my job to convince him. He was the bird I had to free.

"What if I said I want to break up?" I asked.

"I wouldn't believe you," Dex said. "You'd just be saying that because you think it's better for me."

"Well, isn't it?"

Dex turned to look at me. Even through the darkening sky, I could make out the exasperation and affection in his pale-eyed gaze. "Miranda. Don't you think I should get to make that decision? About what's right for me? What's best for me?"

My lips twitched up into a half smile. "No."

"No?"

"You'd stick with me because you thought it was the right thing to do. Even if your heart was somewhere else," I explained.

"My heart is right here," Dex said. He tapped my chest, just over where my heart was thumping away.

"Will you at least think about it?" I asked.

"No," Dex said. "Like it or not, I'm yours. No matter where I am. No matter where you are."

"Are you sure?" I asked.

Dex nodded. He held my hand up to his lips and kissed the knuckles. "I'm sure," he said.

And then he leaned forward, cupping one hand behind my neck, and kissed me. It was the perfect kiss. Sweet and warm, it caused my entire body to feel as though it had turned to liquid. In the tiny part of my brain that was still able to form thoughts, I realized that this was a kiss I would remember for a long, long time.

Dex drew back, his lips inches from mine.

"See you later," he said softly.

"See you later," I said.

About the Author

Photo by Marie Langmore

Piper Banks lives in South Florida with her husband, son, and smelly pug dog. You can visit her Web site at www.piperbanks.com.